Devil's Trace

Devil's Trace

RC White

Copyright © 2008 by RC White.

Library of Congress Control Number: 2008901334
ISBN: Hardcover   978-1-4363-2265-2
               Softcover   978-1-4363-2264-5

All rights reserved. No part of this book may be reproduced or transmitted in any form or by any means, electronic or mechanical, including photocopying, recording, or by any information storage and retrieval system, without permission in writing from the copyright owner.

This is a work of fiction. Names, characters, places and incidents either are the product of the author's imagination or are used fictitiously, and any resemblance to any actual persons, living or dead, events, or locales is entirely coincidental.

This book was printed in the United States of America.

To order additional copies of this book, contact:
Xlibris Corporation
1-888-795-4274
www.Xlibris.com
Orders@Xlibris.com
47976

Dedication

Devil's Trace owes its existence to one person, one who wears a multitude of hats. Whether he's serving as editor/idea man, business manager, chef extraordinaire, best friend, or traveling partner, Greg remains the love of my life. His encouragement persisted through times when I sent the manuscript flying across the room and when the world seemed to conspire against me. Most importantly, however, he keeps me focused on the God who makes all things possible. Thank you, Greg, for being you.

FOREWORD

In the late 1700s, at the inception of commerce in the South, adventurous men floated merchandise down the Mississippi to Natchez and New Orleans, the largest settlements along the river. Lacking a navigable reverse route, however, they abandoned their simple flatboats and returned by land, thus beating a pathway that became known as the Natchez Trace. Beginning in Natchez and extending north to Nashville, this now famous footpath once offered as many as fifty crude inns along the way to provide basics for men with a thirst for adventure and pockets lined with gold.

Armed with a rifle and at least one bottle of whiskey, these boatmen made the grueling trek north as they risked all for the profits that waited at the other end of the trail. Ruthless bandits, territorial Indians, wild animals, disease-carrying insects, and relentless weather tested men to their limits and earned for the trail the name "Devil's Backbone."

The hardy, more often the lucky, survived. Their stories abound, but this rough and rowdy lot left behind something else. There remains a spirit that can still be felt when you park your car at one of the remote picnic areas and walk a winding trail through a forest so thick it captures your very breath. Spanish moss hangs like ratty hair in witches' havens, unearthly birds call across silken black bogs, and tree frogs watch with piercing eyes. The trace is far more than a place. It's a dimension. And some say, anything can happen on the Devil's Trace.

ONE

I spotted it from a long way off. At first I thought it must be some sort of animal, but it never moved. Unable to tear my eyes away, I squinted for a better look and slowed the car. Lucky for me there wasn't anybody coming from either direction because by the time I got to it, I'd almost come to a complete stop in the middle of the parkway.

I pulled off, thankfully onto a level shoulder, and stopped, then turned slightly in my seat to get a better look. No doubt, it was a suitcase. Upright and perpendicular to the length of the road, it couldn't have been more at odds with those halcyon surroundings.

Still mine was the only car in sight. People had warned me that this part of the Natchez Trace was little traveled, especially since the inception of the interstate a few miles away. But I was there on assignment for *American Byways*, and I searched out the remote, the offbeat that would send my career skyrocketing.

I turned all the way around in my seat. It couldn't have fallen from a truck or car. No way it would have landed upright like that. On either side of the road, a thick forest of oaks and sweet gums dripped with Spanish moss and cast a gray glow, more pronounced because of the cloudless blue overhead.

To the right, the young green earth rose slightly, then leveled off. Judging by the glare, I assumed there must be a lake, or at least a pond, at the top of the hill. On the other side of the road, the ground tapered downward until it disappeared entirely beneath suspicious water that guarded cypress trunks and who knew what else. A pervasive quiet enveloped everything, only the sound of my car's engine breaking the stillness. I turned it off.

What the hell? The possibility of somebody's leaving the suitcase there by accident was out of the question. It had to have been on purpose. But why?

I opened the car door, checked one more time for traffic, and took a step toward the suitcase. From somewhere in the recesses of my memory, warnings reared about hijackers who plant things to get their victims off guard before moving in for the attack. I stood there with my hand on the door until an involuntary chuckle rose in my throat. *Don't hijackers live in cities where there are places to hide out?* If anybody was hiding there, he had to be either part fish or alligator, in which case probably not interested in me.

Still laughing at myself, I took the few steps to the center of the road. The suitcase had no markings on it, but it had seen some use. Basically, it was the standard mossy green variety that you used to see going round the carousel if you waited long enough.

"Go for it, Reagan," I said aloud and picked it up.

Those standard hard-cover issues, designed to take the weight of an elephant, were fairly heavy to begin with, making it impossible to tell if it contained anything. Still, I carried it back to the car and laid it across the passenger seat. The locked side faced me, but I ran my hand around all four edges, as if my brain wouldn't accept what my eyes told it. No identifying tags. My mother's voice grew louder. The suitcase wasn't mine, and I had no business whatsoever looking inside. But how was I supposed to find out whose it was?

Then I remembered something else. People these days hide bombs in all sorts of weird places. But who would want to blow me up? And who knew I'd be coming by there at that particular time? I had no exes desperate enough to exterminate the source of their worries, and even if I had, nobody could know for sure I'd really pick up the stupid thing.

Oh, for crap's sake. I slid both metal locks outward, and the case sprang open. Nothing exploded, but nothing glittered either. Once more I looked around. I half-expected to see the perpetrator sniggling behind a tree, but there was no one. Only me and a suitcase that contained a handful of photographic negatives.

They were fairly dark and wider than the usual, different from any I'd ever seen. I held one up and turned it to catch the full light that poured through the sunroof. Fine details were too difficult to discern from the negatives, but the woman, on the far side of a picnic table, looked a lot like me. She wasn't skinny, but slender, the way someone who enjoys the outdoors is. Her long hair, light in the negative, was pulled back into a no-frills ponytail.

The child—a little girl, her hair dark in the negative—sat nearest the camera, her feet drawn up under her on the bench and half-turned toward whoever was taking the picture. She grinned and offered up what looked like a sandwich.

I held up a second negative, turned it to catch the most of the rays, and reached for my reading glasses stuck in that little space over the radio. The negative looked like maybe a double exposure because it appeared to hold parts of two pictures. The little girl faced the camera and held on to someone's hand, but the arm attached to the hand vanished just above the elbow. The remainder of the person was missing, as if two pictures had melded. I wondered where the other half was and briefly rummaged through the case, looking for the man that belonged to the arm.

Sunlight penetrated into my scalp and made me feel as if an army of biting ants had invaded, so I turned the engine back on and aimed the vent toward me. As cold air spread across my face, I looked back at the negative. Who might be looking for these negatives? Who might value these scant souvenirs of a family's time together?

A white car, one of those unidentifiable luxury models, approached from the way I'd just come, and its lone male driver slowed and glanced my way. Before somebody stopped or, worse yet, called the park rangers about a woman in distress, I wanted to get out of there. I eased my own car back onto the road and headed again for the town called Kosciusko.

Looking for signs that might point me to the nearest ranger station, I remembered something Ray once told me. By pushing *hp on my cell phone, I could conjure up the highway patrol or, in this case, a park ranger. That's what I really wanted. These pictures must be in their domain. I started to dial, then spotted a sign telling me that the next ranger station was only two miles ahead, at the exit I'd planned to take. I drove there and pulled into the parking lot.

June in Mississippi is still for the most part a pleasant month, but whisperings of what was to come were everywhere. Here, sweet gums and maples that vied with each other for breathing space over the rustic ranger station formed a little copse of protection from the heat. The station had been built of native woods and stained a dark brown, no doubt to blend in with the surroundings. But in summer's state of vestal green, it stood out like a beacon. Had it been large and modern, it would have been ugly; as it was, primitive save for an antenna that pushed up through the forest and a droning window unit, this small station appeared quite at home.

When I pushed open the door, a young man wearing the standard brown issue of park rangers crouched over an ancient desk made of gray steel. He was apparently deep into some other train of thought, and I'd been there for several seconds before he squinted up through wire frames and adjusted his eyes to the light that followed me through the door.

"Can I help you?" he asked in the unmistakable pace of the region.

He was young, but I wasn't so far up the hill myself that I couldn't help noticing his good looks. His sloping brown eyes held a kindness that always attracts me, not unlike the way spotted puppy dogs do.

"Yes, I hope so," I admitted. "I'm Reagan Wilks," I said, offering my hand.

He stood behind the desk and returned the handshake. "Don Stroud. Pleased to meet you, Ms. Wilks. What can I do for you?"

"I came by to see if anybody reported something lost on the parkway."

"Have you lost something?"

"No, actually I found something."

His brows raised, and a shock of dark brown hair fell onto an otherwise unmarked forehead. I started to feel a little foolish and said, "Why don't I just go get it and bring it in?"

I left the door open while I retrieved the suitcase from my car, and when I turned back toward the building, he was watching me. His brows raised once again, this time accompanied by a question.

"You found that suitcase on the parkway?"

"Yes, between French Camp and here. Actually closer to here."

He remembered his manners and eyed the gray steel chair standing like a castaway in a corner. "Here, have a seat," he said and dragged the chair up to the side of his desk.

I thanked him and gratefully sank into the cool vinyl, forming my explanation. Because I wanted to make it perfectly clear that I had nothing to do with the placement of the suitcase, I began with when I first spotted it. By the time I got to the opening of the case, I could see he was intrigued.

"I finally opened it to see if I could find some identification. But there wasn't anything."

"What was in the case?"

I told him.

"Negatives?" he asked.

"That's it." I slid the case toward him.

He took it out of my hands and laid it across the desk in front of him. Then he slid open the locks, as I had done, and stared down at the negatives. Without comment, he picked up the one on top and held it beneath the crook-neck lamp's glare. He studied it for a moment, then picked up a second negative and studied it as well. He shook his head vaguely as he reached for a third.

I could see from my chair that he was looking at the superimposed negative, what I assumed to be one image atop another. He leaned farther across the desk and held it closer to the light. "What in the world? Looks like something's wrong with this one."

"I know. I saw that too. Must be some sort of double exposure."

"Yeah, I guess so." He managed a smile for me, all the while unable to tear his focus away from the negative. "I really appreciate your bringing this in. We haven't had any requests for missing suitcases, but I'll send it along to Jackson just in case. Let them take a look at it."

I stood up and offered my hand again. "Well, thanks for your help. I really didn't know what to do with it. Maybe you can find the owners."

"Hopefully. Thanks again." He came from behind the desk and followed me toward the door. "So are you heading on down the trace?"

"Yes, I'm eventually going all the way to Natchez, but I'll probably spend the night somewhere nearby." I couldn't help smiling myself now. Finally somebody to tell this to. "I'm doing a piece on the Natchez Trace for *American Byways*, and I'm taking my time."

His face lit up. "That right? You're a writer then?"

"Yes, mostly freelance, but after I finish this project, I want to try my hand at fiction."

He stood a bit straighter, and I realized he was taller than I'd thought. "I think you'll find lots of people around these parts interested in fiction. You know, we're kinda proud of our writers."

I grinned back. "It's hard to ignore this state when it comes to writers."

"We've had our share," he said, shoving his hands into his pockets. "Well, I guess you need to get going."

"Probably. But I wonder about something."

"What's that?"

"Do you think you could contact me when you find the owner? This suitcase has really got me intrigued, and I'd like to know the rest of the story."

We both laughed at my unintentional allusion, and he said, "Sure. That's not a problem. Besides, I wanted to ask your name so I can look for your work. It would be so cool to know a real writer."

He turned back to his desk and shuffled through the stack of papers, then produced a small lined tablet and handed it to me. "Here. If you'll write your name and a contact number, I'll call you when I know something."

I gratefully accepted his offer, wrote the information, and handed it back to him. "I'd appreciate that, Agent Stroud."

"Don. Just ask for Don. I'm the only one around."

"Okay then, Don. Thanks for all your help, and I'll look forward to your call."

Returning to my car, I had that feeling that I always have when something's hanging over my head, but I don't yet know what. I told myself that I was being superstitious, that those negatives were lost some time ago, probably dropped by a truck taking stuff to a dump, and never thought of again. Still, that feeling was there.

TWO

The motel I selected could have been anywhere in the United States, and I made a mental note about doing better next time. The mountains of research I'd done before beginning the trip told me that Mississippi offers a variety of accommodations ranging from quaint to bizarre, so why was I staying at a chain? Determined to do better from that point on, I checked the room one more time and walked out to my car.

I had breakfast in a local café, along with some personalities that would make great interviews. The place reeked of characters. An older man, heavyset with the kind of permanent smile that said he knew things no one else did, held court around a corner booth. Three younger men, all in jeans and tee shirts, focused on his words, occasionally exchanging glances among themselves. Every few minutes, a waitress appeared to refill their cups, ending each round with, "Anything else, darlin'?"

These were the types of folks my article needed, but before I could think of a way to introduce myself, the party started to break up. Each younger man made sure to pat the monarch appreciatively on the back before heading out the door. I did my best to finish a biscuit about the size of a dinner plate, backed up by ham and scrambled eggs, took one last swig of black coffee, and asked for my check. Next time I wouldn't let such an opportunity pass.

I'd driven nearly an hour when the cell phone interrupted my reverie. After my breakfast of champions, I felt sleepy, but not so much that I didn't recognize the voice from the afternoon before.

"Hey, I'm glad I caught you. This is Ranger Stroud. Remember me?"

"Sure, Don. I remember you. How are you?"

His voice held a tone of concern. "Good. I hope you haven't gone too far."

"No, I'm," I began, looking for a marker, "I'm on the way to Jackson. I must be about halfway."

"Good. I'm glad I caught you."

"What's going on?"

"My supervisor came in after you left and took a look at the pictures, and he just about split a gut. He had me take it in to Jackson early this morning."

"Jackson? Why?"

"To the police department. And they want to talk to you about it."

A tinge of apprehension nudged at me. "Why do the police want to talk to me? All I know is what I told you yesterday."

"I understand," he assured. "It seems that there's more to this suitcase than either of us knew about, and they just want to talk to you. Maybe some detail that means something to them but not to you."

Now he really had me intrigued. "Okay. But where do I go?"

He gave me directions and a name to ask for when I arrived. The remainder of the drive into Jackson should have been spent looking and talking to people along the way. Instead, I drove straight into town, taking the most direct route from the parkway into the heart of the city. By the time I found the promised parking and entered the building, I began to feel a bit like a character in a Nancy Drew mystery. What in the world could possibly be so exciting about photographic negatives?

I took the elevator to the fifth floor and exited as two men and a woman, all wearing police force blue, got onto the elevator I'd just left without giving me a second glance. Apparently one more thirty-something redhead made no impression on them. The chief's office was well marked, but I could have found it anyway from the number of people buzzing around it.

An older man at the reception desk stared at a computer in apparent disgust as he pecked at the keyboard with pudgy fingers. I waited for a few seconds, hovering a few feet behind his screen until he looked up at me from beneath shaggy brows littered with more salt than pepper.

"Yes, ma'am. Can I help you?"

I gave my name and was about to state my business when his internal alarm went off. Frustration with the keyboard evaporated, and a more serious demeanor appeared. He stood up and ordered, "Wait here, Ms. Wilks. I'll be right back. The chief wants to see you."

He returned in seconds, followed by the chief himself. Resisting the urge to turn and run, I swallowed hard and stood my ground. In his pin-stripe suit, the chief looked more like a politician than any image I'd ever had of mere policemen, chiefs or otherwise. He was taller than the man who'd introduced me and much, much smoother.

Get a grip, I told myself. He was handsome, maybe not movie-star handsome, but close. He had black hair, not shoe-polish black, but the real thing, and blue eyes that paralleled an Arizona sky. The only thing imperfect about that face was a nose that took an awkward angle about halfway down, but the result did little to hamper the overall effect.

I gripped the firm hand that he extended toward me. "Jess Loden," he said as he placed one hand on my back and motioned me toward the door of his office with the other. "Let's go in here where we can talk, shall we?"

I had no choice but to follow, and even if I did, I wouldn't have objected. If the contents of the suitcase hadn't collared me, this man surely would have. He offered me a chair in front of his desk and glanced back at the officer waiting in the doorway. "Coffee?" he asked.

I shook my head and dropped gratefully into the black leather chair. "No, thanks."

As the door closed, the noise of the outside office subsided, and the calm of this room sank in. This was the center of it all in a city. What in the world had suddenly brought a writer doing a piece on the tranquility of the Natchez Trace into the office of the chief of police?

He sat down behind his massive desk and looked solemnly across at me. "I guess you're wondering why we wanted to talk to you."

"As a matter of fact, I am." My thumbnail clicked uncontrollably across the tip of my index finger, a habit I'd tried for years to break.

He sat back in the tall leather chair, nodding as he spoke. Fluorescent overhead lights had turned his tanned face slightly yellow, and I could see now the black hair beginning to edge into silver. "Ms. Wilks, that's right, isn't it?"

"Yes. Reagan."

He nodded. "Ms. Wilks, that suitcase you brought in has some really interesting pictures in it." He leaned forward and dropped his voice a bit. "Are you from anywhere around here?"

"No. I live in Charlotte. Why?"

"So you don't have any idea who the people in those pictures are?"

Once again I answered no, although I was beginning to want to scream my answers. After all, he was the one who'd dragged me all the way down here and into his office.

He turned in the chair as again his eyes darted to a point just over my head, then back to me. "Ms. Wilks, the people in those pictures disappeared twenty-three years ago."

"Disappeared?"

"Yes. The parents and their eight-year-old daughter were heading from their home in Florence, Alabama, to see relatives in Natchez. Relatives said they were making a vacation of driving the trace, and when they didn't arrive, family contacted the police. The whole state searched for them for months, but nobody found a clue. Park rangers, police, even the FBI talked to hundreds of people, but nobody saw a thing out of the ordinary. The last contact was at a little grocery store where they stopped to pick up food for a picnic. The case was finally closed for lack of any evidence—until now."

I was pretty sure he could hear my heart pumping, and my voice grew louder. "You mean I found a suitcase with pictures of people that disappeared twenty-three years ago?"

"That's exactly what you did."

I wanted to run, but now I couldn't move. I had a thousand questions, if only I could find the words. Finally I asked, "But how did, I mean, who put it there?"

"I don't have the faintest idea. We thought maybe you did."

"You don't think I had anything to do with this, do you?"

A faint smile crossed his lips. "You're certainly not a suspect in their disappearance, if that's what you mean. My calculations say you would have been about the daughter's age at the time they disappeared."

"Thanks for that, but you're close."

"So you saw nobody near the suitcase?"

"No. In fact, only one car passed the whole time I was parked on the side of the road."

"Did you see who was in the car? Was it more than one person?"

I shook my head, trying to remember. "The driver was a man. I didn't see anybody else."

"Do you remember what kind of car he was driving?"

"It was some kind of luxury model—Mercedes maybe. And white. That's about all I remember."

"Did you get a look at the driver? Anything you can tell us about his appearance?"

"About all I can tell you is that he looked like a businessman—trim-cut hair, looked like he was dressed up. I think I remember a tie."

"Did he slow down?"

"Yeah, somewhat. But it all happened so fast, and I really didn't pay much attention. I just wanted to get out of there before somebody stopped and offered to help the lady in distress."

"Probably a good idea." He made a note on a yellow pad beside his phone. "Doesn't sound as if he had anything to do with it, but we'll keep asking around. Somebody's bound to have seen something."

"Chief Loden, may I ask you a question?"

"Sure. If I can't answer, I'll tell you."

"Who were these people?"

He visibly relaxed, and his tone lost some of its formality as he said, "Family name's Weir. The father's name is Danny, and his wife is Stephanie. The little girl is Lauren. She was about eight when they went missing."

"So we'd really be looking for somebody close to my own age." The image of the child in the picture drifted behind my eyelids. "Who were they going to see in Natchez?"

"Grandparents. The mother's parents."

My stomach sent an uneasy warning, as the picture expanded to images of my own mother in Charlotte waiting for her family that never arrived. I looked more seriously at the man across the desk from me. "Were you working here then?"

"Yes, I was a brand-new detective, but I do remember the case. All of us do."

I nodded in agreement. How could anyone forget that scene? "Must have been tough on everybody, especially the family."

"No doubt. For years, the woman's mother called us the first day of every month, asking the same questions. The sad part is we never had any more answers."

"Does she still call?"

"No, not for several years now. I'm not even sure the parents are still alive."

"How sad. For everybody."

"Yes, it is." I felt myself sighing as I stared at a neutral spot on the desk between us. "Do you plan on telling the parents about the negatives?"

"Eventually. But first we'll want to track down any connections we might find."

That scenario played out in my mind. What would they do after all those years? Wouldn't it be cruel to perhaps raise their hopes again, all for nothing?

His voice broke into my thoughts. "Well, Ms. Wilks, thank you for coming in. We really appreciate it."

"Of course. I'm glad to help, but I'm afraid I haven't added anything helpful."

"On the contrary. I'd say you've reopened the case."

"Do you mean you're going to reopen the investigation?"

"Looks that way. We still don't have any real evidence, but the appearance of those negatives tells us that somebody's still interested. Who knows, maybe the person responsible for their disappearance in the first place."

I felt a surge of relief mixed with yet more questions. "Have you developed the negatives?"

He opened a folder in front of him and took out several pictures, then pushed them across the desk. I'd seen the first one before, but in color, its subjects looked far more real. The mother's hair was a shade of copper close to my own, and it glistened in the sunlight dappling through trees over their picnic table, but little Lauren's glistened like the sun itself. A breeze lifted blond wafts from her shoulders and gave her an elfin appearance. Both smiled back at the camera's holder in the way that only love can smile.

The writer in me wanted to be a part of the investigation, to uncover the one clue that would find these lost people. At least I could help the grieved parents find some type of closure. I wanted to say so much, but restraints of what was really my business and what was not stopped me. Then there was the matter of my deadline. I couldn't afford to screw up this chance.

Still, I asked, "May I possibly have one of these photographs?"

"For what?"

I shook my head as I wondered the same thing. "To remember these people, I guess. I feel connected somehow."

"I'm afraid they're evidence right now. Come back after we've had a chance to decide what we're going to do with them, and maybe we can share then."

"I understand." I closed the folder and stood up, feeling my purpose coming to a close. "Chief Loden, I'm a writer, doing a piece on the Natchez Trace. That's why I was there when I was. Call me superstitious, but that's enough for me to believe I was supposed to find the suitcase. And enough for me to feel responsibility for the missing family. What can I do to help?"

"I don't know how much the lay person can help in this case, but I do appreciate the offer."

"Sure." I had no choice then but to thank the man and take my exit. I opened the door and looked back at him. "Would it be okay if I talked to the parents?"

"I don't suppose I can stop you if you really want to, but I don't know what you'll get from them."

"I realize that, but if I had a phone number, I could at least offer my condolences."

He nodded and dutifully wrote the number, then passed the paper over to me. "Remember, these people have been through a lot."

"I'm sure. But maybe someone who wasn't there at the time can see a fresh link."

"I guess anything's possible."

"Can I tell them about the negatives?"

His eyes drilled into mine, and I could practically see the wheels of his mind turning. "No. I'd better do that."

"Okay, I understand. I just thought that maybe I could give them something to hope for. Some type of closure."

"Ms. Wilks, as much as you want to help, you might actually make things worse if you raise their hopes for nothing. Let us handle that detail, will you?" His voice softened. "Believe me, those people would do anything to get their family back, with or without us."

"I can only imagine."

Armed with the latest information Loden had on the family, I left the police department with a vague notion of what I was doing. I'd come to Mississippi on a dream assignment, and here I was ready to abandon it and go looking for a lost family. I fully intended to drive straight to Natchez in search of them, but knowledge that I shouldn't just pop in on people who'd already been through hell gnawed at me. After all, I was a stranger. What right did I have to pry into their lives with more questions after all these years?

That question and a plethora of others swarmed in my head. It had become difficult to discern what my real intentions were. Was I genuinely trying to help these people, or had I become a rubberneck at a ghastly wreck? The more I tried to separate fact from fiction, the more I needed time to think; so when I spotted the turnoff to Port Gibson, I took it. My original agenda had me spending several days there, but for now an hour or two would have to do. Immersion in history always clears my thought process.

I took Highway 61 into the old town and, before long, spotted the ten-foot gold hand atop the church. Story says that the Reverend Zebulon Butler had labored alongside construction workers to place the wooden hand atop his tribute to God, but unfortunately, he died before completion. And the first service held there was his own funeral. Talk about irony.

Later, the original hand had to be replaced with a metal one finished in gold when the town's woodpeckers failed to understand the importance of this symbol. By the time I parked in the visitors' center and headed out on foot, I'd made up my mind.

I took out my cell phone and punched in the number Chief Loden gave me. These nice people at least deserved the chance to tell me no, but I'd begun to think that I wouldn't have that choice when a male voice finally answered.

"Mr. Suttle?"

His voice sounded matter-of-fact, nearly devoid of emotion. I explained who I was and why I'd called him. The ensuing silence made me wonder if I'd lost the connection.

Then a tentative voice asked, "Who'd you say you were?"

I repeated it, tempted to give the name of the magazine, but I knew that would be wrong since my meeting with Mr. Suttle had nothing to do with my assignment. I stuck to the basics. "I've just come from the police chief in Jackson, and he gave me your number. Would it be possible for me to come by your home for a short while to talk with you?"

"About what?"

"About your family's disappearance twenty-three years ago."

I heard a familiar sigh, the same one I'd heard before when people are confronted with a buried past, and his voice held the flatness of resignation.

"Ms. Wilks, I don't know that I can tell you a thing hasn't been said too many times already."

"That may very well be true, Mr. Suttle, but I'd really like to meet with you anyway, just for a few minutes."

"Do you have something new?"

I held my breath, wanting desperately to tell him about the pictures. "No. Not really. Guess I just hoped to see a clue that the others missed." I paused, waiting. "I promise not to take much of your time."

Again he sighed. "Do you know how to get here?"

He gave me directions, and after doing my cursory tour of the church and completely avoiding several other buildings that would normally have made fascinating fodder, I left Port Gibson and made as straight a line as possible to Natchez.

The Suttle house sat on a couple of acres in the middle of a much larger neighborhood of small brick homes, every fourth one exactly like the first. Urbanization had encroached, but it hadn't eaten this property entirely. Theirs was a lovely old white two-story house, tall and narrow, with a wide covered porch across the front. When I pulled into the driveway, I could see someone sitting alone in the swing on the front, partially hidden in shadows. I pulled into a driveway covered with river pebbles the color of Mississippi clay and stopped beneath an arch of huge oaks. I got out and waved toward the figure on the porch.

"Mr. Suttle?"

Slowly and deliberately, the tall, angular figure rose from the swing and came out of the shadows to the top of the stairs. The hand he offered was rough and strong. He wore jeans, old but clean, and a plaid shirt in green and red, tucked in and ironed to perfection. Few wrinkles marred his deeply tanned face, and his hair was still mostly black and remarkably thick.

"Reagan Wilks," I said in introduction, waiting for the invitation to proceed.

"Everette Suttle. Glad to meet you, Ms. Wilks." He nodded slightly and half-turned toward the swing. "Like to join me on the porch?" He pointed toward a rocker positioned beside the swing.

"That would be nice. I love being outdoors whenever I can."

I sat down in the rocker and accepted his offer of iced tea. When he returned from inside the house carrying two tall glasses, he handed me one and resumed his place on the swing. He took a long draught of the icy beverage and eyed me over the rim of his glass.

"So, Ms. Wilks, why don't you tell me what's on your mind."

My fingertips were wet from the sweat of the glass, and when I touched the back of my neck, a slight breeze evaporated the moisture into coolness. The tea was sweet, the way it's supposed to be, and I nearly forgot my purpose in the visit.

I said, "Mr. Suttle, I really appreciate your seeing me. I can only guess how you and Mrs. Suttle must feel."

The stoicism flickered momentarily. "It's just me now. My wife Janie died about four years ago."

"Oh, I'm sorry. I didn't know."

He nodded. "Pancreatic cancer. From the time they found it, she was gone in three months."

"I'm so sorry, Mr. Suttle. If you'd like, I can leave. I don't want to impose on you, especially after all you've been through."

He set the glass on the little wicker table between us and leaned back, letting his shoulders relax against the wooden slats painted the same shade of green as the house's shutters.

"You're not imposin', Ms. Wilks. I don't mind talking. Just wanna know why you're here."

Good question, I thought but said instead, "I'm a writer, Mr. Suttle, working for the magazine *American Byways*. I'm doing a piece on the Natchez Trace, and when I heard about your tragedy, I thought it might somehow fit in with what I'm doing."

"You're gonna tell the whole country about what happened to my family?"

"Oh, it wouldn't be about their disappearance so much as it would be about who they were before they disappeared. What I'm trying to do is to show the rest of the country what kind of people live along the trace, and who better than your family? It would be sort of like a memorial to them."

He stared silently at me while wrinkles around his mouth deepened. For a moment, I thought he would tell me to get off his porch and out of his life. Finally, he said flatly, "That'd be nice. That'd be real nice. They'd like that."

I took out the traditional yellow pad and began to ask questions, while for nearly two hours, this kind gentleman made me privy to the beatings of his family's heart. The Suttles had once been cotton farmers, but economics forced the latest generation into a different type of farming. Everette turned to growing flowers and landscaping and had enjoyed quite a bit of success maintaining antebellum mansions scattered throughout this small city.

Janie never worked outside their home, but Stephanie had other ideas. With a keen interest in fashion, she'd gone off to the big city of Atlanta where she soon met Danny, who, in turn, convinced her to marry. Within the year, Stephanie was pregnant. With Lauren's birth, she discovered a new love, one even more enticing than the fashion industry. She soon quit her attractive job in a department store chain to be a full-time mother to Lauren. Shortly after that, Danny moved his family back to his hometown, Florence, Alabama, to take over his father's insurance agency.

The trip down the Natchez Trace had been planned for a long time. They waited for Lauren to finish her school year, and the three of them took off down the trace for several days of unplanned picnics and side trips across Mississippi's back roads on their way to Natchez. Danny and Stephanie wanted to teach little Lauren the values associated with the simpler life, one they themselves enjoyed.

"The trip had a purpose too, Ms. Wilks." He paused, and I looked up from the tablet. "She was coming to tell Janie that she was expectin' another baby."

"She was pregnant?"

"Yep. Only reason I knew was she never could keep anything from her old dad." He looked down at his hands, turning them as if the answer lay there. "Truth is, I guessed it, but she didn't deny, so I knew that's what this trip was all about. I never did tell Janie. Guess I thought she couldn't take any more."

"Mr. Suttle, did you tell the authorities about this?"

He shook his head. "Nope. Only reason I'm tellin' you now is this may be my last chance to do somethin' for that grandbaby I never got to see."

I wanted to weep. How much can one person hold in for a lifetime without exploding or going berserk in a shopping mall? I closed the tablet and looked down at my own hands in the growing darkness on the porch, unable to make eye contact with this kind of grief.

He must have sensed my uneasiness and broke the silence. "Janie'd like what you're doin'. She always was the one to talk to folks, so you can just talk for her I guess."

"I'll do my best, Mr. Suttle. That's a promise."

Last of the sun's orange light colored the tiny brick houses around his now, and I stood on the first step, thanking him yet again when he stopped me in mid-sentence. I could hardly see his face in the shadows.

"Ya know, there is one other thing I liked to forget about."

"What's that, Mr. Suttle?"

"There's one of those private detective fellas up in Jackson you might wanna talk to."

"Oh? Is this somebody you hired?"

"Yeah. Like I said, nearly forgot all about it. There was some good ole boys up around Greenwood that reported seein' a car bein' pushed into a lake, but when the police went to talk to 'um, they figured it was just some kinda prank to get their names in the papers. So we hired this detective to take a look for himself."

"Did he find anything?"

Everette shook his head. "Nothing to speak of. I'd have kept him hired forever if I'd thought there was a point in it, but I finally had to tell him to let it go."

"I understand. They don't work cheap, even twenty-three years ago. Mr. Suttle, would you give me his name?"

"Sure. Remember it well. Rand McArdle. Reason I remember it so is that it was an unusual name."

"Yes. It is a bit unusual." I opened the tablet one more time and wrote the name as he pronounced it for me again.

"You shouldn't have too much trouble findin' it in the book in Jackson."

"I'd say you're absolutely right, Mr. Suttle."

I thanked him again and left him watching me from the porch. How long had it been since he'd watched a visitor leave his house? I could do nothing about the sadness in this man's life, but there was something I could do. As I drove away from this lonely man, I reached for my cell phone. My editor would have to give me a little more time. This project might take longer than I'd thought.

THREE

Lucky for me, my editor Katie had already left her office, so my message would have to be interpreted without me on the other end to yell at. I told her I'd found more human interest here than I'd imagined and I needed more time. At that point, I figured the less said the better.

Darkness was by then complete, and I realized how very tired I was. Beginning to feel as if I'd traveled the entire state in less than twenty-four hours, I stopped at a gas station restroom, and one look in the mirror confirmed my suspicions.

I still remembered the vow to find the unusual accommodations available across the state, but that would have to wait for another day. Standard rooms near the interstate beckoned with hot water and, if I was lucky, a soft bed.

True to form, the room offered plenty of hot water, but the bed was only thinly disguised as an instrument of torture. By the time daylight finally filtered through the pair of heavy drapes separating me from street traffic, I was up. I borrowed a tiny tray from the lobby's breakfast area and carried enough black coffee back to the room to get my motor running. By seven, I was on my way again.

The day could have served as a poster for life in the Deep South, with a deep-sea-blue sky, and only a stiff breeze from the northwest relieved temperatures already surging toward eighty. Any other time, I'd be driving the parkway, stopping every few miles to talk or crawl around some quaint shop; but this time, I opted for the faster route of connecting with I-55, which put me back in Jackson soon after the morning rush. I stopped at a convenience store and headed for the phone out front, luckily not in use at the moment. Yellow pages hung suspended inside a scratched metal folder, and although some of its pages had been ripped out, the ones I needed were there. After twenty-three years, McArdle Investigative Services still existed.

His office was out in Ridgeland, which in itself told me something. In the movies, the private detective always had a rundown office over a Chinese laundry, but this end of town held no resemblance whatsoever. If all his clients hailed from this neighborhood, the man was doing all right.

McArdle Investigations occupied the corner portion on the bottom floor of an attractive office building arranged around a central courtyard. Huge crape myrtle bushes bearing a profusion of white and deep-rose blooms alternated with red maples and decorative wrought-iron benches. What a pretty place to spend lunch, I thought, remembering some of the windowless lunches I'd spent during my big-city days.

I expected to be greeted by a receptionist, and I must have shown surprise when a handsome male face looked up from the desk near the door. Somewhere around fifty, he wore a white polo shirt that accentuated his tanned muscular arms. Dark brown hair bordering on black, although close cropped, still tried to curl all over his head and gave him a boyish appeal.

Deep brown eyes smiled back at me as he greeted, "Hi. Can I help you?"

"Yes, I hope so. I'm looking for Rand McArdle."

"That'd be me." He smiled broadly. Silkiness in his deep voice reminded me of some actor, but I couldn't remember which one. "My secretary's out today, and I'm trying to figure out what I did with some files." He looked back at the pile of folders laid out on the desk, then gave a resigned grin. "Well, what can I do for you?"

"Sorry about not calling," I began. "I'm Reagan Wilks. Somebody referred me to you just last night, and this is the first chance I've had to contact you. Do you think we can talk for a few minutes?"

He came out from behind the desk and gestured toward a doorway across the room. "Sure, Ms. Wilks. Let's move into my office."

I followed him into a larger room lined with bookcases on two sides from floor to ceiling. Each shelf brimmed with every size volume, with pictures scattered throughout. Most were pictures of McArdle and a little girl who grew older as the photos progressed, with the latest apparently a high school graduation in white cap and gown. Not only had the girl grown progressively more beautiful, but she had also grown more like her father. The dark hair and flashing deep eyes were unmistakable.

A third wall was made entirely of glass and allowed unlimited view of the courtyard garden. Two bird feeders hung from a large maple just outside the window where cardinals and house finches dined on sunflower seeds.

He walked up behind me as I watched the feeder. "You like birds?"

"Love 'em. I don't know a whole lot, but they're fascinating. And beautiful."

"Yes, they are. Relaxing too." He took his seat behind the desk. Then after offering coffee, he asked, "Who referred you to me?"

"Everette Suttle," I said, watching his expression.

His eyes widened as he leaned back. "Everette Suttle. How's he doing?"

"He seems to be okay. Or at least as okay as possible after all that's happened to him." Testing the waters seemed pointless, and I continued. "I'm afraid he's lost his wife now though."

"Janie's gone?"

"Yes. He said she had pancreatic cancer about four years ago and died very quickly."

McArdle shook his head, trying to digest the most recent tragedy of Everette's life. "I'm so sorry to hear that. You'd think the poor man has had enough."

"You'd think, wouldn't you?"

"Well, I appreciate Everette's recommending me. He's a good man. So, Ms. Wilks, how can I help you?"

"Reagan, please call me Reagan."

He smiled, and I began to tell my story, starting with the suitcase containing the negatives. His eyes widened again.

"You mean it was sitting in the middle of the parkway?"

"Exactly. Sitting there upright, as if somebody wanted it to be found. But believe me, there couldn't have been anybody around where I found it. I was surrounded by swamp and really thick woods."

"And the suitcase contained pictures of the Weirs?"

"Negatives."

"Damn! No idea where they came from?"

"I'm sure I don't know. Neither do the police."

"So you took it to the police?"

"Actually, I took it to a ranger at the station, and apparently he showed it to his supervisor. The supervisor must've known what the pictures meant because he had the ranger take them in to Jackson to the police."

"And so you talked to the police in Jackson?"

"None other than Chief Loden himself."

"Huh. Do you still have the negatives?"

"No. Sorry. The police chief has them. That's where you come in."

"How's that?"

"I'm hoping maybe you can help me put the pieces together."

Sympathy spilled from his eyes. "You know, Ms. Wilks, you're not the first person who's wanted to solve this case."

I'd begun to feel more than a little bit foolish. What made me think I could come in many years later and find answers that professionals by the score had been unable to find when the event was recent?

"I guess that sounds naïve, doesn't it?"

Once again his smile drew me in, and for the first time I noticed the dimples in his cheeks. "No, it sounds like you really care about people. Now if you'd been one of those trash writers who print anything for a buck, that'd be a whole different ballgame."

"Thanks. I appreciate that. So you'll help me?"

"I'll help you if I can—which I doubt. But I'll try. What do you want to know about?"

"Everette said that some locals up around Greenwood called in the police with a story about a car being pushed into a lake. Did you ever talk with those guys?"

"I did. I've got all that in the files if you'd like to see it."

"Would you mind?"

"Not as long as Everette gives permission, which I'm sure he will since you just came from there. But I'm also sure you understand I'll have to get his permission."

"I'd expect you to," I said and got up from my chair. I walked to the window and stood watching a pair of cardinals as they perched on the feeder. They expertly opened sunflower seeds, dropped the shells to the ground, and occasionally glanced toward the window, as if also waiting. Rand's voice behind me sounded cordial and familiar.

He chatted briefly, offered condolences, and promised to be in touch.

When he called my name, I turned around. "Everything all right?"

"No surprise there. Everette gave us the go-ahead. So. You ready to take a look at this?"

I sat down across from him, and he opened the folder. He thumbed through several sheets, then stopped. "Here it is. I remembered the Billy Ray part, but I'd forgotten the Slocum. He did most of the talking, and scary as it seems, he was probably the brains. The other one was Eugene Bittle."

"What exactly did they tell you?"

"If I remember correctly, they'd changed the story for the fourth or fifth time by the time they talked to me, so I didn't put too much stock in it. But what they essentially said to get everybody all worked up was that they were out gigging frogs late one night when they stumbled on a man pushing a car into one of the lakes around the Delta. But like I said, by the time I got there, they'd changed it to a lake in town, then they said they actually didn't see a man doing it, just the car already in the water. Whatever, I think the only thing they might have seen was dollar signs. You know, in search of their fifteen minutes of fame or some such."

"So the police searched where they said they'd seen a car?"

"Actually, they dragged two lakes. Only thing they found was a refrigerator and the kink of junk you'd expect to find at the bottom of the lake."

"Did anybody else in town see anything?"

He sat back and crossed his arms over his chest. "Funny you should ask that because there was one other person I talked to who might have known something, but he was scared."

"Of what?"

"What I suspected was that he was hunting alligators. Without the proper authorization, killing them carried a stiff fine at the time, so he wasn't about to say where and lead authorities to his kill sight."

"Did the police talk to him too?"

"I don't think so. I did most of my poking around in local establishments. I seem to learn more that way. I ran into him playing pool. When I brought up the subject, he backed away like a scalded dog."

"Do you have his name?"

"Yeah. That I did get. From somebody else, but I got it." He turned a page in the folder and ran his finger down the lines. "Here it is. Ricky Byers."

I felt the adrenaline start to pump. "Do you think he'll talk? Surely he can't be brought up on charges now."

"There's always a possibility he'll talk. If he's still around."

"I keep forgetting how long it's been." Searching for another avenue of attack, I asked, "By the way, Mr. McArdle, do you have any pictures of the family that you can let me borrow?"

"Yes. I had some. Should still be here."

He turned to the back of the folder and removed a large manila envelope and passed it over the desk to me.

"These were copies I made from Everette's pictures, but we still need to hold on to 'em."

"No problem." I removed the small stack of pictures and began looking through them. One included the entire family, Everette and Janie, along with the couple and their new baby. It had been taken on the same porch where I'd sat talking with the bereaved grandfather. Others were of the couple alone, then of the child as she grew up. The final picture showed a dressed-up Lauren with her parents. Judging by Lauren's age, it must have been taken near the time they disappeared.

"Thanks, Mr. McArdle. I promise to take good care of these." I slipped the pictures back into the envelope. "Was there anything else you discovered that might help my search?"

"Unfortunately, not much. You probably already know about the grocery store where they stopped before lunch, and the people there really didn't know anything else. I'm sorry, Ms. Wilks, but I don't have much to tell you. Everywhere I went, I ran into the same blank walls."

His eyes gave away the frustration he'd felt all those years before, and I found myself feeling sorry for him, along with the Suttles. But something else gathered strength inside me. It was the same amorphous feeling I always had when my life was about to change course sharply.

"Mr. McArdle, I really want to thank you for sharing what you have. I'm not sure what, if anything, I can do that hasn't already been done, but I've got to try."

"I understand," he said softly. "I don't think anything's ever happened in this state that affected so many people, but I'm afraid only God knows what happened to that family. I wish you luck."

I thanked him again and started to leave, then stopped. "Oh. Let me give you my cell phone number so you can contact me if you need to."

"Of course. I'll need that, Ms. Wilks."

"Reagan please."

"Reagan it is. And I'm Rand. Fair enough?"

A blush began on my cheeks, and I hurriedly called out the number. "Thanks again. I'll keep you posted if I find anything."

"I'd appreciate that. Oh, and, Reagan, I don't want to sound like your father, but watch your step if you're gonna go asking questions around the Delta, will you?" He tried to smile, but it wound up looking more like a grimace. "It's a bit of a different world up there, especially for a woman and a stranger. Just be careful."

I couldn't help grinning at his concern. "Thanks, Rand. I promise."

I was turned to buckle my seat belt when a tap on the driver's window startled me. Rand stood there with an embarrassed grin on his face. I rolled down the window.

"Sorry. I just couldn't let you go without telling you one more thing."

"What's that?" I asked.

He rolled his eyes and shrugged. "Actually, what I came out here to tell you was that I can't let you go up there all alone, but now I realize how stupid that sounds. So how about if I ask if I can go with you?"

Surprise would hardly describe what I was feeling. "That depends on your motives."

He tugged at his earlobe now and stood up, grinning as he looked out over the parking lot before he turned his eyes back to me. "Look, Ms. Wilks, Reagan, this may sound like the lamest line you've ever heard, but it's not a line at all. This case has never left me. Only reason I quit in the first place was that I couldn't afford to keep going without pay, and well, you met Everette. He couldn't afford to keep paying me. I want to go with you if there's any possibility that we might find out what happened to the Weirs. It's as simple as that."

Something about his demeanor told me this was no lie. "You'd do that?" I asked.

"If you'll let me. I've got a little time right now, what with my secretary off and all that. How long do you plan to stay?"

"A day or two. It depends on what I find."

"Perfect. I could take my car and follow if you'd rather."

I thought about that. I surely wouldn't mind his company. And he had a lot more experience in this kind of thing than I did. "No. That's not necessary. Why bother?"

"Well, if you're sure."

"I'm sure," I admitted. I had begun to doubt my sanity, but I liked the feeling in my gut. It had never failed me. I just didn't always listen.

"Great then. Can you give me a few minutes?"

I promised to meet him at the restaurant down the street in an hour and turned out of the parking lot. Well, I thought, who knew I was going to have help on this project?

FOUR

The drive to Greenwood made me feel as if I'd left that state and entered another realm entirely. Within a couple of hours, flat earth covered by oceans of cotton plants in bloom spread in every direction, the sameness broken only by sporadic clusters of trees huddling in relentless sunlight. Visible sheets of heat shimmered over the two-lane highway and created little ghosts that hovered just out of reach. Rand in the passenger seat gazed out over the unchanging landscape, apparently lost in thought of his own, quiet for the first time since we left Jackson.

A few hours before only two strangers, we so far hadn't had any problem finding things to talk about. But now I had a bit of trouble holding in my laughter. My mother's image kept reappearing, along with a scolding about not being "brought up that way." I was on my way to one of the South's most infamous areas, the Delta, with a man I had known for a matter of hours in search of persons responsible for the disappearance of an entire family. She'd never understand, but then she'd also never tried to earn a living, not to mention a reputation, as a writer.

As we approached Greenwood, Rand sat up straighter and began taking note of familiar landmarks. Traffic picked up, and we finally stopped at the intersection where we either continued on into Arkansas or delved farther into land officially known as the Delta.

"That way." He pointed.

I turned and followed the road up into the only hills around. I'd never seen a stranger sight than these hills that rose out of the flatness, like some kudzu-green monsters lifting themselves from a primordial lake. I'd done enough reading about the area to know that what I was looking at was the demarcation between flatland and the first stirrings of the Appalachians, but the writer in me saw it differently.

That road eventually led us through what could generously be termed an unkempt section of the city, again flat and unremarkable. I had slowed because he sat forward, reading street signs as we passed. He finally directed me into the parking lot of a barbecue place with a neon pink pig dancing overhead.

He turned around in his seat and looked back toward the direction we'd just come from. "Yep. It's back there. Sorry we missed the turn."

"No problem." I backed up and headed the car east again. "It's been a while, hasn't it?"

He made a sound like a grunt as he stared intently down a side street. "Stop," he ordered, then turned to look behind us again. "Sorry. That's the street back there."

Again I turned the car around, and we took off in a new direction, bordered on both sides by shotgun houses painted in different shades of pastels. Had they been in more charming surroundings, they might have looked remotely like the Caribbean; but as they were, mingled with carcasses of automobiles and relentless trash, they appeared more comical and sad.

Within a few blocks, the houses gave way to a scattering of small businesses and nightclubs, with the occasional house holding its own after the many decades of encroachment. We were about to give up when he spotted what he was looking for. The house sat fifty or so yards off the street to the left. It had been painted a dark green some time ago and thus blended with untamed bushes and overhanging trees that nearly met in front of the screened porch that crossed the front of the house.

"That's it," he muttered. "I remember the screened porch."

As I eased the car onto the ruts connecting the house with the street, the screened door flew open, and a hundred pounds of black muscle raced toward us. I stopped, afraid of hitting the dog if I continued, but far more afraid of what this creature might do were I stupid enough to get out. For a while, it pranced back and forth in front of us in the driveway, alternately snarling and barking, ready for its next meal. Then it circled the car and bounded to my side, planted huge paws on my window and peered back at me while issuing a low growl through huge bared teeth. My own breath nearly stopped, awaiting the sound of broken glass.

Near panic, I looked back toward the house where the screen door had opened once again. This time, a lean unsmiling figure held open the door and stared unflinching at our predicament.

"Frog! Git back here!"

At the sound of his master's voice, the growling calmed, then stopped altogether as the massive head turned, slung a string of saliva across my window, and looked back at the source of the voice. Paws still planted near my head, the dog looked one more time at me, licked his lips and slid off my car. As he trotted back toward his master, I could finally speak.

"Now that my life has flashed before my eyes, is this the right place?"

Rand laughed out loud. "This is the place. I couldn't ever forget it. Mr. Byers?" he called, getting out of the car.

The man's face showed no emotion as he bent to pat the dog that had returned to his master, pleased no doubt with his achievement. "Yep. Who're you?"

Rand walked toward the man, extending his hand as he approached the top step. I could hear only the tone of their voices and an occasional word, but it was enough to know that the meeting was going okay so far. In a few more seconds, he turned and motioned for me to follow.

I took a deep breath and headed for the front porch. Frog returned to his dirty, worn spot on the dark-green wooden floor, growled a last low warning, and thumped his massive body beside his master's chair. Beneath heavy foliage, the porch offered some respite from the afternoon's heat, but the air was still muggy, mixed with the stench of permanent nicotine and formaldehyde. Constant traffic on the street made our words sound faraway; Ricky's voice blended in, almost as if it, too, were a machine.

He was no taller than Rand, but a lot thinner. He was lean, the way people get after too many years on a diet of beer and smoke, and his jeans looked as if he'd been born in them, molded onto his body and just as rock hard. On his once-white tee shirt, a woman with really big hair recommended a particular truck stop.

Ricky Byers offered us our choice of lawn chairs scattered about the porch and stared openly at Rand, while he waited for some form of explanation.

"Mr. Byers, you been doin' okay?" Rand asked for starters.

The glint of his eyes softened a bit, but his only answer was a slight nod. He reached for the cigarette smoldering in an ashtray and inhaled noisily as a long trail of ash fell onto the wooden floor.

"Yeah. I'm doin' fine. What you here for?"

Rand squinted through the haze. "Mr. Byers, since you remember me from the Weir case, you probably figure I'm here to ask you some more questions."

"Man, I'm tellin' you. I didn't know nothin' then, and I sure as hell don't know nothin' now."

Rand grimaced through the smoke and tried again, this time including me. "Mr. Byers, this is Reagan Wilks. She's a writer doin' a piece on the Natchez Trace Parkway. She heard about this story, and I'm tryin' to introduce her to some of the people involved in the case. We hoped you'd share what details you remember about the whole thing."

I joined in. "That's right, Mr. Byers. I'm trying to make this story seem real. And since you're part of it all, whatever you can tell me would help make it come alive for the readers."

For what seemed an eternity, Byers was silent. Even Frog shifted uneasily and turned questioning, brown eyes up to his master. Byers finally said, "Lady, like I said, I don't know what I can tell you hadn't already been said, but I reckon there ain't no harm in talkin'."

"That's great." I drew in as much air as I dared from the thickness around me. "How about if you just tell us anything that you remember about that night."

Lines furrowed across his forehead, and I thought for a minute we'd lost him.

Rand added, "Mr. Byers, you must know that whatever happened that night can't possibly be held against you now. There are laws about how long you can hold somebody responsible—for anything except murder."

Byers leaned forward and propped his bony elbows on his legs as he drew once again from the cigarette. "I guess you're right. Nothin' can come of it now." For the first time, he looked directly at me. "Ms. Wilks, you ever seen an alligator?"

"Sure," I gulped. "But not up close."

"Well, they're mean as can be. And real good eatin', if you know what you're doin'." A tiny smile curled his lips. His eyes then left mine as he looked somewhere past me to the busy street outside. "The night you're talkin' about, I was out there in the swamp huntin' for gators. Wasn't nobody with me, but I saw what I saw."

I asked softly, "What did you see?"

He shook his head, as if to clear cobwebs implanted long ago. "I saw this little girl. At least part of one."

My heart froze. "Was she in the water?"

"Nope. On the bank. I was comin' in off the lake. I liked ta stepped on her."

"Was she alive?"

He scowled, and he snapped, "What kinda monster you think I am, lady?"

"I'm sorry, Mr. Byers. I didn't know if she died while you were there."

He slumped back and shook his head. "Wadn't much left of her—just 'bout the top half."

Trembling, I asked the next question. "Mr. Byers, what did you do then?"

"I puked. Then I got the hell outta there."

"And so you didn't tell anybody what you saw that night?"

"Nope."

Rand asked, "You never told anybody?"

"Mister, you already know the answer to that one. Fine for huntin' gators woulda put me under for life."

It was Rand's turn to nod. "I see your point. I guess I was thinking that maybe you made an anonymous call or something."

"What good would that a done?"

I continued, "Did you see anybody else out there?"

"Nope. That was enough. Believe me, I've had plenty a dreams about that one."

"I'm sure you have," I sighed. "Mr. Byers, do you think you could tell us exactly where you were hunting that night?"

"Course. A hunter's gotta know where he is."

"Would you take us there?"

He glanced at Rand, then back at me. "Don't see what good it'd do. That little girl's been gone a long time now."

"Yes, unfortunately, she has, but I'd still like to see the place. You know, so I can describe it."

"I reckon I could take you there, but I'm tellin' you, it won't do no good. There's a bunch of houses sittin' on top of what usta be a swamp."

"Houses?" The remaining air rushed from my lungs. "I thought you said it was a swamp."

"Usta be."

Rand and I exchanged a glance. "Mr. Byers, I'd really appreciate it if we could see the spot anyway."

He stared back, and I waited for the rebuff when he said something that nearly blew me off the porch. "That ain't all there is to it, Ms. Wilks. Somethin' else's happened out there."

"You mean since then?"

Ricky reached for another cigarette, took a match from a box and struck it noisily across the strip, then inhaled. Smoke curled about his head, and he sat back, soaking in the cloud.

"Few days ago, some folks that live out there was diggin' up the yard for a pool, and they found some bones. Paper said it looked like a woman, but they were gonna send 'em down to Jackson to be sure. Way I figure, it's gotta be connected someway."

"Did they find any other bones?"

"Not that I know of."

"And do you think that's the place where you saw the body?"

"Hard to tell. Guess I'll have to go there myself to be sure."

By the time we left Ricky's front porch, I felt the effects of our long day. Darkness had descended onto the Delta. I wanted food, and I wanted sleep. Almost as much as I wanted a long, hot shower and clean clothes that didn't reek of smoke.

Rand and I made plans to pick up Ricky early the next morning, and we left his house in search of a motel. As exotic as that may have sounded at another time, I'm sure nothing of the sort entered either of our minds. After crossing back through the center of town and seeing nothing that remotely looked out of the ordinary, we stopped at a chain motel and asked for two single rooms. The Middle-Eastern man behind the desk hardly blinked at our request, especially in light of the fact that he was selling two rooms instead of one, but I caught a certain glimmer in his eye as we left. He could watch our adjoining rooms all night if he wanted to, but all he'd see would be closed doors. I was in no mood for explanations or for come-ons either.

I eagerly used my share of hot water, changed into a long white linen dress and sandals I'd brought along for the heat, and thought about burning what I'd worn earlier. Instead, I slipped the slacks and top into a plastic bag and sealed them up until time would allow me to find a laundry somewhere. One thing at a time.

Another thing that has become a certainty in America has to be the presence of Mexican restaurants. Not only did we find one just down the street from our motel, but we even had our choice. Thank goodness my dinner partner had the same feeling I did about those things and opted for the mom-and-pop version. Somehow, kids wearing cute little sombreros and conversation forced to compete with a strolling mariachi band weren't what I had in mind.

After a really good margarita and salsa drenched with fresh cilantro, I perked up. We had spent the day talking about nothing very personal, and I thought it might be time to break the ice.

"Rand, I appreciate your dropping everything and coming along with me. For some reason, I doubt that our friend Ricky would have been too eager to share without you along."

He grinned sheepishly. "Kinda hard to talk with a big black dog snarlin' in your face?"

"Something like that," I admitted readily. "But it's more than that, and you know it. Folks like Ricky don't immediately take to girls not from around here. So thanks. I really appreciate it."

He stared down at his margarita and idly traced a pattern through moisture collected on the base of the glass. "You're more than welcome." He looked up at me. "Truth is, I never got those people out of my mind. And when you popped into my office like you did . . ." He grinned sadly and continued, "Hey, had to be an omen or something. That family's waited a long time for some sort of closure."

"Yes, yes, they have. Maybe we can finally help provide that."

"I hope so. But, Reagan?" His expression turned somber. "It's been a long time. Believe me, this whole state, not to mention the FBI, couldn't find them. I don't know how much we can expect to do."

I wanted to cry, not just for the Suttles, but for him too. What I said was, "I understand. Do you think you can handle going through it all again?"

He nodded almost imperceptibly and added, "As it turns out, your timing is pretty good."

"How's that?"

He looked out across the parking lot. A young couple got out of a pickup, laughing and holding hands. When he turned back, I saw a vulnerability I hadn't seen before. "I've got a little time on my hands right now."

"Oh?"

"Yeah, my daughter left for school a couple of weeks ago. She and I've been partners for about twelve years now, and I guess I'm feelin' a little lost."

"Um. That's rough. Where did she go to school?"

"Went up to South Carolina, to a culinary school. Supposed to be one of the best." The pride on his face was obvious. "She always wanted to be in the kitchen. When her mom died, she was too little to reach the counter, and she'd stand on a stool I gave her." He shook his head, remembering. "That girl could make one hell of a mess, but by golly, she caught on. Now she makes food you just wouldn't believe."

"So she's going to be a chef. How wonderful. Does she want to buy her own place?"

"For now, she just wants to learn the business. I guess the rest will come later."

"I'm sure it will," I agreed. "So is she your only child?"

"Yeah. How 'bout you?"

"Never had the chance." I felt the familiar lump in my throat, but it wasn't time yet. "Trying to get a break in this writing business doesn't leave a lot of time for anything else."

"How about your family?"

"Oh, my parents still live in Charlotte. I've got a brother who's a big-time lawyer there. He's done all the right things—Harvard, kids, country club. But I think they've finally admitted I don't fit the mold."

"Good for you." He lifted his glass toward mine. "How about a significant other, as they used to say?"

I wasn't ready to go there yet either, so I answered as innocuously as possible. "I'm afraid that at the present, the written word is my sole companion."

"That's too bad. Well, let's drink to not fitting into the mold."

"Hear, hear," I agreed, clinking my glass against his. "So be it. And while we're at it, may we find the answers to all of life's great questions."

FIVE

The burial place of some unfortunate soul now supported suburbanites, who until very recently had no clue about secrets that waited beneath their houses. Gated communities have become a ubiquitous part of our society, but I hardly expected to find one so far removed from a city of any size.

Rand had made use of a contact in Greenwood, and before long we were inside what amounted to the most exclusive neighborhood in that part of the state. Huge houses occupied most of the two and three-acre lots, dwarfing what little shrubbery had been hauled in to soften the newness of the neighborhood. Occasional willow trees thrived in the terrain, but it would be years before this neighborhood resembled anything like the thick forests that had been destroyed to create it. The sky was ripe with moisture, and the sun felt much closer, more intense than it had been only a few days before.

When we reached the far side of the circle that enveloped the neighborhood, one house stood out from all the others. Police cars and unmarked vehicles bearing the familiar blue license plate of government workers filled the winding driveway and spilled over onto the street. No self-respecting country-clubber would welcome this intrusion.

"That must be it," Rand suggested, and I agreed, stopping the car across the street where we could still see the enormous house. It perched on a slight rise, probably dirt hauled in to give its owners a vantage point, but it provided more in the way of a view for envious visitors and other neighbors. Its ivory walls of stucco rose into the sky like an Italian palace transplanted onto foreign soil. Complete with a colonnaded balcony at the front, it presented a regal façade.

In the backyard, a backhoe stood idle beside a huge mound of earth. People in uniform, and some in plain clothes, milled about the yard. "Looks like we're in the right place," I said. "Now if we can just get in for a look."

"Huh," Byers grunted. "I can already tell you that's the place."

I turned around to face him. "How can you tell?"

"See that rise over yonder?" He pointed. "Right back of their fence?"

I followed his hand to a sharp rise three or four feet high that ran behind the house in question. It seemed out of keeping with the otherwise flat landscape, almost like a giant mole had left his mark.

"Yes. What is that?"

"That usta be a levee. When the Yazoo ran over, it kinda protected the town. But since they put in those drain ways, they don't need it no more."

"Oh. I see." Actually I didn't see at all, but I wanted to find out what his point was. "So that ridge was where you were hunting?"

"Yep. That's the place all right. Can't never forget it. Never went back there either. That's where I saw her."

Rand and I looked at each other, but he asked first. "So you think we ought to try to get in to take a look?"

"I think we should, don't you?"

"Yeah, I do." He turned back to Byers. "Wanna go with us?"

"No way, man. I'm stayin' right here."

We left him in the car with the engine and, more importantly, the air conditioner running. We tried to appear as if we belonged as we made our way up the driveway, but before we got even with the house, a uniformed officer came out of nowhere and stood between us and the backyard.

"Sorry, folks, can't go back there."

I introduced ourselves, then began explaining why it was important to me to see the actual sight.

His expression never changed. "Too bad, lady. We can't allow sightseers. This is private property. And it's a possible crime scene."

"I understand that, Officer, and I appreciate your position. But what I'm trying to say is that I have some information you could use."

"That so?" His official expression turned sour.

"Yes. I do. You see, I was the one who found the pictures of the family that disappeared twenty-three years ago. Now there's a very good chance that the bones you have in that backyard belong to a member of the same family."

He looped his right thumb through his belt and shifted weight from one foot to the other. "Are you tellin' me that you think what's goin' on here has to do with those missing people?"

"That's exactly what I'm telling you. So if you'll let us in, we can explain what we know about their identity." The officer's disposition was not improving, but I thought he might be weakening. "So can we just go around to the backyard for a minute? I promise we won't get in the way."

Before he could answer, a tall, slender man in an expensive fawn-colored suit and starched white shirt appeared from the rear of the house and walked straight toward us. The officer glanced over his shoulder and beckoned the taller man forward. "These folks wanna have a look around. They say they know somethin' about who's buried back there."

Oh god, I thought. *We're done now.* The suit, probably six-four, maybe five, with an impeccable complexion of café au lait and an imperturbable air produced a badge from his inside pocket and held it up for Rand to read.

"FBI. I'm Special Agent Alfred Mullen." Sweat beaded on his forehead, and after he put the badge back into the pocket, he loosened the striped tie around an already wet collar. "You know something about what's back there?"

"Actually, I'm the one responsible for wanting to go in," I interrupted, and he changed focus to me.

"Okay, ma'am. So you're the one who knows what's going on here. That right?"

"Agent Mullen, did you hear about the suitcase of pictures found on the Natchez Trace Parkway?"

He frowned behind the sunglasses. "Pictures?"

"Negatives, actually. I found a suitcase two days ago on the parkway, between French Camp and Kosciusko, and it had in it negatives of a family that disappeared twenty-three years ago. I took it to the ranger station, and they took it to Jackson, to the police chief." My breath grew harder to collect, as if I was trying to breathe underwater. "Mind if we move over to the shade?"

He didn't answer, but instead took off the coat, draped it casually over his shoulder, and led us into the shade of the house where we huddled in the scant respite.

I started again. "So. I found those pictures, and nobody knows how they got there. And now"—I glanced back toward the car on the street—"we've talked to a man who said he saw a body right here just a few days after the family disappeared. We think the bones in this backyard might be one of the missing people."

Agent Mullen's dark, military-style glasses reflected my own puzzled image. He said, "I think you'd better slow down because I still don't see what business you have being here."

I had to admit he had a point, especially since I might have even questioned my motives. But what I said was a repeat of what had transpired in the past two days. This time when I finished, his expression changed. He was about to answer when a voice from the back of the house called his name.

"Excuse me for a minute, folks." He left us there while the second man met him in the driveway.

They talked briefly. And when he returned, gone was the casual stance, and instead he strode purposefully toward me. "How many people were in this family?"

"Three," I told him, "the parents and a little girl about eight years old."

"Looks like you may be onto something," he finally admitted. He removed the glasses. "We found another one."

I didn't really want to see what I saw at that point. Agent Mullen escorted us to the backyard and stopped beside the idle backhoe. There on the ground, atop a heap of soil, lay bones that to my untrained eye looked human. My college anatomy was minimal, but even I could recognize what had to be the remains of someone's legs.

Sun pressed down on my head like an iron. Agent Mullen gazed down at the little heap of what had been a human being, as if trying to put them into some logical form, and I felt Rand's hand on my elbow.

"Let's get out of the sun," he suggested as he guided me into the shade of the patio.

I sank into a wrought-iron chair, still cool to the touch. "This is getting real, isn't it?"

Rand sat down beside me and, after a moment said simply, "I suspect the whole family may be buried here."

My brain whirled from the heat of the sun, but also from the possibilities. "Greenwood's nearly two hundred miles from where they disappeared. How did the killer get them all the way over here without anybody noticing?"

"I don't know," he answered quietly. "But who pays attention to a family on vacation? If somebody held a gun and made them drive here, who would know?"

"It's so sad," I said. "And to find them like this."

"Yeah, I know. Not a nice concept, is it?"

Agent Mullen came over to where we sat, towering over us. He said, "Okay, folks. I guess it's time we did some serious talking."

"About what? I've already told you everything I know." I was getting uneasy. I'd stumbled on something that had gone unnoticed for twenty-three years, and that made me a suspect somehow. "Good lord! You don't think we know anything about how they got here, do you?"

Mullen's voice remained steady. "I'm not accusing you of anything, if that's what you think. We just need to talk,"—he looked around the backyard—"somewhere else."

We followed him into town where he had set up a temporary office in the local police station. Instructed that he, too, had to be in on the conference,

Ricky grew surlier by the minute. I hoped beyond hope that this town had adopted a no-smoking policy. I didn't think I could stand another episode with Ricky's addiction.

After the heat of the afternoon, dark clouds gathered, and huge drops of rain now splattered irregularly on the heated sidewalk and created instant steam. We parked behind Mullen's car on the street, and by the time we got to the entrance to the station, individual drops had melded into a steady stream of water pouring from the sky.

I shivered as we entered the air-conditioned red brick building and looked around for a place to talk. Mullen led us to a small office where a middle-aged man in uniform laughed into a phone.

Mullen asked, "Mind if we use your office for a few minutes?" Somehow there was no hint of question in his voice.

The uniform nodded and mouthed into the phone, "Get back to you."

When he was gone, Mullen took his place behind the desk. His eyes bore into mine as he instructed, "Ms. Wilks, why don't you start at the beginning."

"Agent Mullen, I've already told you everything I know. Nothing's changed."

"Okay. But let's just do it one more time, if you don't mind. Sometimes people leave out things that may prove important later. Relax and tell me exactly what happened."

Relax, yeah, right. I started the story again, this time including every detail that I thought might have some significance. I wanted to find these people, but more importantly, I wanted to find out what happened to them. But something else had changed inside me. Now, more than anything, I wanted to bring their killers to justice.

My part of the story thus far was uncomplicated, and Mullen listened without interruption. But as I brought my actions up to the present, something stirred in my own consciousness, something that I began to suspect might have direct bearing on finding the mysterious killer.

"Agent Mullen," I asked, "do you think it would be possible for us to have copies of the pictures I found?"

"What do you want them for?"

I shook my head, trying to figure out exactly what I did want with them. When I answered, it was the truth, as I knew it. "Agent Mullen, all I can tell you is that I feel some sort of responsibility for those people. After all, for whatever reason, I was the one to find the first evidence in twenty-three years. And if, for some other mysterious reason, I'm supposed to help find the killer or killers, then I'm going to need those pictures."

I could practically hear my internal clock ticking as he stared at me from behind the desk. Then without a word, he picked up the phone. "Chief Loden please. Agent Mullen calling. I need to speak to him right away."

Rand and I were more than happy to deposit Ricky safely back into his environs, but probably not nearly so happy as he was to learn that he was not a suspect in the case. At least not yet. Then, anxious to see the photos, we picked up our belongings at the motel and headed back toward Jackson. Mullen had assured us that we'd have copies by morning, but neither of us really wanted to wait. Any time spent on the road might take us closer to finding the killers.

Nighttime on the highway lends a sort of coziness to people trapped in a vehicle, sort of as if visitors to a foreign planet had to stick together. We began to talk like old friends, at least the friends we were rapidly becoming. I told Rand about my efforts to break into the writing business and that I'd enjoyed a modicum of success, particularly in getting this latest assignment on the Natchez Trace. But I went on to admit that I felt certain now that I'd found my real interest—people. Places are great, but people are where the real stories lie.

He listened quietly, leaning against the headrest and staring ahead into the darkened highway. Finally, he agreed, "You're right. People are the most important. That's what Shelley always said."

He must have heard my unspoken question because he glanced at me and added, "I'm sorry. Shelley was my wife. You feel like a friend already, and I kinda forgot you didn't know her."

"Thanks. I take that as a compliment. And I wish I had known Shelley." The flat countryside rolled by as it recovered from the day's heat. "Do you feel like talking about your family?"

"Sure. I love to talk about them." He ran a hand through his hair. "Shelley was my high school sweetheart. I wanted to marry her when I graduated from high school, but she was still a junior, and our parents blew a gasket. So we waited till I graduated from college for the official day. What our parents never knew, though, was that we got married during my junior year at State and kept it a secret. When the big church wedding happened two years later, we made it official."

I could hear the smile in his voice across the darkness. He continued. "Oh, we made it a celebration all right. We got married a week before Christmas and finished it off with a balloon ride over the Mississippi."

"Wow! That's some way to start a marriage—official or otherwise."

"Yep. That's how Shelley was. All or nothing. After all that waiting, we figured we may as well start a family right away, and apparently Noelle was conceived on Christmas Day. That's why we called her Noelle."

"I love that story," I said, meaning it. Then I waited. I wanted to ask what happened to Shelley, but I was afraid to intrude into such an intimate area. He saved me from having to ask.

"We were married for nearly seven years when she died."

"I'm sorry, Rand. Marriages like yours shouldn't have to end that way."

"Thanks." He faced the window, then lay back against the headrest again. "You're right, but they do. Like I told you, Shelley was just that kind of person—all or nothing. She could have never endured a long, boring life, but I don't think it ever seriously entered her mind that she could get killed doing something she loved."

He tried to appear casual, but the pain was still there. "She always loved the water. We all did, but especially Shelley. So for her thirtieth birthday, she talked me into taking us all on a diving trip to Mexico. Ever been there?"

"Cancun, Cozumel?"

"Yep, Cozumel."

"Once. It's gorgeous."

"We thought so too. Anyway, we were diving with some real pros. No way the accident should've happened, but it did. She wanted to go down for one last dive for the day. I was tired, and she wanted me to stay on the boat with Noelle anyway, so I did. But something happened down there. I'll never know exactly what, but something scared her, and she came straight to the top. When she did, she hit her head on the prop. It was just a fluke. If we'd been able to get her help at a hospital here, she would've made it fine. But their hospital was too far away, and by the time we got her there, they couldn't do anything except watch her die. It was the most horrible day of my life, and Noelle was right there, going through it all too."

I didn't know what to say, so I mumbled something about how sorry I was. He nodded as if he'd heard it all a thousand times, then closed his eyes. By the time we reached the outskirts of Jackson, he was snoring gently. I hated to wake him, but I had to ask where he wanted me to go.

SIX

One fifteen in the morning, and Jackson's Police Headquarters was as alive as it had been on my previous visit. Apparently criminals don't take nights off. It was also apparent that rank has privilege because Chief Loden was nowhere in sight.

However, good to his promise, he had left the pictures with a young woman on duty in his office. When I produced identification, she handed over a sealed manila envelope. I thanked her and immediately sat down in the chair across from her. I couldn't wait any longer.

"Something else I can do for you?" she asked.

"No. Mind if I sit here for a minute?"

She shook her head and turned back to the computer. "Take as much time as you need."

My hands felt clammy in spite of the cold air that blew over me with a vengeance. Rand sat down beside me and watched as I tore open the envelope. The picture on top was the one I'd first seen, but it was much clearer now. Technology, I guessed. I handed it over to Rand and went on through the stack until I got to the one where someone held on to Lauren's hand. Technology had done wonders there too.

Rand leaned over to look at the picture still in my hands. "What the hell?" he mumbled. "Where's the rest of the person?"

I couldn't believe it either. Everything else in the picture was as clear as a mountain stream. A hand, obviously that of a man, held tightly on to Lauren's. I could even see muscles protruding above the strong wrist, continuing up to where the elbow should have been. Then there was nothing. It was as if the rest of the person had simply disappeared. "Do you think it's her father?" I asked, handing the picture to Rand.

He held it close and shook his head. "No way. Look," he tilted the picture my way. "See that tattoo?"

I pushed my glasses up on my nose and zeroed in for a closer look. "Yeah, it does look like a tattoo. Did Danny have one?"

"Not that I'm aware of. And I looked at plenty of pictures. Besides, Danny was tall and blond. Look at that arm. Whoever it belongs to is stocky, dark. It can't be the same person."

The air conditioner still pumped furiously, but even it couldn't account for the cold shiver that coursed through my body. "Rand, do you think we're looking at the killer's arm?"

"I don't know," he mumbled. He shook his head and pulled the picture closer to his face. "But I'll say this much. It's definitely not Danny and definitely not Everette."

Neither of us had much to say as we made our way back to the car parked beside the police building. But my brain whirred with possibilities. When we got back into town, Rand had asked me to drive him to pick up his car, so he drove now, and I rode with him. And I had plenty of time to think. I had a million questions, none of which I had answers to at the moment. How do you take a photo of part of a person? Why would anybody take a picture of a hostage-taker, if indeed that's what had happened? And even more disturbing for me, how did the suitcase get in the middle of the road in the first place?

The clock was pushing three when he returned me to my car, and I felt every minute of it. I did my best to thank him for his help, already wondering where the nearest motel might be in a mostly residential neighborhood when he laid a hand innocently on my shoulder.

"Reagan, it's too late for you to go looking for a motel. Why don't you follow me home? I've got three perfectly good bedrooms, and the neighbors aren't nosey."

I was more than a little surprised, and I shook my head. "No, but thanks. You've done too much already."

"Aw, come on. I promise to be a perfect gentleman."

I had to laugh at that one. "I'm not worried about your behavior," I chuckled, "just your sleep, or lack of it."

"Believe me, you won't interfere with my sleep. Nobody's ever been able to do that. So how about it?"

I had to admit it made sense, and I also had to admit I welcomed being around this man. Not only did he make me feel secure, but he also stirred up some feelings that I wasn't ready to admit even to myself.

"That's sweet of you," I admitted. "You lead, I'll follow."

Home proved to be not far from his office in a pretty, but unpretentious neighborhood that sat up on a hill overlooking an entrance to the parkway itself. The house, a contemporary two-story with blue-gray clapboard siding, had its own hill, away from the street and at the back of a circular drive. I gladly followed him to the guestroom upstairs and, within fifteen minutes, collapsed onto a marvelous feather mattress that covered the old iron bed in that room. I must have slept the sleep of the dead because when I finally opened my eyes, sunlight had created an outline around the shutters at both windows, and the pale yellow curtains seemed to shimmer around them.

For the first time since arriving, I took a good look around the room. From the handmade quilt draped across the foot of the bed to the antique dresser with its three-sectioned mirror, the feminine influence was apparent everywhere. I just didn't know whose feminine influence yet.

I dressed and made a few perfunctory stabs at makeup, then went downstairs as quietly as possible. Rand already sat at the kitchen table, a newspaper and coffee mug set out before him. Sunlight streamed in through a stained-glass pattern set in the middle of three full windows behind him and cast rose hues over the gleaming white tiles of the table.

"Good morning," I said, trying to sound as if I woke up in other men's houses all the time.

"Morning yourself." He grinned and held up his own mug. "Coffee?"

I gladly accepted and sat down at the table, waiting while he poured me a share. "Black, please." I watched him return with my cup and added, "That's a wonderful bed you've got up there. I slept like a baby."

Again he grinned, as if he knew a secret that I was about to figure out.

"What?" I asked.

"Oh, nothing. I just always thought that expression is kinda funny. I only had one baby, and I sure hope you slept better than she did."

I laughed at my own naivete. "I guess the person who started that never had a sleepless baby."

"Guess not," he admitted. "Well, anyway, I'm glad you slept well."

"Thanks. Did you?"

He nodded, obviously a bit embarrassed himself. "Well, now that we've got that out of the way, I've had an idea about the picture."

"Oh?"

"Yeah, I think so. Do you have them upstairs?"

"Yes, I do." I jumped up from the table, intent on retrieving them from the guestroom, but he beat me to the punch.

"If you don't mind, I'll get them for you."

"Sure. They're on the dresser."

He returned with the pictures and set them out on the table in front of us. Then he did something strange. He began shuffling the pictures from left to right. "Now take a look," he suggested.

I leaned over the pictures and looked for what he apparently saw that I didn't. "What am I missing, Rand?"

He said, "Look at the little girl in each picture. Do you see any differences?"

Again I studied the pictures. In each one, her hair flowed freely. In each one, her little sundress was the same boldly flowered pattern. Then I looked again at the last picture, the one with the mysterious hand, and I saw it. What I had thought was part of the flowers on her dress was something else entirely.

"My god, Rand! Is that what I think it is?"

"I think so."

Now the blood stood out like an evil sign. And the smile that had been present in the other pictures was replaced with a grimace of pain. How could I have missed it?

"How could anybody do this to a little girl?" I asked. "And the worst part is that they must have made her watch."

"I know, I know." He shook his head. "Reagan, I've been in this business a long time, and I've never been able to answer questions like this one. The best I can tell you is that evil exists for its own sake. And whoever did this is evil. Pure and simple."

I felt as if someone had punched me in the gut. I guess up to that point, I hadn't thought about the real horror involved in this little girl's death. But the blood on the dress made it real.

I picked up the picture again. "Rand, who took this?"

He lowered his head and stared at the newspaper in front of him as he answered softly. "I don't know. Maybe there was another one."

"Another one?" The idea proved more and more repulsive. "They took pictures for each other?"

"Could be. They do that sometimes."

I wanted to scream, to rant, and I wanted to throw things. But I did none of those things. Instead, tears fell down my face, and I was incapable of stopping them.

A veteran of women's emotions, he waited for me to regain control. He didn't pat me on the hand and tell me it was okay because he knew it wasn't. I even think he wanted to cry too. Finally, he said simply, "I've got an idea."

"I'd sure like to hear it."

"I've been thinking about that tattoo, and I'm pretty sure I've seen it before."

I blew my nose one more time and waited for him to continue. "You have?"

"I'm sure of it. I think it's some kind of military deal. Tattoos are really common now, but this one's different. It's not the kind you see all the time." He reached for the picture and laid it in front of me, pointing to the arm. "Look, right there."

He placed the magnifying glass over the picture, and I could see an image forming. "I see what you mean. It looks like words on top of the flag. What do you think it means?"

"I'm not sure, but I'll bet I can find out. I've got an old buddy who spent a lot of time in Nam. If anybody knows, Mike will."

Mike Fondren spent the better part of his life as a Marine, and he'd had enough. Although the Piney Woods Country Life School was not intended to serve as a retreat for world-weary adults, what Mike brought to it from his decades of experience more than compensated for the solace its isolation offered him in return. Seeing these troubled kids break their cycles of failure did much to exorcise his ghosts, and Mike Fondren loved his teaching job with the same passion he'd given to the Marines.

On the forty-five-minute drive down, Rand shared what he knew about the school. It was founded in 1909 by Dr. Laurence Jones, who came to Mississippi with small change in his pocket and an idea about how to help poor, rural black children. When some local men caught him teaching classes under a cedar tree, they were ready to lynch the good Dr. Jones for preaching against whites. However, when they discovered what he was really doing, they not only sent him away with good wishes, but they also contributed to the building of a school for his purposes.

Since that time, the school has been the subject of several national television specials and the recipient of fund-raisers by some of Hollywood's greatest. The result is that children from Mississippi, along with inner-city children from around the country, have had a taste of old-time values and country living.

As impressive as the history behind the school might be, nothing could have adequately prepared me for the beauty and simplicity of life in that place. We turned off busy Highway 49 onto an entrance flanked on both sides by enormous pines and stopped at a small wooden guard post hardly deserving the moniker. A kindly gentleman in a brown and tan uniform stepped out of his tiny office to greet us.

"We'd like to see Mike Fondren," Rand said after the men exchanged pleasantries. "He's an old friend of mine, but he's not expecting us. Hope that's all right."

The guard smiled knowingly. "I'm sure that'll be just fine. I know how Mr. Fondren don't like to take calls on the phone."

Rand shared the private joke, and the guard continued, "You should find him up there in the first building at the top o' the hill, to your left." He looked at his wrist, then added, "He outta be 'bout through with his classes now."

"Great then. We'll just drive on up if you don't mind."

"Visitors are always welcome here. That'd be just fine. Enjoy your stay." And he backed away from the car and watched us as we drove uphill toward the school.

The road took us past a small oval lake down a hill on our right surrounded by well-tended grounds covered in grass so green I could feel its coolness. Graceful oaks draped over the lake's edge against a backdrop of the school's namesake pines towering toward heaven. This was the kind of place I could spend a very long time.

When we entered the small congregation of buildings that compromise the school and dormitories, simple white signs with black lettering appeared at odd intervals. "A soft answer turneth away wrath." One Bible verse after the other reminded students of the values of hard work and adherence to godly principles. This was not like any school I'd ever seen.

I was reading the last sign when Rand came to a stop. "There he is," he said and pointed toward a whitewashed building.

The building was old, built almost entirely of native stone, and it reminded me of somebody's grandmother's house. Well-worn but loved. And the man coming down the stairs belonged there.

He was not what I'd expected from Rand's stories of valor. Probably a little shorter than average, this man still walked with all the pride of a lifetime Marine. He took the stairs with shoulders squared and head upright, although he held on to the railing at his side. His silver hair shone in the sunlight. A slight paunch preceded him as he moved down the stairs, but he moved with the grace of a much younger person.

Rand rolled down his window. "Mike Fondren! Wait up!"

The silver head turned our way, and as recognition dawned, a slow smile spread from his eyes to the rest of his face. "Well, I'll be a son of a gun," he said, grinning as he walked toward our car. "Would you look at what's come home to roost?"

Rand got out of the car, and the two men embraced, patting each other affectionately on the back. Mike then looked past Rand to me, waiting in the car, and Rand followed his gaze. "Mike, I brought a friend to meet you."

I got out and walked around the car to offer my own hand. Mike's eyes glimmered with fun as introductions were made. "I'm very glad to meet you, Reagan," he said sincerely. "Lord knows, this boy needs all the help he can get."

Rand dropped his chin onto his chest, yet his dimples deepened into a wide grin. "It's true, Mike. You always knew me. But you're actually the one we came to for help."

"Help? Sure. But what can a retired Marine possibly do to help the big-city investigator?"

"Mike, we've got a picture we'd like for you to take a look at. I think you may be able to identify something really important."

The fun in the man's face turned serious, and he glanced toward the lake. "Let's take a little walk. Shall we?"

The three of us followed the stone pathway down to the lake's edge where a concrete bench secluded from passers-by awaited us. Mike waited until Rand and I had made ourselves comfortable before he took the third spot.

"Sure is pretty down here, isn't it?" He sighed deeply and looked out over the water. "I believe this is my favorite spot on earth."

"I can see why," I readily admitted.

"This is what all that fightin' was about," he said. "Always is. Somebody wants to take away what we got in this country, and we can't ever let that happen."

"I agree," Rand admitted. "I guess there always have been greedy people who want it all. Always will be."

Mike's eyes lit up. "Well, they'll have to step over this old man to get it."

"Thank God for people like you," I added.

"So. What's this about a picture?"

Rand placed the picture in Mike's hands, and he held it close to his face, peering at the strange juxtaposition of ghost and reality. He looked questioningly at Rand, who then handed him a second photo, a blow-up he'd had made that morning. The arm, although still vague, was plainer.

Instantly, Mike's face registered recognition. "You want me to tell you about the tattoo, don't you?"

"Exactly." Rand nodded. "I knew you'd know."

"'Course, I know. No Malice. That's the code name they used."

"Who were they?" Rand asked.

Mike leaned back and crossed his arms over his chest. "Bunch a renegades in Nam. They were latecomers to the fight. Didn't start up until about the last year or so we were there, but they were something else."

"How's that?"

Mike shook his head and tried to explain. "I guess you might call them vigilantes. They weren't afraid of anything, especially the Vietcong. Said they wouldn't quit till the whole lot of 'em was snuffed out. So when we tucked tail and came home, some of 'em took off. I think it was eight of 'em hid out. Never could figure out what they thought they were gonna do all by themselves when the combined United States Military Forces couldn't defeat the bastards."

"What happened to them?" Rand asked.

"I heard all but two eventually showed up back in the States, wantin' their back pay and all."

"That probably didn't float too well, did it?"

Mike smiled at Rand's suggestion and studied the picture again. "So where'd this picture come from, if I may ask?"

"Oh, you can certainly ask," I said. "That's why we're here." I briefly explained how I'd come by the pictures and what had happened since then.

He listened intently and his expression changed as understanding sank in. "So you think the person in that picture killed this Weir family?"

"It looks that way."

Once again the man's shoulders squared, and his chin jutted forward. "Well, I'll be damned. I knew they were bad asses, but I sure didn't think they would kill their own."

"So you think it's possible that one of them got back and did this?" I asked.

"Anything's possible. But there's not a doubt in my mind about that tattoo. No Malice. I'd know that anywhere."

SEVEN

We spent a couple of hours with Mike while he and Rand revisited times past. When he retired from the Marines, Mike found out about the Piney Woods school from another buddy, and he wanted to teach those kids the good things he knew about this world. The school, too, was very much interested in what Mike had to offer; but as is always the case in the twenty-first century, there had to be a background check. And there was one little thing Mike didn't want to share.

Mike had been married to a beautiful woman from his own home state of Kansas. Four children and twenty-eight years later, Mike came home from his last duty in Afghanistan to find Doris not alone. Shock and anger were too much for Mike, and he exploded.

The other man said Mike threw the first punch. Mike knew otherwise, but by the time the police got there, it didn't matter. If Mike's record had shown an arrest for assault, his job at the Piney Woods would have gone down the tubes. When faced with Mike's solemn avowal, Rand decided on the course of discretion. He told me, "If it had been rape or child molestation, I wouldn't have blinked an eye. But in this case, who could blame him, even if he did throw the first punch?"

I had to agree, especially since I'd met Mike. After spending a couple of years in New York and having had my share of experiences with egotistical men, I'd come to expect the hair at the back of my neck to prickle around the bad ones. Mike had just the opposite effect. I felt good around the man, and that told me he was okay. Listening to my gut keeps me out of trouble.

At any rate, we now had something to go on. We made it back to Rand's house before dark, tired but invigorated mentally. Both of us wanted to get going on the search for the missing vigilantes. Either of them could be our guy, possibly even both, but I doubted that. It just didn't feel right that two men could escape Vietnam, then slip back into the country unnoticed and go on a killing spree. One mind might fall into that absurd darkness, but both at the same time defied too many odds.

Mike had given us a description of the kind of people we were looking for, but he himself didn't have any names. Rand asked for them, but Mike's answer had been firm. Even if he had access to those names, to divulge them could land him in jail. And he hadn't put his life on the line all those years to go to jail now. We understood and accepted it as such. Still, names would have made our job so much easier.

On the way back into town, Rand suggested takeouts for dinner, but my stomach demanded something homier.

"Look, I know you may not believe this, but I'm actually something of an eat-at-home girl. Mind if we buy some groceries and cook? I'll do it all."

He looked at me as if I'd spoken a foreign language. "I didn't figure you for the Betty Crocker type," he laughed.

"I'm not. But it's good therapy. Besides, I haven't had a home-cooked meal in nearly two weeks."

"Then cook you shall. Who am I to argue with a woman who wants to cook?"

We couldn't help laughing at the image of ourselves, only a few days ago total strangers now shopping for groceries. In my past, that step had always come far later—when it was too late to back out gracefully. Now we had this cart way before the horse, but I liked the way it felt. Friends first. I think that's what my therapist kept saying.

Dinner would be simple. Chicken enchiladas, salad, and ice cream with fruit; but I had a few tricks to make them special. While I prepared my simple fiesta, Rand offered to do some searching on the Internet, which sounded like a good idea. For one reason, I needed the breathing room in somebody else's kitchen. Secondly, I still hoped he might find something.

So I wasn't really surprised when he came into the kitchen holding sheets that he'd copied from his search. "I found some stuff about these guys," he began telling me as he sat down at the bar.

"Oh yeah? What?"

"Well, for one thing, there are three of them unaccounted for, not two."

"Great," I moaned.

"It gets better."

"I can hardly wait."

He looked up at me and turned his head to the side, sniffing. "Something smells great. What is that?"

"Basic stuff," I admitted. "Come on. What'd you find?"

He shook his head and looked back at the papers. "Well, it seems that everything about this group went underground once we got out of Nam. No names, no families. Nothing. Like they never existed."

"Why would the military cover up their existence?"

"That's a really good question. You know, as a detective, I have access to some pretty good online information, but I couldn't find a thing."

"In that case, how will we ever get a name?"

"I haven't figured that out yet. But I will." He got up and walked to the stove, opened the door and peeked inside. "Aha! You remembered."

I grinned at the compliment. True enough I had remembered that he ordered enchiladas, but what he didn't know was that these, with cream cheese and tomatillo sauce was something I'd concocted a while ago. They were my own favorite, but he'd just have to go on thinking I did it for him.

We spent that night and the following day looking for something, anything on the group that called itself No Malice. Eventually, we moved to his office in town where he had access to more than a single computer. Rand's secretary, a tiny gray-haired meticulous woman who probably arranged her spices at home alphabetically and could find a can of peas in the dark, returned to field his calls, freeing us to continue our search.

And search we did, but after two days, it still appeared that the group simply ceased to exist when our involvement in Vietnam came to an end. Either that or somebody higher up, much higher up, had decided that they were part of a very bad image and wanted to erase any memories of them.

That would have been believable except for one thing. These men all had families of some sort. They had friends. And if one of them had gone off the deep end and killed a whole family, what was there to keep him from doing it again? Somebody had to know something.

I opted to cook once again, but this time Rand insisted on firing up his famous grill. I certainly had no objections to grilled filet mignon. I sat on the patio with him taking in the last of the day's beauty while he tended to our dinner. He had made my favorite vodka and tonic with lemon, and I sipped at it, trying to make it last without making me drunk first. I watched him standing in front of his grill, wearing a bright yellow apron with chili peppers scattered across the front, his pleasure in the duty apparent. I didn't want to spoil the moment, but I had to tell him something. "Rand, I've made a decision."

He lifted the hood one more time to peek at his charges, then lowered it and came to sit on the other side of the little round table. He picked up his own elixir of bourbon and cola and asked, "So what's your decision? You're going to let me cook all the time?"

I laughed at his attempt to avoid the serious. "No. But that's a good idea." I took another slug of the drink and started over.

"Actually, what I've decided is that if we don't find some clue by tomorrow, I've got to call it quits. This assignment won't wait forever, and we're getting nowhere."

He sipped silently, watching me all the while. When he finally spoke, his voice betrayed no emotion one way or the other. "If you think that's what you need to do, I understand."

"Thanks for understanding, Rand. This opportunity's too good to let it pass me by."

"What else can I say?"

To my surprise, he stood up then and lifted the lid on the grill once again. Apparently satisfied that they were fine, he turned back around to the table and sat down. Still not looking at me, he started talking again. But this time his voice reminded me of velvet rippling beneath my fingers, gentle and familiar. Gone was the impersonal note I'd heard only seconds before.

"Reagan, I won't lie. I've loved having you around these past few days. But I do understand. You have a life to live, and you can't hang around forever hoping to find some clue that may not even exist." He set the glass down and tried to smile at me. "I don't blame you. I'd do the same thing."

I didn't know what to say. Until that minute, my perception had been that he was the one helping me. It had never occurred to me that maybe I was doing something for him too. There had never been so much as the brush of a hand to indicate that he thought of me in any way but as a partner or a friend. Had I read him right?

Not sure how to respond, I just said, "Thanks, Rand. Thanks for understanding."

That night sleep evaded me like the answers on a math test. It's always been that way when I'm avoiding something. But that night, I wasn't sure what I was avoiding. Was it my writing project? Surely enough in itself. Or was it something else—like my feelings for Rand?

Every time I thought about how I'd felt when he registered no complaints about my leaving, I wanted to kick myself. Why didn't I say something like *I'll be back in town in about a week*? No, not me. Always the truthful Reagan, I made it sound as if I was walking out of his life, never to look back.

Even on a feather mattress, I can flop and turn over only so many times, so I finally gave up and got out of bed about four. When the tiny television in the room offered nothing interesting, I changed into a pair of jeans and tee shirt and crept down the stairs as quietly as possible. Rand's bedroom was just off the kitchen, but I figured if I closed his door gently, he'd be none the wiser. I could make some coffee and look through our meager information one more time before he got up. Maybe I could find some clue that we'd missed before.

I slipped through the darkened kitchen and gently pulled his door shut, but before I could move away from it, he called out, "Reagan?"

I opened the door a crack and whispered across the darkened room. "Yes, it's me. Sorry, now go back to sleep." And I pushed the door to once again. A second time he called my name.

"Don't close it. I'm awake." I could see him sit up, then swing his legs off the side of the bed.

"I'll make some coffee," I suggested and turned back toward the counter.

"Mind coming in here for a minute first?" he asked, motioning for me to sit beside him.

My heart fluttered like a schoolgirl with a crush. I quietly entered his private domain and sat down on the side of the bed next to him. As my eyes adjusted to the darkness, I could see that he wore only pajama bottoms and that his bare arms revealed muscles like those of a swimmer.

"Reagan," he said, taking my hand into his, "I think we should have a talk."

"About what?" I asked stupidly.

In spite of his grogginess, he smiled. "About us."

I was glad for the darkness because I could feel my ears burning like they always do at the most inopportune moments. "Us?"

This time he laughed easily. "I may be an idiot, but I think you feel the same way I do—that is, if you're not opposed to being with an old man."

"If I knew one, I might be," I responded. But before I could get anything else out, his hand slipped around the back of my neck, pulling me toward him, and he kissed me the way I hadn't been kissed in a very long time. The way I'd always dreamed about being kissed.

My pulse went wild, and for once my mouth couldn't get me into trouble. I kissed him back, and his arms enveloped me as he pulled me toward his body. I was dizzy, falling, and we collapsed into the warmth of his bed.

By the time I finally made it to the kitchen for coffee, sunlight poured in through the row of kitchen windows, and the stop and start of the city's sanitation department truck could be heard as it made its way up the street.

Rand insisted on making breakfast while I sat at the bar drinking coffee. It was definitely true that our lovemaking gave a very different slant to my leaving, but it didn't change the fact that we still had no clue about the Weirs' killer or where the mysterious person might be, if indeed he was still alive. And it didn't change the fact that I still had an assignment to finish.

At that point, I had to have a plan, and ours was simple. I would finish my project, get the story in to the editor, and then we'd pick up the pieces—both of the Weir case and of our newly found life together. As we sat there at his kitchen table sharing breakfast, I knew that I'd never felt anything so right before. And judging by the way his eyes met mine, I thought he must feel the same. I wasn't exactly looking forward to leaving, but I also knew that he had work to do as well.

After breakfast, I'd be back on the trace and, with any luck, could finish my project within a week. Then when I returned to Jackson, we'd have more time to talk. And lots more time to think.

I put the last of my things into the suitcase when I heard a second voice downstairs, one instantly familiar. Rand and Mike looked up from the conversation when I entered the living room.

"I hope that'll help you," Mike finished.

"Mike, what a surprise," I began.

I reached out to take his hand, but Mike's arms went around me in a now familiar hug. "Good to see you," I told him sincerely. "What brings you into town?"

"Good to see you too." He grinned at Rand, who held on to a medium-size manila envelope. "You're prettier than he is. Besides, I found some information you two might be able to use, and I didn't want to put it in the mail."

"I think you'll like this," Rand said and held the envelope out to me.

I took it and removed several sheets of paper filled with information copied from someone's computer. By the time I got to the third name, I realized what I was looking at. "Is this what I think it is?"

Rand nodded. "Those are the names of everybody associated with No Malice. And look at the last two."

My eyes went to the bottom of the page. "These are still unaccounted for, aren't they?"

"As far as I know."

I read aloud, "Glenn Paul Brister. Harold Wayne Brutkiewicz." My heart raced as I read the last words. "And Brister's from Mississippi."

"Narrows our search, doesn't it?"

"I'll say. But, Mike, where did you get this?"

Mike's lips formed a thin straight line across his mouth, and he shook his head slowly from side to side.

Rand spoke for him. "He can't say, Reagan. He's called in favors, but he'll be in real trouble if this source gets out. It's our secret now."

"I don't have a problem with that," I admitted readily. "But, Mike, are you sure you're okay with this?"

His eyes told me that he'd thought long and hard about his decision. They also told me how very much he wanted to help. "My secret's safe with you."

"I don't know what to say."

"You don't have to say anything. Just find some justice for the Weirs, will you? They deserve it."

"I'll do my best," I admitted, looking at Rand. "This is the break we've been waiting for, isn't it?"

"Apparently so. Soon as you're finished with the project, we'll get on it."

My mind raced with anticipation. "How far is it to Tupelo?"

"Reagan, twenty-three years have passed. Nobody's going anywhere in the next few days."

"I know. I know that. But I don't think I can concentrate until we at least go up there and talk to some people. See if this guy's still in town. Then we can call the police, the FBI, anybody you want. But think about it. If we call the authorities now, he may spook and take off."

Mike, who'd been watching the exchange with mild amusement, chuckled softly.

"I've got the laptop," I continued, trying to salve my own conscience. "I can work on the way up while you drive."

Rand's sigh filled the room. "Just do what you've gotta do, Reagan," he told me. "We'll leave when you're ready."

EIGHT

The parkway is still the shortest distance from Jackson to Tupelo, although probably not the quickest. A speed limit of fifty-five and troopers enthusiastic about enforcing it make the going slow, but after all, I was still on assignment. As a result, Rand offered to drive while I took notes on my laptop as we inched northward. By the time we got to Tupelo, I had a good head start on my article.

The cloudless blue sky of a few days ago had turned ugly, and thunderstorms were moving in from the west with low-flying black clouds that hung over Tupelo like evil threats. The air conditioner in Rand's car pumped out cold air, but ubiquitous humidity turned it into a steady stream of vapor as it exited the vents. I was beginning to see what they meant about summer in Mississippi.

Rand suggested that we'd stop first at a local convenience store and just start asking questions. My job was once again to tackle the local phone book for any listings of Bristers or Brutkiewiczs. Tupelo is still a small enough city that what we couldn't find in the book surely we could find if we asked enough questions. Somebody had to know something. Somebody had to be willing to talk.

Standing outside the convenience store, though, I began to think that maybe Rand had the better assignment. The approaching storm had yet to cool anything down, and the hot air stuck to me like flypaper. I picked up what was left of the listings and thumbed through to the *B*s. My hopes mounted when I found two Bristers. Neither had a first name beginning with a *G*, but I copied the information anyway.

Then I thumbed down to *Bru*. There was nothing remotely resembling that name, but at least we had one lead.

Rand returned shortly, and I could tell that he hadn't had much luck. "Anything?" I asked.

"Nope. Nobody in there ever heard the name. How 'bout you?"

"Found two Bristers. Neither is Glenn, but I copied the addresses."

"Way to go!"

I handed the short list to him, and he reached into the side compartment of his door and took out a map, which he unfolded across the steering wheel. "Here it is," he said, turning the map over. "Tupelo." He studied the small insert of the city, then looked over his shoulder to a street sign that demarcated an intersection. "That should be Choctaw back there. If I'm reading this correctly, that road will take us to the first house."

"Think we should call ahead?"

"Unhun. We don't want anybody to get spooked and run before we get a chance to talk to them."

I watched in amazement as he adroitly drove across a totally unfamiliar town and, before long, turned into a recently built subdivision. Houses on both sides of the narrow street faced each other with a bland sameness. It was a neat, newer neighborhood, and the houses demonstrated a pride of ownership. Given a few years and a few sad stories, however, it would start. Then bland would give way to ugly.

We followed the entranceway to a cul-de-sac that rose slightly from the other houses, giving the short street a bit more personality, but still it lacked something. As we parked on the street in front of 109, I knew what it was. This had no doubt been someone's cow pasture or cotton field in a former life, and trees had yet to grow here. In a land where trees far outnumber people, these houses looked sadly out of place.

Rand rang the doorbell, and inside a small dog answered with a series of high-pitched yelps. We waited several seconds before he tried again. This time, the door cracked open, and a teenage face peered at us through a narrow slit. Behind him a tiny white dog bounced and yelped excitedly.

"Yeah? Can I help you?" A skinny youth in a black tee shirt stared back at us without a hint of real inquisitiveness. Behind him, the little white spotted dog had quit bouncing and sneaked toward the doorway as it eyed us cautiously. A television set blared somewhere within the house, and my olfactory caught the reason for the boy's caution. A layer of smoke filtered into the foyer from the adjoining room. And it didn't smell like ordinary smoke.

"We're looking for someone," Rand began. "This is the Brister residence, isn't it?"

The kid nodded blankly. "What Brister you lookin' for?"

"Glenn Brister. Is this the right house?"

Brown hair that was long overdue on washing moved slightly when he shook his head. "Nope. Wrong place."

"Do you know Glenn Brister?"

"Nope. Never heard of him."

"Well, thanks anyway," Rand added. He started to leave, then turned back quickly toward the boy. "Oh, may I ask what your father's name is?"

The boy stared back for a second, an answer implicit on his lips. "You can ask, but I won't tell you," the boy snarled, and the lock clicked as the door shut once again.

We were back in the car, and Rand glanced over his shoulder as we left the cul-de-sac. "Kid knew something, didn't he?"

"I thought so. Maybe he was just scared of strangers."

"Could be. Maybe he's scared of why we were asking. That wasn't ordinary cigarette smoke, was it?"

"I caught that too." He smiled. "At any rate, let's see if we can get to the second one before this kid makes a phone call."

The second house proved to be more difficult to find. It was out of the city, on a county highway, and quite a different story from the bland little neighborhood that we'd just left. The older house stood off the highway by a good hundred yards and was covered in asbestos siding that had no doubt replaced wood half a century before. It looked as if it hadn't been washed in about that long. Blue hydrangeas nearly covered a row of windows across the front, a strong testament to their hardiness.

Behind the house, an empty barn with gaping holes in its roof leaned tiredly to the right, where a few chickens pecked about in what had once been a corral.

"Lovely place," I muttered as we turned onto the circular gravel drive.

Rand's cheek twitched in a near smile, and he parked as close to the house as we could get without taking the drive to the back.

"Wonder if anybody still lives here."

"Pretty sad, isn't it?"

"Yeah," he agreed as he got out of the car. "Why don't you stay put, and I'll go check?"

I didn't object and watched him climb the dirty brick steps and begin knocking on the door. When no one answered, he looked back toward me in the car and shrugged. He was about to knock again when the door opened. From the car, I couldn't see much, but the voice sounded friendly.

Rand motioned me forward, and I joined him on the stoop while he explained that we were looking for a particular Brister. The tiny woman's face was lined with decades of sun and work, and I suspected sorrow.

"You folks come on in. It's too hot to stand out here on the porch." She held open an oak door smudged with fingerprints that had long ago worn away all traces of varnish and led us into her living room. Everywhere, fake paneling loomed darker than the storm clouds that gathered outside.

She pointed us to a sofa covered in moss-green velvet with raised pattern of swirls that reminded me of huge lily pads. Then she stopped in front of the old television long enough to silence its fuzzy picture and returned to her chair, a darker, more worn version of the sofa. "Now, that's better," she said, satisfied. "TV's nice, but I'd rather talk to people. I don't get much company, you know."

"I understand," Rand said. "And we really appreciate your seeing us. As I said, we're looking for someone with your same name, and we thought you might be able to tell us where to find him."

She steadied her gaze at Rand. "I see." Her words created soft clicking sounds from her teeth, something like tiny raindrops on a tin roof. "Well, I know most everybody 'round these parts, so maybe I can help you."

"I hope so. We're looking for Glenn Brister. Do you know him?"

The eyes turned away, and her chin puckered. "Glenn was my son," she said thinly.

"Oh. I see." Rand gave her a moment, then continued. "Mrs. Brister, I hate to ask this question, but is your son still alive?"

A shaking hand covered her mouth, and her weary eyes filled with tears. "I don't know. I just don't know."

I went to her chair and, stooping beside her, said, "We're so sorry, Mrs. Brister. We didn't mean to cause you any pain." I held out my hand, and she accepted it in her own frail ones. "We wouldn't ask if it wasn't really important. Do you mind telling us what happened to him?"

"Honey," she said, "he went off to fight for his country in Vietnam, and that's the last I ever saw of him."

"You mean he's missing in action?"

Again the tears formed, and she shook her head as if not understanding her own words. "The war ended. Everybody came home. Least wise those that didn't get killed. But my Glenn never came home. Those two army men that came to see me said he was supposed to be on a plane coming home, but he didn't show up." Her hand left mine and reached for a tissue stuffed in her pocket. "I never knew what happened to my son. All I had was my daughter-in-law and my little granddaughter. But they're gone too."

"Gone?" Rand asked.

Her gray head bobbed as she told yet another awful story. "Killed. Shot to death by some monster. He came into their house and killed those precious two people, sure as a hunter'd go out and kill a deer. Just like that."

Rand's face expressed the shock I was feeling, but he kept talking. "Mrs. Brister, did they ever find out who killed your family?"

"No, son, they didn't." She tried to smile, probably still in disbelief after all those years. "They even tried to blame it on Glenn." Then she turned innocent eyes up to Rand. "How could he have done anything so awful? He loved his family."

"I'm sure he did," Rand agreed.

I remained kneeling on the floor beside her chair. I didn't know what to say, and I had no idea how to alleviate the pain this woman felt. All I could do was what I would want somebody to do if the tables were reversed.

"Mrs. Brister, would you mind if I asked you one more question?"

She smiled bravely. "No, honey. You go right ahead."

Rand watched me, too, waiting. "Mrs. Brister, do you have a picture of your son that we could see?"

A smile peeked out through the tears, and she rose from her chair and took several shaky steps toward the mantel. Then she took down a tarnished silver frame and handed me the treasure.

The frame held a faded photo of a young man in the khaki uniform of the army's rank-and-file. His hair had been cut in the customary burr, and his smile held all the cockiness of the young and bulletproof.

"I have some others," she added, turning back to the mantel. "That's the best one of him, but I've got others of the whole family."

One by one, she handed over her treasures to me, and I passed them on to Rand, who held them until we'd seen the entire lot.

"You had a lovely family," I told the woman sincerely. "I'm so sorry about what happened to them. Nobody deserves that kind of pain."

Rand returned the pictures to their place of prominence and added, "Mrs. Brister, I'm going to be honest with you."

Her eyes widened.

"It's very true that we came here to find out if you know where your son might be, but we also had another motive."

"Don't tell me that you two think he killed his family too."

"No. That's not what we're saying," Rand explained. "We just wanted to talk to him about another matter."

"Another matter?"

He sighed, searching for the right words. "We found a picture, Mrs. Brister. One with your son in it."

The gray eyes went from Rand to me. "A picture of my Glenn?"

"Mrs. Brister, do you remember a family that disappeared on the Natchez Trace Parkway over twenty years ago?" I asked.

First she shook her head slowly, then she stopped. "Why, yes. Yes, I do remember something about that. Why?"

"The picture we found had a part of your son in it, but it also had the little girl that disappeared. We wondered if maybe Glenn knew that family somehow."

"What was their name?" she asked tremulously.

"Weir. Danny and Stephanie Weir. Their little girl was Lauren. Did you know them?"

Again she shook her head. Pursing her lips, she added, "I wish I could help, but I don't know them. I don't think Glenn did either."

"Well, it was a thought," Rand said gently. "We really appreciate your help anyway, Mrs. Brister."

"Are you two trying to solve what happened to that nice family?"

"Yes, we are," I answered for us both. "I'm writing about the Natchez Trace Parkway, and Rand is a private investigator. He was working on the case when it happened."

"I sure hope you find them," she said. "Everybody deserves to have answers."

NINE

We left Mrs. Brister standing in the doorway of her home, fully aware that the quiet would envelop her the minute we drove away. But there was nothing else we could do for her, and we certainly didn't need to hang around while she thought of other questions to ask about her son.

I watched Rand at the wheel, and I wondered what he was thinking about and tried to come up with a plan myself. We'd left Jackson with the intent of being away for a few days, and we intended to make use of our time in that part of the state. But the news that Glenn's family had been murdered put a different slant on our thinking.

I asked, "You think anybody in town would still be able to tell us about the Bristers' murder?"

"Something that big, somebody's sure to remember. Even if the people who worked the case are retired, somebody's got to be around. Don't you think?"

"You're the expert here. Do you think they'll talk to us?"

"Only one way to find out."

The Tupelo Police Department—a sixties-style, two-story building made of dirty blond brick—took up most of a downtown block and accounted for most of the activity as far as I could see. I followed Rand through a set of heavy glass doors and on to a desk situated in the center of the room, marked Information.

A tired-looking woman with ebony skin and too many pounds to fit comfortably into the uniform studied her computer screen, while long red fingernails clicked away noisily at the keyboard. Finally she stopped. "Can I help you?"

Rand held his identification out. "I'm Rand McArdle, and this is my partner, Reagan Wilks. We'd like to speak with somebody about an old case."

The woman's eyes floated across his identification, then turned back to his face, vaguely interested. "How old?"

"Twenty-three years."

She sighed heavily and picked up the phone. "Jack, somebody up here wants to talk to you."

After a brief silence, she said into the phone, "Some old case. Since you're the oldest thing around, I called you."

She couldn't hide the tiny smile as she lowered the phone and asked us to have a seat. "Detective Stafford will be out in a minute."

We hadn't even had time to settle into the barrel-shaped wooden chairs that lined the wall when Stafford appeared, glancing at the woman behind the desk as he made his way toward us. He was tall, but his sixty or more years had given him a forward bent that took off a couple of inches. The mass of white hair compensated to a degree, and he still loomed an impressive figure. In his youth, he must have been a giant of a man, but the painful gait told me he'd lost more in the process than height.

Stafford stopped a few feet from us and peered over the thick glasses perched halfway down his nose. "I understand you folks are looking for somebody old," he said with a smile.

Rand grinned back. "Actually, we didn't ask about an old person, just an old case."

"Well then, I reckon I'll have to do since I qualify on both counts. Come on back here to my office."

He led us through a narrow hallway lined on either side with dark wood paneling to the rear of the building where three offices, each with half glass fronts, faced a common hallway. His office was the middle one.

"Now, what can I do for you?" he asked as he settled his large frame behind the desk.

Rand introduced us and began telling our story. He told how I found a suitcase with pictures of the Weirs and that we'd just come from talking with Glenn's mother. By the time he got to the part about the Brister family's murder, we had Stafford's undivided attention. He sat forward and propped his elbows on the desk. "So you think there's a connection between the Bristers' murder and the Weirs'?"

"Yeah, we do," Rand admitted.

"You think Glenn Brister committed all of those murders?"

"I don't know," Rand said, "but we've got something in a picture that might corroborate that theory." Then he took out the photo with little Lauren and the hand grasping hers. Stafford pushed the glasses up on his nose and drew the picture closer. "Where's the rest of the picture?"

"We don't know," I answered truthfully. "That's part of the mystery."

"Huh," he grunted. "Kinda hard to tell anything about him with this little bit, but it could be Glenn. If memory serves, he was a stocky sort, just like this fella."

"Actually," Rand took over, "we're pretty sure it is Glenn. See that tattoo?"

Stafford held the picture up again.

"He got that in Vietnam. Only a handful of men had that tattoo, and all of them are accounted for now except Glenn and one other. The other man was from Michigan, so we doubt he's the one we're looking for."

"I see your point."

Finally Jack tore his eyes away from the photo to gaze back at us over the glasses. "So you wanna know what clues we found that could have made Glenn the murderer of his own family?"

"Yeah, I guess that's what we're asking. We know his mother's had all one person can stand, but the coincidence is too much to ignore."

Jack set his glasses on the desk and wiped his eyes with a worn handkerchief. "I guess you're right. Believe me, I remember this case like it was yesterday. You don't ever forget this kind of stuff. It's still open, but we don't have the manpower to follow up any more."

"I'll bet not," Rand admitted. "Was there anything that pointed directly to Glenn?"

"Of course, his fingerprints were all over the place. After all, the man used to live there. Apart from those, most of it was circumstantial—like motive."

"Oh? What motive would he have had for killing his own family?"

"Well, you see, Glenn was gone for a long time. And the last year or so, nobody had heard a word from him, including his wife Nancy. You really couldn't blame her."

"She remarried?" I asked.

Nodding, Stafford continued, "Nice fellow from the community. Even went to high school with Glenn. From what we could gather, the army said Glenn had escaped into the countryside rather than come home when he got the order, so I guess Nancy thought he didn't want any part of her any more. She was an attractive young woman. She had a life to live. Who could blame her?"

"You think an ex-husband might though?" Rand asked.

"Blame her?"

"Yeah. Makes a good motive for murder, doesn't it?"

"I've seen less do it." Stafford returned the glasses. "Who knows what goes through somebody's mind?"

"No kidding," Rand agreed. "But could Glenn have shown up in his hometown without anybody's recognizing him? Wouldn't neighbors, friends see something?"

"Couldn't figure that one out either. Not then, not now. During the investigation, we talked to everybody we could figure knew Glenn at all, and not a single one of 'em had seen him. Least that's what they all claimed."

"Do you think somebody was lying to cover for him?"

"Coulda been," Stafford said and leaned back, his swivel chair creaking in protest. "He had a cousin in town that might have known something, but he wasn't talking. We didn't have anything on the man, so all we could do was ask questions."

Rand glanced at me. "I think we may have visited the cousin's house today."

Stafford's brows raised. "Yeah?"

"In that new subdivision off Choctaw."

"That'd be the one. Did he talk to you?"

"Apparently the only person home was a teenage boy who was more concerned about hiding his smoke break than anything else."

Stafford smiled tiredly in response. "Yeah, I guess the kid's following Dad's instructions."

"Yeah. Guess so," Rand agreed. "But there's something else I don't understand. Why would a man who'd not seen his family for over three years *want* to remain unnoticed? Why would he even bother to go home if he didn't want anybody seeing him?"

"Now that's the question, isn't it? Never did understand that one."

Something else had been bothering me about Glenn's willful disappearance the entire time, and I asked, "What about his military pay? Did his wife get something when he didn't return? Wouldn't Glenn want that money he'd earned?"

"She got checks for a year or so," Stafford explained, "but after a while, they stopped. When the military finally decided to classify him as a deserter, the pay stopped."

I was still trying to digest that information when a new thought hit me. "What about the new husband? Where was he when the murder happened?"

"That was my first question," Stafford admitted. "But believe me, he had an airtight alibi. He was on a plane headed to Chicago. I picked him up at the airport on his return. There was no way he could have faked the reaction I witnessed."

"Was there anybody else in town who'd want to kill the wife?" Rand asked. "Maybe the little girl just saw too much."

"We tried that angle. But we're talking about a housewife who, as far as we could find, didn't have an enemy in the world. First-grade room mother for the child's school. Drove the carpool. You name it. We couldn't find even a suggestion of an affair." He sighed loudly. "No evidence of anything missing from the house. Credit card still in her purse."

"Was she molested?" I asked, not really wanting to know.

He shook his head. "No, and that's part of the strangeness of it all. In a case like this, when there's nothing taken, it's almost always a case of rape gone bad. But this was different. Somebody just wanted her dead."

"Shot?" Rand asked.

"Yep. Clean through the heart. No sign of struggle either. That's another sign. Must've been somebody she knew."

"Sounds to me like somebody went insane," I suggested. "Who else could kill a little girl?" Thinking of the little girl made me feel sick at heart. "Why would anybody do something so reprehensible unless he was mentally ill?"

"Or pure evil," Rand added. "Let's hope he was mentally ill."

"The bastards usually are," Stafford said. "They usually are."

Rand and I thanked Jack Stafford for his time and returned to our car, both of us quiet as we got into the stifling automobile. While we had been inside talking to Jack Stafford, a cloudburst soaked the city around us and had created a steam bath that rose from the pavement in billows.

"Where to now?" Rand asked.

The sky had begun to fade around the edges, and I felt the same way. "I'm not sure, but I need time to think."

"How about some dinner while we think?"

I agreed, and we headed to one of those generic restaurants found in every town. We were nearly finished when the idea came to me. "Rand, we may be tackling this from the wrong angle."

"Whadda you mean?"

"Well, we've spent all day talking to people about Glenn and his family's murder. But what started all this was the Weir's murder."

"Agreed. We're trying to make a connection. What are you driving at?"

"Do you remember that little grocery store in French Camp where the Weirs stopped the day they disappeared?"

"Sure. I talked to the owner myself."

My exhaustion was lifting with the idea. "Did he tell you anything usable?"

"Just that they had been in the store that day—the same as he told everybody else. Why?"

"Can we go back and talk to him one more time? Maybe after all these years, he'll remember some little tidbit. So many people asking questions, maybe he didn't elaborate for fear of being implicated. Not much chance of that now."

Rand reached across the table for my hand. His face showed the tiredness I myself felt, but there was more. There was real concern. "You wanna go tonight?"

I had to admit he had a point. "I guess it can wait till tomorrow, can't it?"

He nodded and reached for the check. "Not too many places to sleep in French Camp except in somebody's home."

The chain motel we chose still had none of the charm I'd imagined when I set out from Nashville, but then nothing else on this assignment had followed expectations either. I hadn't expected to find pictures of a murdered family. I hadn't expected to chase a phantom all over the state. And I certainly hadn't expected to fall for a man nearly twenty years my senior.

We entered the dark room, and as I turned to flip on the switch beside the door, Rand kissed the back of my neck. Tiny shivers of electricity edged down my arms, and I turned around to meet his kisses with my own. My heart raced as we edged toward the bed that would be ours for the night.

After the loving, we lay facing each other, talking quietly. I kissed his chest and drew in the fresh scent of soap and my own perfume. I said, "You know, this wasn't part of my plan."

He lifted my chin and kissed me softly. "Are you sorry?"

"Only sorry I didn't meet you sooner."

I pushed my body closer to his and lay still, listening to the hum of the air conditioner. I suspected he was dozing off, and there was something I wanted to tell him before I lost my nerve. "You awake?" I finally asked.

His tiny jump told me he wasn't, but he answered that he was.

"I need to tell you something," I said. I sat up and propped my pillow against the headboard, then pulled the sheet up around my chest.

He rolled onto his back, grinning. "Let me guess. You're a werewolf."

"That'd be werewolfess," I corrected. "No, I'm afraid this one's a bit more serious."

"Then I am too," he said and propped his pillow beside mine. "What is it you need to tell me?"

"Rand, I took this job for a couple of reasons. It's true that this is a wonderful opportunity. But there's more to it."

His eyes softened, and he leaned over to kiss me lightly as he waited for me to continue.

"Do you remember my telling you that I spent two years in New York?"

"Sure."

"I was working for a magazine, the fortunate protégé of none other than Ray Williams. Do you know who he is?"

"Yeah, sure. I've read some of his stuff. Didn't he win the Pulitzer Prize for covering some Caribbean revolution or something?"

"Grenada," I nodded. I watched for the customary reaction, but none was forthcoming. Rand was waiting for me to finish my story. "As I said, I was his protégé, but I also became involved with him. Very involved."

The next part was more difficult, and I couldn't look at him. "I was going to have his baby."

Seconds ticked by before he asked, "What happened to change that?"

"It's not what you think," I explained. "I'd never do that." I could feel his eyes on me, but I couldn't look back. "We were going to get married. I'd already told my folks about it, and we'd started making plans. But I couldn't live in New York, especially with a baby. There was no way I was going to bring up my little girl in New York."

"You knew it was a girl?"

"Yes. I'd just seen the first pictures. I was going to name her Laura—you know, after the Lara in Dr. Zhivago, even though I spelled it differently. I guess that was a silly romantic notion of mine, but I thought she was so beautiful."

Thank goodness he didn't laugh. "I don't think that's silly at all. We all want our children to be special."

"Thanks for that." I started again. "Rand, I can't tell you how happy I was. But Ray wouldn't talk about leaving the city. Every time I brought up the subject, he'd get furious and say I was being silly."

"So what happened?"

"We had a huge fight. I told him I was leaving town. I wanted to go home, back to the South where I could think."

"And he let you go?"

"I didn't give him much choice. I should never have left so angry and hurt. I know that now, but I couldn't think. I wanted out of there, and I wanted away from him."

I stopped to collect myself and the tears returned—tears I thought had long ago dried up forever. I had trouble finding my voice over the huge knot in my throat, but I had to finish my story.

"But I didn't get very far. I was on the outskirts of Philly when I came across a wreck that had just happened. There was a car in the middle of the road, and I jerked the wheel to avoid it. My car skidded off the road and flipped down an embankment. That's all I remember until the next day when I learned about the baby."

"You lost her," he said softly, and he pulled me toward him and held me close. Softly, he repeated, "I'm sorry, Reagan. So sorry."

And I cried once again for the little girl I'd never get to know, never see grow up. I had to find what happened to little Lauren. For her sake, for Laura's, and for mine.

TEN

French Camp is really nothing more than a dot on the map, and the store where the Weirs had stopped on the fateful day didn't even exist anymore. But with the name that Rand had taken from his records and a little luck, we might still talk to its owner. Like I said, we needed some luck, due some actually.

We stopped first at the log cabin housing the gift shop for the French Camp Academy, a school founded in the late nineteenth century for children from the most remote, poverty-stricken areas of the state. I'd visited the school on my way down the trace and had even had lunch in the tiny café that helps support it. Inside the shop, the pleasant young woman I'd spent an hour or so talking with on my previous stop recognized me.

"Back so soon?" she asked with a curious smile.

"Yes. Told you I'd be back."

"So how's your story going?"

"Great," I lied. "I knew it would."

"That's good. I'm glad you're enjoying your trip through Mississippi."

"Oh, I am, believe me. But, Trish, I'm looking for a different kind of information today."

"Oh? Well, how can I help?" she asked, glancing over my shoulder to Rand.

"We're looking for the man who used to run a little grocery store here twenty or so years ago. Would you know who that is?"

"Of course. Everybody knows Mr. Purvis. He used to be mayor too. The store's been closed for, hmm, five years or so, but he still lives not too far from here."

"So you can tell us how to get to his house?" I asked hopefully.

"Sure. No problem. But it's pretty far out."

"That's okay. We'd really like to talk to him. Think you might give him a call and ask if we could pay him a visit?"

Her smile widened at the inclusion. "Sure. Be glad to."

She repeated our names to Jimmy Purvis, louder the second time. Although they apparently meant nothing to him, he agreed to see us. When she put down the phone, she added, "I'll draw you some directions. It's a little bit hard to find if you don't know where you're going."

Armed with her hand-drawn map of twisting roads and markers of wooden fence posts and big oak trees, we headed out to talk to Jimmy Purvis. Each mile led us deeper into countryside green to the skies. The sun had returned with a vengeance, and our air conditioner barely kept up. With each turn of the road, the pavement narrowed more until it stopped altogether as it crested a hill. Before us lay a gravel road that dead-ended in the front yard of a farm sprawling across the valley.

The huge cedar house stood on a rise in the middle of rich pastureland surrounded by trees that provided protection from the heat. Trisha told us that Purvis had also run a dairy farm until a few years before when his health dictated he sell the cows and take it easy. True to the profession, the barn behind the house occupied twice as much space as its human counterpart, and that was considerable. I could imagine what this place must have looked like a couple of decades ago, with the constant activity of farm hands and animals being tended. Now its emptiness only mocked its size.

As we approached the house, the front door opened, and a tall man emerged. In his faded jeans and denim work shirt, he projected a powerful image. Not fat, he was still big and, I'm sure in his day, a force to be reckoned with. But age had softened features, giving him a kinder aura, more like that of a Santa Claus minus the beard.

"I reckon you'd be the people Trish called about," he said as he took my hand in his grip. "Welcome to my little farm."

His face was tanned and weathered, and what remained of his thick hair circled his crown like a peppery wreath of snow. Jimmy may have aged, but the blue eyes were still alive with humor and determination.

Rand and I made introductions and accepted the invitation into his home. As my own eyes adjusted to the cool darkness, I could feel others on me—glassy stares stilled long ago by a hunter's good aim.

A stone fireplace at the far end of the room served as a backdrop for yet more animals. On the right side of the hearth, a bobcat crouched next to a beautiful red fox; on the left, a coyote howled up at an imaginary moon. My heart ached for them, but I turned attention to our host.

"What beautiful animals," I conceded.

"That they are," he agreed.

I was familiar with the Bible verse that served as the rationale for hunting. God gave man dominion over all the animals of the earth, but did he intend for us to kill them, I wondered.

Aloud, I said, "Mr. Purvis, thank you for seeing us. We really appreciate it."

"Glad to have the company. My wife's gone into Kosciusko today. Otherwise, she'd be here to offer you cake or something. Can I get you a cold drink at least?"

We declined, and he led us to a pair of tan leather sofas facing each other across a glass top coffee table supported by two huge gnarled tree trunks.

Purvis sank into the other sofa. "You know, son, you look kinda familiar to me. Have we met before?"

"You've got a very good memory, Mr. Purvis. Or did you remember my name?"

He chuckled and admitted, "Little bit o' both, I suppose. You're that detective that came to see me way back when the Weir family disappeared, aren't you?"

"That's me," Rand admitted. "Like I said, you've got a good memory."

"So does this visit have anything to do with those folks?"

Rand sat forward and leaned in our host's direction. "Mr. Purvis, this may be a wild shot, but we believe we have something that you might help us with." He turned to me. "Why don't you tell him about it, Reagan?"

I replayed the incident with the pictures yet again, then went on to include the skeletons uncovered in Greenwood. Purvis's concentration was complete as I led up to the present.

"So you think if I tell my part one more time, you might hear or see the thing that'll solve the whole mystery. Am I right?"

"Mr. Purvis, Rand told you we're playing a wild card. But it's the only one we have."

"Well then, let's play the hand we've been dealt."

I thanked him, and Purvis began his story again. He told us that he remembered this family in particular because of their obvious attachment for each other and for the beauty of the little girl. He even told us what items they had purchased on that fateful day. A loaf of bread, sandwich meat, chips, drinks, and those little round chocolate cakes. He said, "The chocolate was for the little girl."

"I think it's a gender thing," I offered lamely.

"Must be. My daughter's always been the same way. Anyway, that's all I can tell you 'bout that poor family. Only other person not from around here that day was a soldier."

Rand's head jerked up at the word as I know mine did. "Soldier?"

"Yeah. Came in not too long after the Weirs."

Rand's confusion and excitement were obvious. "You never mentioned a soldier before."

"Truth of the matter was, I didn't think of it till everybody'd gone, and I couldn't see where it had anything to do with the Weirs. He was travelin' alone, far as I could tell."

"Was he wearing a uniform?"

"Naw. Nothing like that. Only way I knew he was a soldier was what he said. He bought himself a Coke and a little pack of crackers, and when he was payin', I made a mistake in his change. I apologized, and he answered, 'No malice, man. No malice.' That's how I knew he was a soldier."

"But how did you know that phrase?" I asked.

Purvis didn't answer immediately, but when he did, his eyes had clouded with unmistakable grief. "My son Tommy told me about a group of guys over there that had the same phrase as their motto. No Malice. Tommy said it meant that they were tryin' to do nothing but good over there. You know, no harm to anybody, just free those people from the Communists so they could live their lives the way they wanted to. The way they'd always done. Tommy really took a liking to the Vietnamese people, and with all the bad press goin' on back home, he figured these guys could use all the support they could get."

It suddenly made sense. "Mr. Purvis, is your son living in the States?"

His eyes searched mine for understanding. "I still can't believe it. Tommy made it through thirteen months in Nam. Even won medals for savin' a couple of buddies. And then he got killed on the highway two months later, not a hundred miles from this house."

"I'm so sorry," Rand and I both told him, "So sorry." I waited before I continued, but I had to know. "Mr. Purvis, I hate to ask anything else about such a painful subject, but this is really important if we're ever going to find the killer."

The genial host returned, along with his composure. "That's all right. If it'll help find a murderer, I'm glad to talk. What is it?"

"Was Tommy still alive when the soldier came into your store?"

"No. How'd you know that?"

"Just a thought," I admitted. "I figured that if Tommy was still alive, you would've probably asked the man how he knew that phrase. And asked if he knew your son. You know how it is. When a loved one is far away, any stranger that's met him suddenly becomes a friend. But if Tommy was gone, you may not have wanted to open up that subject with a stranger. It would have been too painful." I watched my words hit their mark and added, "That soldier came home, but yours didn't."

Purvis nodded in agreement, and I continued, "I know this is painful, Mr. Purvis, but how long had your Tommy been gone when this soldier came into your store?"

"A little over a year. I remember because his mother and I had been to the cemetery a couple a days before. To put fresh flowers on the marker." He looked at me again for understanding. "You know how it is."

"Yes, yes, I do," I answered. "I think we all do."

Rand added, "That means Brister had enough time to get back to the States. Glenn Brister could've been the soldier in your store that day, Mr. Purvis. He could be the murderer."

"Mr. Purvis," I continued, "did you notice any tattoos the man might have had?"

"No. I didn't see anything, but I really wasn't looking. When he said that about no malice, I kinda blocked out everything else." He sighed heavily, then went on. "I wanted to ask him about Tommy. Believe me, I was aching to ask him about Tommy. But when he said that, it was all I could do to give the man his change."

"We understand," Rand told him. "Anybody who knew about the group would've been shocked to hear that phrase. And with your own grief so fresh, I'd have done the same thing."

"Thanks," he said quietly as he sat staring at the work-hardened hands in his lap. "Thanks for that."

We thanked Purvis profusely for his help and promised to keep him informed of our progress. Here was another person who'd suffered silently for many years over the fate of the Weirs. Only this man's suffering had been guilt. Undeserved, but guilt nonetheless. Of all people, I know something about that.

ELEVEN

Sunshine was slowly losing its battle with night as we headed south on the parkway toward Jackson and home as I was rapidly coming to know it. We'd decided that there was nothing else to be done in that part of the state for the moment, and Rand's access to Internet databases in his office might turn up a clue as to Brister's whereabouts, particularly if he still lived in the state of Mississippi.

Already we were approaching the spot where I'd found the suitcase, where it all began. We passed it once on the way up, but as longer shadows now fell across the trace, an uncertain dread rose in my throat. What was there about that spot?

On the trip up, Rand had slowed the car to give me time to look around. Satisfied that no ghosts lurked in the roadside swamp, we had a good laugh and continued on our way. This time, however, he wasn't slowing. I'm not even sure if his mind was on our location, but for whatever reason, I was alert. So when I saw her, I instantly knew why.

The little girl in a flowered sundress was alone at the very edge of the woods, not far from the picnic tables. Nearly engulfed in shadows, her pale hair still glimmered as though sunlight washed over her head, and she held something in her hand, something that she held out to me as we passed by.

I screamed for Rand to stop. He stepped instantly on the brakes.

"What? What is it?"

"Turn around. We've got to go back."

He slowed to turn the car around in the wide exit, then headed back in the opposite direction before he asked, "Why are we going back?" His eyes darted continuously back to me.

"I saw a little girl. Please, Rand. Turn in there at the picnic area."

"A little girl?"

"Yes. That's what I said."

"What little girl?"

"I don't know, just keep going, will you?"

The car crunched onto the gravel and finally came to a stop near a pair of concrete tables in a clearing. I got out of the car, aware that I was shivering in spite of the heat. Rand soon joined me and put his arm around my shoulder. He didn't say a word, but I could tell what he thought. I was losing it.

"Rand, I saw her. I know I did."

His grasp tightened and he asked, "Who did you see, Reagan?"

"Lauren."

"Lauren?"

"Yes. I saw her. I know it was her." I pulled away and headed toward the woods where little Lauren had stood. He followed, calling softly after me, "Reagan, it's almost dark. Are you sure it wasn't a mirage?"

I didn't answer, but stepped into the thick undergrowth. I pushed back tiny limbs that blocked my path and made my way deeper into the woods. Darkness there was nearly complete, and I couldn't see more than a few feet ahead of me. The thickness of the trees threatened to take what air I had left in my lungs, and only sounds of animals disturbed by my presence broke the stillness. I swatted at a wisp of what I hoped was moss touching my cheek and took another step.

"Reagan! Come on back!"

A bird flushed from the grass and skittered close by my head in its escape.

"Come out of there. There's nobody there."

I turned. I could see only his outline in the semidarkness at the edge of the woods. What was I doing? Something pulled me farther into the woods, but the voice behind me urged me back.

I started making my way back toward his outline, but only when I could touch his face, feel his very real presence, could I find the words. "I saw Lauren. I know I did."

"Okay, Reagan, I believe you." He put his arms around me, and I shivered violently. The tears I'd held in for days found release, and he held me closer.

"I believe you," he repeated softly. "You've been thinking about her for so long, it's only natural that you thought you saw her."

I pulled back and looked into his doubting eyes. "But I did see her. How can that be? Am I going crazy?"

"No, you're a long way from crazy. People do stuff like that all the time when they're under pressure."

"You believe me, don't you?"

"Yes, Reagan. I believe that you saw what you thought was Lauren. You wanted to see her so badly that you actually did. And as long as you know that's what happened, it's okay."

"So you do think I'm nuts."

"That's not what I'm saying, and you know it," he said, drawing back.

I took a deep breath and backed away myself. "I know you're right. I didn't mean to take your head off."

"No apologies necessary," he answered softly. "But it's really dark out here, and I think we should leave." He turned toward the parkway as lights from an approaching car came nearer. "Probably not a real good idea to be out here alone in the dark."

I agreed. It was getting to me too. I turned to follow him to the car, but as I did, something else caught my eye, and I said, "Wait a minute, Rand."

He stopped, and I crunched across the gravel toward the table. I couldn't really identify the object until I held it in my hand, but I knew instinctively what it was. I held the still-moist purple iris to my face and drew in its freshness.

TWELVE

I held on to the flower all the way back to Jackson. Neither of us wanted to talk much, I guess because neither of us could begin to explain what had happened. The one thing I did tell him was that this flower was most special to me and that only someone who knew me could have possibly known that.

Later, as we entered town, I was still searching for possible explanations. I knew all the while that there was no real one, at least in the way I'd always thought of that word. Lauren was reaching out for someone, and for whatever reason, I was her choice. I had to think that my Laura had told her I'd be a good one. But then I'd never really believed in ghosts or the possibility of communicating with the dead.

Probably Rand was going through a similar litany in his own head because he was inordinately quiet as we pulled into his driveway. Days before, I'd abandoned my bed in the upstairs guestroom, and all I wanted at the moment was to fall into Rand's. We'd sort out some meaning the next day.

But as we entered the house, that was not yet to be. I'd turned off my cell phone somewhere in Tupelo, and I knew it was time to check for messages. Sure enough, the box was brimming with them. Katie's was first on the list.

Katie, my editor, was known for her fiery temper, although I'd never been the recipient—until now. Her first message was stern. I was to call her back immediately. The second became more imperative, and the third made my blood run cold. I had an ultimatum. Either I produced the promised story within the week, or I would have to look for employment elsewhere, and she promised I'd need a lot of luck doing that.

Katie could, indeed, ruin me. My face no doubt blanched. Rand pretended not to watch, but when I turned off the phone, he said, "That bad, huh?"

"Oh, you could say that. I'm about to lose a job and a career at the same time."

"Then we need to do something to keep those from happening, don't we?"

"I've had this day of reckoning coming, I guess. Mind if I use your office tomorrow?"

I was up early the following morning, hard at work, but each time I stopped writing, my mind flashed to the roadside and a little girl who'd left me a flower. It was unnerving, but before long, something else started to happen. I had begun writing about the history of the Natchez Trace. Created by bands of rough and rowdy river men collectively called Kaintucks, the trace served for years as the main route from south to north. With enterprising boldness, these river men loaded flatboats with goods and floated down the Mississippi to Natchez or New Orleans, where they would sell the goods as well as the lumber from the flatboats. The return trip, by necessity on foot, soon carved out what we know as the Natchez Trace.

Besieged by breath-sucking heat and humidity, this terrain also offered up an assortment of bandits, savages, and various other discards from polite society, always on the lookout for unsuspecting victims. What neither the river men nor those awaiting them could have possibly imagined is what the trace has become today, a bountiful portion of pristine America unmarred by advertising and Indy speed limits.

Those who want to attempt a re-creation of life along the trace need only to visit Mount Locust, near the entrance outside Natchez. This house, belonging to the same family since its construction in the late eighteenth century, is the last of fifty inns that once dotted the trace. There, for a small sum, travelers could sleep on corn shuck mattresses in dormitory style and have a hot meal before resuming their journeys.

I finished that section of the story and sat staring at the computer screen. Then words began to flow through my fingertips. Words that talked about a Mississippi few people know, much less care about. Words about a family that disappeared long ago from the trace, drawing an entire state together in a futile, but never-ending search.

I had set out to write about a place, but I had found it to be so much more. For the people of this state, the Natchez Trace is a bond, not unlike the one that brings people back to the ocean. It keeps them intact, a people apart, but united.

By late afternoon, I'd nearly finished the piece. I was tired to the bone and ready for company. Rand had secreted himself at his office for most of the day to catch up on the ton of work that had accumulated in his absence. Now I wanted to share my article with him, but more importantly, we needed to share some thoughts.

Nothing further had been said about my sighting, but the subject was still there, silently waiting in the wings. This relationship we'd begun was so far based on solid truth, and I didn't want that to change.

I waited until we'd had dinner. We poured out two glasses of dessert wine and took them onto the patio where a soft breeze stirred. He asked how my article was going and seemed genuinely surprised when I said that it was probably finished.

"I'll need to sleep on it tonight and give it one more going-through in the morning, but I think it's ready," I told him. Then I broached the subject I really wanted to talk about. "Rand, I think we need to talk."

"I figured that was coming," he said, winking as he smiled at me.

"Yeah, well, we've been nothing but honest with each other so far, so I don't see any reason to change now. Do you?"

"Not at all." He reached out for my hand. "So what's this deep subject you want to talk about?"

"For one thing, I want to make sure you don't think I'm some kind of nut."

"Never did," he said blankly. "Let's face it, Reagan. You've had some real changes in your life during the last few days." Then he chuckled and added, "We both have."

I laughed along with him on that one. Here we were acting as if we'd known each other forever when in reality, it had been little more than a week.

"Good point," I admitted, "but you know as well as I do there's more to it than our relationship."

"Yeah. I agree."

"Rand, if it weren't for the flower, I'd say it was all my imagination. How do we account for the flower?"

"We don't." He shook his head slowly. "Your guess is as good as mine how the flower got there. But I can tell you this much. You've got some sort of connection with that little girl. And that's what we need to concentrate on."

"You mean follow my instinct?"

"Exactly. Reagan, I've never been a big believer in instinct, but I must admit you've changed my opinion. I can't account for what happened. Nobody could. All I know is that we need to follow up on your instincts."

"I'm so glad you understand that. Every time I ignore my instincts, I screw up. And when I listen to them, like when I came to you for answers—well, something good happens." I could feel my ears turning a deep pink. "So I'm determined not to screw up this time. Lauren's too important to me."

He smiled and leaned over to kiss me. Then he sat back. "Do you have any instincts about where Brister is?"

"You'll laugh."

"I doubt it. Didn't I just say I trusted your instincts?"

I knew he was right. "Well, since you asked, I think the answer's in Greenwood. Don't ask me why or how we'll find it, but I think we need to go back there."

"Then Greenwood it is," he answered. But before we could firm up our plans to make the return to Greenwood, an answer came in a form we hadn't expected. The phone's insistent ringing took Rand back into the house, and when he returned, he looked as if he himself had seen a ghost.

I watched him walk back onto the patio and return to his seat beside me. I wanted to ask, but I waited for him to volunteer.

"You're amazing," he finally said.

"Why's that?"

"That was the police in Greenwood. They found the third skeleton. I held my breath while he added, "A child. That's all they could tell for now."

Goose bumps rose on my arms as I realized how close I was again. Something was definitely directing me, and I suspected I knew what it was. FBI had discovered Lauren's remains.

Rand picked up his glass from the table and finished the last of the wine. "We'll leave in the morning. As soon as you're done with your story."

THIRTEEN

Summer had not taken a full grip on our last trip to the Delta, but this time was different. Waves of heat hovered above the cotton fields, and the skies looked ready to burst. We pulled into the city before noon and headed straight for the police station where Agent Mullen said he'd be waiting.

We found him in the same office where we'd talked to him before. He recognized us immediately and stood up to come around the desk to meet us.

"Good to see you. Sorry it has to be for this reason."

"Me too," I admitted. "But at this point, we know the family's dead. We just want to find the killer or killers."

"We're with you on that," he agreed and perched on the corner of the desk. "We've already run the DNA on the first two remains, but of course, we don't have any basis for comparison. The best the lab can tell us is that the bones belonged to a man and a woman."

"Can you compare to Everette Suttle?" Rand asked.

Mullen was already nodding in agreement. "Yep. We've got that under way. But then we found the third set of remains. That ought to give us another clue since if it is the little girl, there'll be a definite match with the parents."

"If only those bones could talk," I said more to myself than anybody else.

Mullen said, "Believe me, they will. In the meantime, I understand you two have done some talking on your own."

I glanced at Rand, and he nodded as if to give me the go-ahead. "Yeah, we've been fairly busy."

"Like to fill me in?"

I couldn't tell if the irony in his voice was real or faked, but I knew better than to try to dissuade him from this line of questioning. I told him that we'd gotten information about the tattoo in the picture and investigated it on our own, including a name that went with the tattoo.

"How'd you find about that?"

Rand explained that he had a friend in the Marines who'd done two tours in Nam, where he met a member of the group, and he remembered the tattoo.

Mullen's face registered nothing. "Do you know who these men were?"

Rand shifted in his chair. "I got one name. Brister. Glenn Brister."

Mullen couldn't hide the surprise this time. "Were you planning to share this information with us any time soon?"

"We're sharing it now. Remember we haven't had a name ourselves but a few hours."

"Have you talked to anybody about this Brister?"

I thought I could see Rand flinch a bit as he told about our trip to Tupelo and our talks with Brister's mother and with Jack Stafford.

"Well, that certainly puts new light on developments, doesn't it?"

Mullen took a seat behind the desk. As he crossed his arms over his chest, I could see the holster below his rib cage. "Anything else you two want to share with the FBI?"

I touched Rand's arm. "Let me." Mullen's face turned my way, and I told him about the soldier in Jimmy Purvis's store.

"He did what?"

I finished telling the last part, including the motto of the group of renegades. "So we think Brister may still be alive."

Rand added, "And we suspect he's living somewhere in Mississippi."

Agent Mullen looked from me to Rand, speechless for once. "I'd say you've been busy. When did you plan on letting us in on your discoveries?"

"We knew you were busy with things here," I answered. "We haven't done anything wrong, have we?"

His eyes betrayed nothing. "I hope you haven't. But you're just going to have to leave it to us from here on."

"No problem," Rand answered. "I'm afraid we don't have the resources to take it from here anyway."

I watched him from the corner of my eye as he lobbed the ball back into Mullen's court. Then I asked, "What will you do from this point?"

"We'll try to find Brister. If he's anywhere in the United States, we'll find him. Believe me, we want to talk to this man as badly as you do. If he's evaded the military, not to mention the government, all this time, I've got more than a few questions to ask him."

"Don't we all?"

I asked, "Will you let us know when you get the DNA results?"

"That shouldn't be a problem. We both know what they'll reveal, but why don't you give me a call about this time next week? And in the meanwhile, do you two promise to let the professionals handle it from here?"

I expected Rand to flinch at the comment, but he didn't. Instead, with calm reserve, he thanked Mullen for his help and promised to be in touch if we uncovered anything else. Once out the door, however, he exhaled slowly. "Gee, and all these years, I thought I was a professional."

I couldn't help laughing at the way he'd defused an insensitive comment, and I told him, "Only a true professional could have handled that insult with the aplomb that you did."

Tension drained from his face, and the dimples deepened. "Oh well, lots of those guys have control issues. Guess it comes with the job."

"Yeah, well, maybe the academy ought to spend more time teaching manners and diplomacy."

As we got back into the car, though, my thoughts had turned to Everette Suttle. He was, after all, the true victim in these recent events. He'd be asked to submit to yet another form of interrogation, knowing all the while that it would yield nothing of value to him. In his heart, he already knew his family was dead. And he already knew too well that the pain of their death would never be far away. All we might hope to offer this man was closure and a final resting place for his family's remains. I didn't know if that was a good thing or not, but it was the best we could do.

We left the city and headed back onto the highway. Neither of us had spoken about the obvious, that Lauren had beckoned me again. Neither of us had to. But as we neared the turnoff leading to the neighborhood where Lauren was found, I caught him watching for it. I know because I had been too.

"Think we ought to go out there for a minute?" I finally asked.

Without a word, he slowed the car and made the turn. We passed through the entry gate and found that, adding to the irritation of its residents, all kinds of cars bustled to and from the house. We got as close as we dared and stopped on the opposite side of the street. Nearest us in the drive, behind two other state vehicles, a large black van that had been parked at the end of the driveway started to back out, then turned onto the street toward us.

On the opposite side of the drive and parked parallel to the spot where the van had been sat a dark green pickup truck. It looked as if it had been used regularly for work, and that probably accounted for the apparent invisibility of the man who sat at the wheel. A blue and red baseball cap was pulled down low on his forehead, but something still looked familiar about the stocky build and the square shape of the face. As the van moved away from the house, the driver glanced toward us, only for a second, but in that second, I knew. The face under the cap was familiar.

In that instant of recognition, the truck roared to life. In a single motion, it backed out of the drive, turned, and took off in the opposite direction. As I screamed, "It's Brister," Rand slammed the car into gear.

We followed the green truck around the circle enveloping the wealthy, only feet behind a probable murderer. Everything happened at fast speed, leaving little room for error. One car pulling out in front of us, and we'd lose him forever. One mistake, and we'd pay dearly.

Our tires screamed in protest on curve after curve, the entrance now in sight. I strained to decipher the dirty plates on the truck as the elderly gentleman at the entrance looked on in horror, his mouth agape, then fell back into the safety of the guardhouse when the truck roared by. With a steady flow of traffic from both directions, we could do nothing more than watch.

The green truck plunged into the traffic and wove its way through nearly nonexistent openings. Rand pounded the steering wheel, and horns blared all around the intervening truck. Some vehicles swerved, and others left the road altogether. But within seconds, the green truck had powered its way out of sight.

When it was all over, Rand asked, "Did you get it?"

I nodded and reached for my pen. That license plate belonged to someone, and it wouldn't take us long to find out to whom.

FOURTEEN

The Department of Motorized Vehicles back in Jackson listed only one owner of the green truck. As unlikely as it might have seemed, we still expected to find Glenn Brister's name as that owner. People do get lost in the shuffle.

It didn't take long for the identification to come up on the screen, and we had our answer. The truck belonged to someone named Harold Brutkiewicz. "Isn't that the other missing man?" I asked.

Rand reached for the file Mike had left with us and turned to the names belonging to No Malice. Harold Brutkiewicz was the last name on the list. At the time, we hadn't paid much attention to it because his last known place of residence was somewhere in Michigan, and it seemed unlikely that somebody from that far away would murder the Brister family. But this time we took note. Harold Brutkiewicz lived in Natchez, Mississippi.

"My god, Rand. This is unbelievable. Do you think he knows?"

"That he lives in the same town with Everette Suttle?"

"What kind of a monster would want to live where the family of his victims lived?"

"I doubt he even knows who Everette Suttle is."

"You don't think he read or heard any of the news when the search was going on?"

"Whether he did or not, he probably still wouldn't connect the dots to Everette. Reagan, anybody who's kidnapped and killed an innocent family couldn't be thinking clearly. Besides, if he'd just killed his own family too, then he'd accomplished his warped purpose. Everette didn't have anything to do with that."

I had to admit he was right, but something still bothered me.

Rand closed the file and turned back to the computer. "Hold on a minute. I wanna see something." He opened the white pages and typed in the name of the town Brutkiewicz had listed as home. Three Rivers, Michigan. Then he typed in the name. Nothing came up for Harold Brutkiewicz.

"That's what I suspected," Rand said, scrolling down one more time. "Not even a Brutkiewicz there at all anymore."

"So what does it mean?"

"Probably that Harold Brutkiewicz is really Glenn Brister."

"But I mean, if this is Brister, how'd he get Brutkiewicz's identification?"

"It's fairly easy. Happens all the time. All you need is a social security number and some pertinent information. Who'd have better access than someone he'd served in the military with?"

I was stunned. Even though finding Brister alive would have been shock enough, knowing he'd also taken someone else's identity made the story all the more implausible. "So you think Brister's been living all this time under somebody else's name? Right here in the same state?"

"That's the way it looks." He punched the Start button on the printer. "Only one way to find out. That is, if you're up to it."

"We're going to Natchez?"

"Yes. Tomorrow. We've had enough for tonight." The printer finished, and Rand scooped up the papers.

"Are we going to call Mullen?" I asked.

"In time." He added the papers to Mike's folder. "Let's take a look-see first. I don't wanna risk losing him till we're sure."

I nodded agreement, and that tugging worry finally came into focus. "Rand, do you think he might go berserk again? I mean, we know what triggered him the last time, when his wife remarried, but what if something else triggers him this time?"

"I'm not an expert, Reagan, but I'd say the chances are fairly good. We just don't know what the trigger might be."

"That's why we have to find him soon, isn't it?"

"That's one good reason. And I just thought of something. Would it make you feel better if we talked to a professional who deals with people like Brister all the time?"

"Well, yes. But who?"

"There's somebody in the department I've worked with a couple of times, a real dynamo. I'll give her a call in the morning."

I could tell by the way that he spoke on the phone that this woman was a friend, but I was hardly prepared for the striking figure who strode across the restaurant to meet us. Heads turned as the petite blonde caught sight of Rand and headed toward our table.

Every bit of her frame exuded energy as the long blond ponytail swished to and fro with her purposeful gait. "Barbie, thanks for coming," he said, leaning to kiss her cheek.

"Glad to do it." She smiled. "It seems to be the only way I get to see an old friend."

"Could you leave off the adjective?"

"If you're old, then so am I, my friend. Besides," she said, flashing hazel eyes on me, "you certainly don't act old."

Rand's dimples deepened, and he draped his arm around my shoulder. "Barbie, this is Reagan Wilks. She's helping me try to make some sense out of this."

"Hi, Barbie," I said as I offered my hand to her.

Her grip was strong and personal, and her voice carried warmth along with authority. "Glad to meet you, Reagan. I'm Barbie Rodriguez."

"Rand tells me you're the best profiler in the Southeast."

"He's prejudiced," she said, "but I'll do my best. Now, who is this person you're looking for?"

He asked, "Barbie, do you remember the Weir family that disappeared from the trace back in the eighties?"

"Yes! Funny you should ask about them. There was something about them on the news this morning. Did you see it?"

Rand and I exchanged glances. Were we out of the loop?

"No, we didn't see it. Something new?" he asked.

"I was only half-listening since I was busy getting the kids out the door, but I did hear something about finding some bones up in Greenwood that are probably the Weir family's."

"Oh, yeah."

"You knew that, didn't you?" Barbie surmised.

"I guess we're a little ahead of you there. Reagan and I just happened to be in Greenwood talking with one of the original suspects when workers digging for a pool uncovered the first set of bones. Now they've found all three."

"I'm glad somebody's finally found them. The rest of their family's waited long enough for some closure." Her face clouded. "But how can I help you then?"

Rand leaned in closer. "No, no. That's not the part we need help with. We think we're on the track of the killer."

Her eyes widened. "You're on the track of a killer all by yourselves?"

"Don't worry. We're working with the feds."

"Well then, what do you need me for? They have all the resources in the world."

"But they're not you."

"That's a nice compliment, but, Rand, you've been around long enough to know what dangerous ground you're on here."

"Don't worry, we won't get too close. We just want to be sure this is our man before we call for help."

Barbie sat back, sighing. "I'm beginning to get the picture. You want me to tell you whether this person is a good candidate."

"That's part of it," I added.

"What's the other part?"

"We need to know if something might trigger another killing."

"That does seem to be the question, doesn't it? But I really can't answer it till you give me some more on this person. In the first place, what makes you think he murdered the Weirs?"

Rand looked at me for approval before he began telling our story. He told her about the suitcase with the pictures, including the missing person in one of them. Although her face registered all kinds of questions, she waited until Rand had told her about No Malice and the subsequent murder of the Bristers.

"Wow," she breathed. "I'd say you two have already had some interesting encounters with this man. So you think he's using Brutkiewicz's identity?"

"It appears that way," Rand answered. "They were both part of this No Malice bunch, so it would've been fairly easy for him to steal an identity. We have no idea what happened to the real Brutkiewicz, but what we're interested in is whether his behavior fits any particular pattern. What's he likely to do now?"

"I'm not a seer, Rand. But I can tell you that you're right on target about his having another episode. I'd almost guarantee it."

"Is there any one thing that's likely to trigger it?" I asked.

She hesitated. "I'd say it's already happened."

I answered, "The skeletons. Right?"

She nodded again. "If I'm right, this guy was a loner by high school. And then he went to Vietnam where he joined forces with another bunch of loners, who were probably self-medicating with drugs to block out the pain. At least, they were using a ton of alcohol and nicotine, all of which exacerbate someone predisposed to schizophrenia."

Rand said, "We talked to his mother, but we didn't ask about his earlier years. The poor woman's had all she can take."

"I'm sure. What I'm seeing is fairly classic symptoms. Of course, I'm flying in the dark without actually seeing the man, but it wouldn't be unusual at all for someone with his particular illness to snap under those circumstances. Most of the men called up to fight in Vietnam were just trying to live their lives. They had no desire to murder people, Asian or otherwise. So those who made it back often carried a truckload of guilt. Turned inward and left untended, that guilt sometimes exploded rather violently. So many of those men didn't necessarily believe in what they were doing over there, but they felt bound to uphold their patriotic duty. Then they came home and got spit on. It made for some real crazy cases."

"I remember," Rand agreed, "and I can sure understand."

"So let's just suppose that Brister had the makings of a mental illness already. And when he got to Nam, he eventually joined up with another group of outcasts, who excused what they were forced to do by creating their own rationale. Didn't you say that Brister avoided his flight home?"

"That's the story," Rand affirmed.

"So he misses the flight on purpose, probably in his mind, to fulfill a higher mission. When he finally gets home, he discovers his wife with another man. See how he feels betrayed all the way around?"

Rand and I could only nod. It was beginning to make horrible sense.

She continued, "My guess is that he killed his own family out of that sense of betrayal, then found another similar family and tried to make them his own. When that didn't happen, he lost it again." Her voice became almost a whisper as she concluded the cycle. "Finding the bones of that family brought it all back. He's starting to repeat the pattern."

"That's what I was afraid of," I admitted.

"Have you met this man?"

"No, we didn't meet him. We got a glimpse of him before we chased the truck, but I don't know whether he saw us or not."

"I hope not," she said. "His reasoning skills are negligible at this point, and whoever gets in his way might be in some trouble."

Rand asked, "Do you think anybody else is in trouble?"

"Anybody who reminds him of his own family."

My mind went back to something I'd seen in the folder. "Rand, didn't Brutkiewicz have a family back in Michigan?"

"Yes. Wife and two kids, I think. Why?"

"Because if the trigger sets him off again, he might think Brutkiewicz's family is his own."

Barbie nodded agreement. "Exactly. At this stage, he can't think straight. And at this point, I'd say it's a safe bet that his world is probably filled with things we can't see or hear. People like him aren't usually violent. But when violence does occur, it's almost always at home."

"And in Brister's case," I added, "he's got two homes."

FIFTEEN

We spent the rest of the afternoon searching sites to locate people and discovered that while it was easy enough to find where Brutkiewicz had lived in Three Rivers, even to determine where his children had gone to school, it was another matter entirely to locate them now.

A people search finally yielded a new address for Valerie Brutkiewicz, now Valerie Hutchison. Not long after the war ended, Harold's family moved from Three Rivers to Ann Arbor where Valerie apparently spent some time studying at the university. Then four years and a name change later, she moved to Gainesville, Florida and, subsequently after another five years, to Baton Rouge, all major university towns. Dr. Donald Hutchison, Professor of Engineering, was apparently in demand within the world of academia.

Children Natalie and Christopher were still listed as relationships, but they seemed to have dropped out of the picture some time in the early nineties. The bottom line was that we knew little about Valerie Hutchison apart from computer-generated facts. She had indeed finished her education at Ann Arbor, with a major in education. Since that time, she'd taught in several different systems, all in elementary education. For all appearances, she was still married and living in Baton Rouge. What we didn't know was whether she had any idea that a murderer might very well be stalking her for a crime she didn't even know about, much less commit.

However, we knew for sure that she had to be warned. Although Brister was unlikely to have the same easy access to computer information that had led us to Valerie, there was nothing to prevent him from hiring another unknowing investigator who did. We agreed it was time to make the call to Mullen. While we might be a step ahead of him on paper, when it came to insuring someone's safety, we couldn't compete. And Valerie deserved all the resources the agency could provide.

I left Rand working at the computer, and I went to call Mullen. He sounded a bit surprised and not totally happy when he asked, "So what have you turned up now?"

I drew a deep breath and decided on discretion. "I'd rather not say too much over the phone, but yes, we've turned up some interesting facts. Some innocent people may be in danger, and we could really use your help."

There was a silence before he answered, and when he did, his voice had assumed a faraway quality. "So you're ready to share information with us now?"

"I called you, didn't I?"

"Look, Ms. Wilks. We're not playing mystery games here. Either you want to talk or you don't, in which case, I can probably arrange something to change your mind. How does interfering with a federal investigation sound?"

"Agent Mullen, apparently you're not listening too well. I called to tell you what we've discovered. And to ask for your help. If that's a problem, perhaps I should call someone else."

"That won't be necessary," he answered crisply. "Give me an address. I'm on the way."

I didn't feel a bit better about calling in Agent Mullen, so I went back to Rand's office to check on his progress. As I stepped through the door, he motioned me toward him at the computer. "Come here and look at this."

I leaned over his shoulder and started reading about someone named Christopher Hutchison. I was halfway down the page when I realized why the name sounded familiar. Donald Hutchison had adopted Valerie's children, and they took his name.

I kept reading, and as I did, a wave of cold fear rushed over me. Of all the places on the planet that someone can live, Christopher Hutchison had chosen Natchez as his home.

"This is unreal. Do you think Brister knows?"

"Probably not. If he did, he'd have lost it a long time ago."

"Yeah, I guess you're right. But I'm still trying to figure out why Brister's living in Natchez in the first place."

"Gotta be a job."

"You'd think. I guess we'll find out when we get there."

Rand turned back to the computer. "Speaking of jobs, I found something rather interesting here about Hutchison. His last address was in Biloxi. He was there for five, nearly six years."

"So? I don't get it."

"I forget you're not as familiar with the politics of the State of Mississippi as I am." He smiled patiently and began to explain. "I guess you'd call this the age of casinos. The first ones came to Biloxi some time around '92. If memory serves, they didn't get to Natchez until four or five years later, but by then, they had a fairly well-trained force to open up in other parts of the state. The way state laws are written, they have to operate on the water, so wherever you find a large river or body of water in Mississippi, you're also likely to find a casino."

"I see. So you're wondering if he went from a casino on the coast to one in Natchez."

"Could be. At any rate, we'll look him up too when we get there." He turned back to the screen. "Oh, did you get Mullen?"

"Yeah. I got him. He's on the way."

Rand's brows raised. "Not your favorite person I take it."

"That would be a safe statement. It's not so much I don't like him as it is I don't want somebody who has no personal stake in all this telling us what to do. And he's really good at that."

"I understand your point, Reagan, but if Brister's gotten the same information we have, we'll need Mullen's help to stop another murder."

I had to agree that what Rand said made sense, but something was still tugging at me about Mullen. I wasn't sure whether it was what I perceived as arrogance or chauvinism or what. Even though my gut is usually right, I also knew we didn't have time to deal with my personal dislikes at the moment. The man would be at Rand's house in a few hours, and I had to put the issue on the back burner. We had more urgent matters to tend.

Like a relative, Mullen showed up as we sat down to dinner. We'd promised Mullen that we'd wait for him, so we set another place and Rand began filling him in on what we'd discovered so far. He told Mullen that Brister was living in Natchez under another soldier's name. Then he told him which name. Rather than the surprise we expected, Mullen barely flinched. "And who is this Brutkiewicz?" he asked.

"He was in the same unit with Brister," Rand explained. "He's the only other one still unaccounted for."

"I see. Do you think he's somewhere nearby?"

Rand admitted, "I have no idea. I don't really care at this point. All we're concerned with is catching the person who murdered two families before he has the chance to do it again. And that means concentrating on Brister, or Brutkiewicz, or whatever he calls himself now. If the man he stole a name from is still alive, I doubt he has any idea what Brister's doing."

"And that's the agency's concern as well, Mr. McArdle, but it seems to me that if Brister assumed the other man's name, maybe he knows something about him that we don't. Like where he is right now."

I could see the fringe of red creeping up from Rand's collar. "Agent Mullen, that may very well be. But to quote a famous Southerner, I frankly don't give a damn. We can sit here talking all night, or we can get to Natchez and find Brister before he finds Valerie Brutkiewicz. Are you with us on that?"

It was the first time I'd seen a break in Mullen's composure, but it came not a moment too soon. If Rand hadn't broken the ice, I would have gladly done it. At any rate, we were ready to leave the house within the half hour. After calling in other field agents to meet up with him in Natchez, Mullen left ahead of us, promising to keep in touch via cell phone. Rand and I were just glad to have a chance to talk without Mullen.

We chose to take the trace back to Natchez, in spite of the fact that it might take a little longer. We wanted time to talk, and we wanted privacy. Few other places on earth now offer both. As we entered a long stretch canopied by thick hardwood forest, I felt as if we'd entered a velvet tunnel, one that mesmerized with its beauty and isolation. The constant motion and lights of the interstate were a million miles away.

"Why do you think he's so interested in Brutkiewicz?" I finally asked, more to break the stillness than anything else.

"You caught that too?"

"How could I miss it? We kept trying to find out if he knew anything about Brister, and he kept going back to Brutkiewicz. He's either hard-headed, dense, or he knows something that we don't."

"That's kinda the impression I got too."

I tried to look through the thick forest surrounding us, but got about as far as my reasoning was taking me for the moment. I finally verbalized what bugged me.

"Rand, from what I've read about the FBI, their resources are practically infinite. Why wouldn't Mullen already know about Brister having taken Brutkiewicz's identification?"

"I thought about that too."

"If that's the case, why's he hanging around us? It just doesn't make sense."

"I agree with you on all of that. Maybe we'll figure it out as we go."

We exited the trace and turned onto Highway 61 about the time the local news would be issuing its weather forecast for the next day. I could already tell them what it'd say. Hot, humid, and more of the same. Brister, AKA Brutkiewicz, had an address not too far from the river, and we headed that way. We were a few blocks from the turnoff when Mullen's call came through.

"Where are you?" he wanted to know.

Rand answered in staccato, "Still on 61. Be there in five minutes."

He told us that he was parked outside Brister's house and was awaiting backup. If we wanted to see the bust, we'd have to watch from the street.

"What makes you think Brister's there?" Rand asked.

I couldn't hear Mullen's response because Rand silenced the phone before he was finished. "This is bullshit," he muttered and tossed the phone into the glove compartment. "We do the groundwork, and we're supposed to sit in the car."

I nodded my agreement and pointed to a street sign. "That's it. Turn up there."

We turned into an older neighborhood not far from the river, some valuable property in today's market. Sixties-style ranch houses sat far apart on huge, well-tended lots, draped by oaks and locust trees that snuffed out any lights from the city. By all appearances, whatever Brister had been doing in Natchez, he was doing okay.

We could see Mullen's car waiting in front of a darkened house. A second car approached from the opposite direction, switched off its lights and parked behind Mullen. Two figures emerged from the car. One rounded the house, while the other followed Mullen to the front door. Mullen's loud knock shattered the peace of the middle-class neighborhood, but still no lights came on inside.

Rand and I waited in the car as we'd been told, watching while our suspect perhaps watched us from a window. Again Mullen knocked, this time louder. Finally, a light appeared from the far-left side of the house, and soon a porch light came on.

We could hear Mullen's voice, along with a second one. But the voice belonged to a woman, not to Brister. They conversed for a moment, and then Mullen raised the phone to his lips. Finally, he turned back toward the car and beckoned us forward.

Lights now blazed in Brister's house. A very slender woman with thick dark hair sat on a worn, but handsome leather sofa the color of a fawn I'd once seen standing on the side of the road. And like the fawn, her eyes were wide with fright. She wore a silk robe in muted shades of turquoise and pink, which she pulled closer as we entered. Mullen sat on the edge of a matching recliner to direct his line of questioning.

The other two agents remained in the doorway at the far end of the room, silently watching the proceedings over a large oval dining table, surrounded by armchairs covered in faded tapestry. Mullen looked up as we entered but continued with his questioning.

"Ms. Brutkiewicz, these people have been on the case for a while. I hope you don't mind if they hear what you have to say."

"Reagan Wilks," I said, reaching out to grasp her cold hand. "Thanks for talking to us."

She attempted to smile and responded weakly, "Ellen Brutkiewicz."

As her questioning eyes turned to Rand, I explained, "This is my friend Rand McArdle. He's a private investigator."

She nodded briefly, deep lines furrowing her brow. "Sit. Please."

Rand and I took the remaining seats, and Mullen continued. "Ms. Brutkiewicz says that her husband disappeared a couple of days ago. She thought at first he'd gone to her brother's place on the river to fish, so she didn't think too much about it. He does that quite a bit. But when he didn't come home today, she got worried and started making phone calls. It seems her brother hasn't heard from Harold either."

Her eyes filled with questions. "Why do you want to talk to Harold? Has he done something?"

"We just need to ask him some questions," Mullen repeated, giving no real answer. "Do you have any idea where he might have gone?"

"Agent Mullen, don't you think if I did I'd call him myself?"

"Yes, ma'am, I suppose you would. But since the most ordinary things we take for granted often yield clues, why not just think this through with me?"

She sighed heavily and nodded acquiescence.

"Where does your husband work, Ms. Brutkiewicz?"

She appeared puzzled by the question, but answered simply, "The casino. He's a dealer."

"How long has he worked there?"

"Since it opened in '96. Why?"

"How long have you two been married?"

"Harold and I got married three years ago. I met him at the casino."

"So this is your house?"

She nodded again.

"Do you know where he lived before that?"

"Yes. Of course I do," she bristled. "He lived up north. In Michigan. Who could blame him for wanting to get away from the winters up there?"

Rand interrupted. "Mrs. Brutkiewicz, is it possible that Harold's job has taken him somewhere else? Louisiana maybe?"

Fear flashed across her face. "What makes you ask about Louisiana?"

"It's close by. Has he said anything about going to Louisiana?"

She sank back onto the couch, and tears welled in her eyes. "He mentioned Baton Rouge. He has an old friend there that he's been wanting to see."

Mullen glanced at Rand as he asked, "Do you know the friend's name?"

She shook her head, averting Mullen's gaze. With shaking hands, she turned the gold ring on her finger absently. "Agent Mullen, what do you think my husband did? You owe me that much."

"We're not sure if he did anything. I'm really sorry, Ms. Brutkiewicz, but that's all we can tell you at this point."

"This is so frustrating. I've been so worried, and now," she stopped in midsentence. "I just thought of something. There is one place you might look."

"Where's that?" Mullen asked.

"He has a friend down on Lower Woodville Road. He and Harold are pretty close. I would've called, but Pete's kind of a recluse, and he doesn't have a phone. Maybe Pete knows something."

"Yeah. I'll bet the two of 'em got to having a few beers and forgot all about time. Does this Pete have a last name?"

"Kelly. Pete Kelly."

"Do you think you could give us directions to his place?"

Her eyes were wide, and she turned the ring faster now. "I've never been there. All I know is what Harold told me about it."

"Have you ever met Pete?" I asked.

Again she shook her head. "But I can tell you how to get to Lower Woodville. And what Harold told me about the place. That's all I know."

Mullen answered, "That's a start. Tell us what you know, and we'll do the rest."

Lower Woodville Road took us ten miles away from the city as it curved back and forth between steep clay banks where centuries-old oaks and maples draped over the roadway, creating a canopy not unlike that of the trace itself. Our little caravan slowed as we neared the marker Ellen had given us. She'd visited White Apple Farms before, a small place that produced gourmet jellies and jams to ship around the country. Pete's house was supposed to be a half mile past the farm on the right side of the road.

In the darkness, we might have missed the house if we hadn't known it was there, so well was it hidden by bushes that grew nearly up to the tin roof. We turned up the steep gravel drive behind Mullen's car, the other agents' car following us in. Lights streamed through the tall but narrow windows in the single-story frame house, and a dog barked from some distance behind the property.

Rand and I again waited in the car for Mullen to give us some signal. "Do you think Brister's here?"

"I don't know what to think. Why would he come out here? I mean, what possible connection could this guy named Pete have with Brister?"

Before I could answer, we could see Mullen's figure reach the porch and stand to the side of the door. I could make out the glint of steel as he reached across the doorway and rapped loudly.

"Pete Kelly, open up. FBI."

"Oh, that'd make me open the door," Rand muttered.

We could see no movement behind uncovered windows, and we heard nothing save the dog, responding in kind to Mullen's insistent rapping. When no one answered his demands, Mullen moved his partners away from the door, took aim, and the door splintered as light spilled onto the dark porch.

We watched them enter the house, and when no sounds of gunfire followed, Rand urged me forward. "Let's go."

Agents Dowell and Mitternite were completing their search of the small house, guns still drawn in anticipation of the fight that never happened. The five of us rejoined in what had probably once served as a living room. Now the only furniture was a large rough-hewn table and a wooden straight-backed chair shoved under it. Overhead, a single bright bulb dangled from the ceiling; and from the table, wires trailed down to a surge protector that connected the computer and printer to the outside world.

Styrofoam cups held various levels of old coffee, and cigarette butts spilled from an ashtray and fell onto the table. Judging by the stench, somebody had spent a lot of time there, and not too long ago.

"Don't touch anything," Mullen reminded.

"Don't worry," Rand mumbled, equally mystified. "We wanna find this guy at least as much as you do."

"You think there is a Pete?" I asked.

"We'll know soon," Mullen said, pointing to the items spread out on the table. "Got to be fingerprints here. If one of 'em belongs to Brister, or Brutkiewicz, or whoever, we'll know soon."

"Is there any chance of a DNA match?"

"Oh, we could get a profile all right. The problem is, they didn't know about DNA when Brutkiewicz was in the service. We wouldn't have any point of comparison."

"So where do we go from here?" I asked.

"We'll take prints, and when we catch up with him, he'll have some explaining to do about this little command post."

Mullen turned to the other agents. "And we'll take his computer back into town, see what he's been up to. Who knows? Maybe he's left us a map."

"That'd be nice," Rand added.

"And in the meantime, we'll get local police down in Baton Rouge alerted. Get a close watch on the Hutchison family."

"Anything we can do?" I asked.

Mullen's smile appeared more bitter than sweet. "No, you two need to stay put now. Brutkiewicz is running out of time."

SIXTEEN

Rand and I agreed that going back to Jackson would be a waste of time since we still wanted to be around when Brister was brought in. Perched high on a hill overlooking the bridge that connects Mississippi with Louisiana, the motel we found wasn't much to look at itself, but the view was spectacular. The Mighty Mississippi filled the landscape and filled my mind with visions of a time in our country's history when towns like Natchez were little more than frontier outposts. Perhaps some day I'd write about that. Some day when I wasn't chasing a killer.

By the time we checked in, the sun had started to cut through a thick fog that settled in over the river during the night. I could tell it was going to be another hot one, but we'd certainly miss part of it. I craved sleep, and Rand looked about the same.

By the time I finished showering, Rand was snoring lightly. I pulled the heavy drapes shut and lay down beside him. I still struggled with how easily we'd slipped into this relationship and now acted like a couple who'd spent years together. It was scary, but it was also comforting. As soon as we saw Brister taken into custody, I vowed to straighten out my feelings, but for the moment, my brain could no longer function. I soon drifted off to sleep.

It seemed that I'd slept only a few minutes when I sensed somebody moving about in the room.

"Hi, Sleepy." Rand grinned. Dressed in fresh khaki slacks and a crisp patterned shirt, he held out a real cup with steam billowing from it.

"Where'd you get that?"

"Restaurant. Thought you might prefer the real thing over the Styrofoam version."

I dragged my aching body into a sitting position and took the hot cup into my hands. "You're a man after my own heart."

When I'd taken a few sips, my consciousness began to return, and I told him, "Rand, I've been thinking about something."

"In your sleep?"

"Sort of." I grinned. "I was thinking about it last night, but now it's coming into focus."

"And what's that?"

"You know how Mullen keeps mentioning Brutkiewicz? Did you also notice he wasn't even surprised when we told him about Brister using his name?"

"Yeah. I had to notice."

"Well, I've got a theory. Help me out here. If Brutkiewicz is still alive somewhere, could Mullen be looking for him under the pretense that he's looking for Brister?"

"But why bother covering up who he's really looking for?"

"I don't know. But let's just suppose. We had information on Brister, and he joined up, thinking that would lead him to his real target."

"Then that would mean he had some reason to go looking for Brutkiewicz. Doesn't make sense unless he has some sort of personal vendetta."

"Yeah, and it might also mean that Brutkiewicz and Brister had a connection we don't know about. Something other than No Malice."

Rand considered my words and took another sip from the cup in his hand. "I gotta admit that makes sense. A lot of things went on in Nam." He sat down at the table and reached for the phone. "I think it's time we talked to Mike again. If anybody can find out what the connection is, Mike can. Somebody's bound to talk."

"It's worth a try."

I could tell by Rand's end of the conversation that Mike didn't promise much, but having met the man, I was willing to bet we'd have an answer back from him soon. We both thought that once we discovered the connection between the two men, we'd be much closer to finding our killer, and that thought provided all the motivation I needed.

Mike had told us that he'd do some checking on his own and get back with us as soon as possible. Happy to help catch the killers of the Weir family, Mike was still saddened to find yet another link between his comrades in Vietnam and the seemingly endless reverberations of the war that tore our country apart. According to Rand, Mike was calling in markers he'd kept for many years. I hoped this was the last time we had to ask.

True to his word, Mullen called within the hour to let us know that he'd set up protection for the Hutchisons in Baton Rouge. As of yet, no one had seen or heard from Brister. As a result, Mullen assumed Brister to be either still in

Natchez or somewhere in between and, as such, had his agents scouring the town as well as putting out bulletins to all law enforcement between the two cities. Sooner or later, somebody would report seeing him. In the meanwhile, Mullen was going back to talk with Ellen Brutkiewicz and set up a trap should Brister attempt to contact her.

Rand and I had our own agenda. Before the day was out, we wanted to return to Everette Suttle's house and bring him up-to-date on the search. The man who'd suffered the most certainly needed to be included in the loop. But first, we wanted to find Chris Hutchison.

With a loose cannon like Brister out there, Hutchison had to be warned. Mullen promised to find Brutkiewicz's son and put out the warning. "It's under control," Mullen told us, adding that we should stay put.

Something, however, didn't sit right. Within minutes of connecting with his assistant in Jackson, Rand found out what we needed to know, and we set out to talk to the man ourselves. Chris Hutchison managed the casino hotel. If we'd found out that easily, we had to assume that Brister—although on a different level, also an employee of the casino—surely could have easily come by the same knowledge.

We left the motel and drove down the steep hill leading back onto the main highway through town. But as we waited for the light to change, the wail of sirens in the distance grew louder as they approached.

Oncoming traffic merged into a single lane to the right, while first paramedics, then police, even a fire truck, followed the lead vehicle almost all the way to the bridge, then turned right onto the street running parallel with the river.

"Isn't that where the casino is?" I asked.

"Yeah, the hotel's right around the corner. Wonder what's going on."

I turned to look as more emergency vehicles swerved their way through traffic. "I don't know, but something tells me we're about to find out."

By the time we got to the hotel, small by casino crowd standards, the usual gathering of rubbernecks had assembled, making our entry into the parking lot nearly impossible. We parked down the street and walked toward the hotel. People stood around the ambulance that blocked the entryway, eager for any glimpse of what was going on.

Since these people probably didn't know any more about what had really happened than we did, we walked around to the back of the building where a guard was stationed at the rear entrance.

"Mornin'," Rand greeted with a smile. "Mind if we go in this way?"

The young thin officer returned Rand's smile, but he moved to block the doorway. "Sorry, sir. Can't go in here."

"Why? We're registered here."

The officer's face remained impassive, but his eyes told us something big was up. "There's been a little problem, and we can't allow you to enter the hotel right now. If you'll just move back, I'm sure you'll be allowed in shortly."

"But we need to get to our room," I insisted.

"Sorry, ma'am. I understand, but you'll have to wait. As I said, we'll let you in just as soon as we can."

"How long will it be?"

"Hard to say, ma'am. But if you'll just wait a while, I'm sure everything will be fine, and you can go back to your room."

Apparently we were fighting a losing battle there, so Rand and I moved around to the front of the hotel, where by now even more people had gathered. As we inched our way into the crowd, paramedics exited the hotel double doors and raised a gurney into the waiting ambulance. We couldn't see much from our position, but judging from the tubes held aloft over the gurney, whoever lay there was still alive, at least for the moment.

"What happened?" Rand finally asked to no one in particular.

The elderly couple in front of us had watched the proceedings with great interest, and now they seemed eager to share what they knew with us.

"Somebody's been shot," the man said.

"Oh no!" I knew the answer, but I asked anyway. "Who was it, do you know?"

"Somebody who worked here."

"Was it an angry spouse or something like that?"

"Nope." The old man shook his head and continued, eager to share what information he'd acquired. "I heard somebody with the ambulance crew say it was the manager of the hotel. Apparently some nut just walked in and started shooting. Before anybody had sense enough to try to stop him, he was long gone."

A chill coursed through my body. Brister was off the deep end, and anybody could be his next target. We thanked the couple in front of us and left the crowd, practically running back to our car. I was furious. And I wanted answers. Where was Mullen when this happened? Didn't he have any kind of guard on Hutchison?

"So what do we do now?" I asked as I closed the car door.

Although his voice sounded calm, I could tell by Rand's expression that he was as angry as I was. "We're going to Everette's place. I can't imagine why Brister would go after Everette, but I'm not taking any chances. We're gonna get him out of harm's way."

"What then?"

"I'm not sure. Maybe by then we'll have heard from Mike."

Our call to Everette found him about to leave the house, but he seemed glad to postpone his plans for the chance to visit with an old friend. It seemed that years had gone by since I first met this kindly gentleman, and I looked forward to seeing him again. So much had happened. I wanted to see for myself how it had all affected him. I wanted to tell him myself that I had actually seen his granddaughter, but I didn't know if I could, or even should.

We drove out Highway 61 to the big white house I'd visited only a few days before. When we pulled into his driveway, I had that feeling I always have returning to an old friend's house. Only in this case, we hadn't been old friends—just privy to knowledge that neither one of us ever really wanted.

Everette stood on the porch about the same place he'd been the first time I saw him. But this time, there were no shadows, only sunlight that seared into my eyeballs. And this time, thankfully, I wasn't alone.

Everette invited us into his house, a cool respite from the blistering sun. While Rand and his old friend caught up on what time had done in the intervening years, I had the chance to look around his living room.

It was not the shrine I might have expected. I had expected to find pictures of the lost family in every niche. Instead, there was only one, a large one, maybe a couple of feet tall, in a lovely gilt frame over the mantel. Danny, Stephanie, and Lauren had been frozen in time at perhaps the apex of their happiness as a family. Lauren looked exactly as she had when I saw her that night on the trace. And in her hand, she held a purple iris.

How many times had Everette looked up at that photo and wished them alive again? I stared up at the picture and imagined the sound of their voices while the conversation around me may as well have taken place on another planet. I could hear nothing but what Lauren's voice must have sounded like when the picture was made. I could see nothing but the little blonde girl on the side of the road, offering me a gift from the past.

"Reagan." Rand's voice beckoned me back to the present. "Don't you think it's a good idea for Everette to be away from the house until Brister's in custody?"

I turned toward Everette, who waited for my response. "Yes. Yes, I do."

"Is there a relative or friend close by you might stay with for a few days?" Rand asked.

"Yeah, there's a fishing buddy up close to Port Gibson. Nobody'd ever think to go lookin' there. But I'm not leavin'. This is my home. It's all I got left."

"I really wish you'd reconsider, Everette."

"Look, Rand, I appreciate what you're trying to do, but nobody's gonna make me run and hide. This fella's already done his worst by me. If he wants me, let him come try it."

"If that's the way you feel, I understand," Rand admitted. "But will you at least call us every day and let us know you're okay?"

"Sure. If it'll make you feel better."

"It would. Thanks."

I couldn't wait any longer, and I asked, "Everette, may I ask you a question?"

"Sure," he said, following my eyes to the picture above his mantel. "What's that?"

"Was the iris always Lauren's favorite flower?"

Surprise registered, he repeated what he'd no doubt replayed in his memories a thousand times.

"I don't know what it was about that flower for her, but for as long as any of us could remember, she loved that flower. Her mama even put up wallpaper in her bedroom that had irises on it."

I nodded my understanding. "I thought so." I glanced at Rand, then chose my words carefully. "Everette, the reason I knew about the flower is that I saw Lauren."

The memory turned to confusion in his face. "You saw her before she disappeared?"

"No, Mr. Suttle. I saw her on the parkway. This week." I had begun to regret my decision, but the door was open. "Rand and I were coming back from French Camp, and at almost the same spot I found the suitcase, I saw her, standing near the edge of the woods. We turned around and went back to find her, but she'd gone."

It was obvious that Everette's wariness vacillated with his desire to believe, but he asked, "Did she say anything?"

"No. By the time we got to where we'd seen her, she'd disappeared. But, Everette, she left me her favorite flower on the picnic table."

All signs of composure left the man, and he dropped his head into his hands. After a moment, he looked up at me. "How can that be?"

"I have no idea. I'm not a believer in ghosts or that sort of thing, but I know what I saw."

Rand added, "And the flower was quite real, Everette. We don't know how it got there. Something happened that we can't account for logically."

"Some how, some way," I added, "Lauren wanted us to go there. First, she wanted me to find the suitcase, then she wanted us to know that we're on the right track. Some how, some way, she wants us to find Brister."

"So you think this Brister is the one that took my family?"

"Brister, Brutkiewicz, whichever you wanna call him," Rand explained. "We're working on the relationship, but we think the two of them were in cahoots on some scheme back in Nam."

The old man looked pleadingly at Rand. "But why'd he kill my family? What did they ever do to him?"

Rand answered simply, "Nothing. He probably didn't even know who they were."

Everette sank back into the worn recliner. "You mean he just wanted to kill somebody, and Steph's family was available?"

"I don't think it's that easily explained. Everette, anything we tell you about his motives is conjecture, but we did talk with a profiler who's spent years studying minds like his. She figures that what probably triggered him was coming home and finding his wife married to somebody else. Here's Brister expecting a joyful reunion, and instead he finds his wife and daughter part of another man's family, no matter that he never contacted them during all that time.

"Brister was probably well on his way to schizophrenia even before he went to Nam, and something happened over there that pushed him further into a psychotic state. Let's face it. No sane person would have avoided a transport leaving for the States. So he killed his family in a rage, then just started driving. Somewhere along the trace, he encountered your family, and he went off again. In his sick mind, he may have associated your family with his own. Maybe he thought he could bring back his family through yours."

I added, "And when he realized that that couldn't happen, he went further into this psychotic state."

Everette couldn't speak. For long seconds, sorrow hung in the air, as tangible as water falling from the sky. Then Everette lowered his head again, and this time he wept.

When we felt reasonably assured that Everette would be all right, we rose to leave. Ever the genial host, he followed us out onto the porch, trying valiantly to smile. "Thank you both for coming. It means a lot for me to know that you care so much about my family."

"It's going to end," Rand assured him. "Soon."

Everette's reply was barely audible. I thought at first I was wrong, but the look on Rand's face told me he'd heard it too. "Get the bastard before I do," he said and retreated into his house.

SEVENTEEN

We left Everette's house with a new fear, but before we could talk about the ramifications of Everette's disclosure, Mike Fondren called to share some good news. Through channels known to a select few, Mike had searched for and found somebody eager to help in the search for the killer that once again had made news in the state of Mississippi.

Like everything else, there was a down side. This veteran resided in Biloxi, a good four or five hours from Natchez. "What if Mullen finds him before we get back?" I asked.

"I really don't think we can find Brister any faster than Mullen can, do you? Besides, Reagan, we may as well face the fact that we're not equipped to deal with somebody like Brister. He's dangerous. Better leave it to the pros."

I had to admit he was right. Still, the thought of leaving the town where Brister was probably hiding went against my grain. I wanted to be there when he was found. But I also wanted to find out what had gone on in Vietnam. And even further, I wanted desperately to know for sure that Glenn Brister was really that person, not Harold Brutkiewicz. And if he was, what happened to Harold?

"Okay. Let's go," I agreed. "But let's call Mullen first. Make sure he'll let us know as soon as he gets word on Brister."

Rand made the call, and we were soon on our way to the veterans' hospital in Biloxi. Mike had warned us that Allan Webster was in the hospital for a purpose. A veteran of two tours of Vietnam, Allan had survived, but his emotional state was only slightly less precarious than his physical one. Mike had kept in touch with his old friend over the years and had watched Allan deteriorate and dwindle to a portion of the robust man who'd served as Special Forces for his country.

"I can't guarantee that he'll be having a good day when you talk to him," Mike warned. "But if he's thinking coherently like he was when I talked to him, he's got quite a story to tell. He says he knew both men. Knew them well."

Mike questioned his former buddy, but got no further. Allan said he didn't feel comfortable talking on the phone, that there was too much at stake. Suspecting that Allan's avoidance was a ploy to garner a visit from his old friend, Mike nevertheless said he'd be there the next day. And we agreed to meet Mike on the grounds of the hospital.

I'd never been to Biloxi, and Rand tried to prepare me for the devastation done by Katrina. Having grown up in the state and having spent many vacations in the area, he was heartbroken. Of course, I had no point of reference from the past, but still signs of struggle remained everywhere.

In glaring contrast, huge casinos had reopened, each sign grander than the last, and each proclaiming the chances of winning better there. Busloads of retirees swarmed around casino entrances, many of them arriving to see the latest attraction in from Las Vegas or New York or Hollywood. High-rise hotels accompanied the casinos themselves, but missing were the small businesses and motels that once shared this gorgeous coastal space.

Most of all, my heart ached for the centuries-old oaks. On some trees, new growth emerged from limbs ripped off like rag dolls, while others would no doubt meet a crueler fate before much longer. The reality was that away from the glitter, things were not so pretty. Rand had told me about the row of old homes that lined the beachfront. From Biloxi to Pass Christian, these gorgeous homes, many older than the state itself, faced the ocean that would one day be their demise. For over a century, they had withstood whatever nature dished out to them, and that had been plenty. But then, on that horrible day in August, a wall of water demolished nearly everything that man had ever built on the coast. An occasional home still stood, but all were in various states of massive repair. Only the very wealthy would be able to duplicate what they'd once had, and none could bring back the history.

Neither of us talked much as we drove down that highway, and when Rand finally turned away from the beach and onto the narrow road housing the veterans' hospital, I had to admit a certain relief. Although this concrete building had all the personality of a Styrofoam cup, it was an improvement over the sadness left by the storm.

Rows of identical, faceless windows could have been anything. According to Rand, only a few years before, quite a controversy ensued when the government announced the closing of another older hospital in Gulfport, a few miles away. Stories of people waiting as long as a year for appointments blazed headlines across the country, but the apparent lack of funding won out, and the hospitals closed anyway.

"So this is what veterans can look forward to after serving their country?" I asked aloud. Bare concrete walls extended six or seven stories into the cloud-filled summer sky. "Not much, is it?"

"I've never been here," Rand told me. "But there are lots of sad cases."

Mike was already walking toward us across the parking lot, and he joined up with us to enter the lobby, equally sterile and devoid of personality. I wondered how a hospital known to be the last resort of people with no other resources could be any other way, but I kept that thought to myself.

Hospitals as such always depress me, and this one proved no exception. The clinical smell permeated the entrance, and my stomach lurched so that by the time we found Allan's room, I was literally reeling.

When we entered his room, however, I did a double take and reread the nametag on the door. Somebody must have given us incorrect information because the man sitting in the chair in front of the window couldn't possibly be the one who'd volunteered for a second term in Vietnam. No way this faint shadow of a man could have literally jumped into the heart of battle. His frailty nearly took my breath away.

Allan gave us his best vestige of a smile. Dressed in gray pajamas, he reminded me of the ghastly pictures of concentration camp victims. His voice sounded as if it came from far away, from some place still remembered, but too distant to bring with it much energy.

"Mike, old buddy," he mumbled thickly as he tried to stand.

Mike's healthy arms embraced the smaller man, and he said, "Hey, buddy. How're you doin'?"

Allan's eyes lifted slowly up to Mike's, as if that motion in itself required monumental effort. "Great. I'm great. Good to see you, man."

After the awkward introductions, Mike told him how much we appreciated his seeing us, while Allan made sure we all had a place to sit. Then in slurred, slow speech, he asked, "You wanna know about Glenn Brister, don't you?"

Mike answered, "Always were the one to get down to business, weren't you?"

"Yeah," he nodded. "Wondered how long before somebody'd ask."

"That right?"

"Yeah. Those two were trouble."

"Those two?" Mike asked.

Each syllable came out with painstaking slowness, and I was hanging on each one. I tried to make sense of what this ghost of a man was telling us.

"Brister and Brutkiewicz." The *R*s stuck thickly against his tongue, and they came out with agonizing slowness.

Rand and I exchanged looks. How had he known that we'd want to know about both men? Mike told us he'd only inquired only about Brister.

"Were they bad news?" Rand finally asked.

Allan's quivering hand reached for the glass of water beside him, but Mike reached to steady the glass, then held it to his friend's lips.

"Thanks," he said, swallowing. Mike offered more water, but he shook his head. "No. They weren't really bad guys. Just confused."

"How's that?" Mike asked.

Allan's struggle was painful to watch, but he wanted to share something with us. And we certainly wanted to hear it.

He spoke again. "Fell in love with the same woman."

"Vietnamese?" Mike asked.

He nodded, and for a moment I thought he was going to sleep. Then he started to speak again in a voice so low I strained to hear.

"It's an accident I knew about 'em at all. I got off course and wound up in a certain village. That's where I stumbled on Brister. He was keepin' house with a woman in the village. He found Brutkiewicz there with her one day. Killed him on the spot."

"Brister killed him?" I asked.

He nodded. "He knew if he came back to camp, he'd be court-martialed."

I looked at Rand. "So that's why he didn't show up when it was time to go."

"It makes sense now," he agreed. "But, Allan, did any of this have to do with the group that called itself No Malice?"

For a second, Allan looked puzzled, and I thought we'd lost him. Finally, the hint of recognition glimmered in his eyes.

"No Malice. Haven't heard that in a long time."

"Do you know about them?" Mike asked.

"I know, all right. Buncha losers."

"Do you think No Malice had anything to do with Brutkiewicz getting killed?"

"Unhuh. No balls."

"So you think the only reason Brister killed Brutkiewicz was because of the woman?" Rand asked.

Again he nodded, adding, "That and Mullen."

Rand's surprise equaled mine he as blurted out, "Mullen?"

Allan repeated, nodding, "Mullen."

"What about Mullen?"

Allan reached for the glass, but his hand fell back limp at his side. A hideous cough issued from his chest, and his head dropped forward. Mike wrapped his arms around his buddy and literally picked him up from the chair, then laid him onto the bed. Allan's eyes closed, and his chest barely moved.

"You gonna be all right?" Mike whispered into his friend's ear.

For a moment, the nearly lifeless eyes opened, and a faint smile crossed his face. Then he returned to sleep. While Mike left the room to look for someone to tend to his friend, Rand and I stood guard, fearing each breath would be the last. But by the time we left his room, the former paratrooper was sleeping, apparently at peace for the moment. The nurse said that he did so with increasing frequency and that "his cancer" would win soon.

Mike followed us out to our car, and we stood talking beneath a huge oak that offered only minimal respite from the heat.

"Who's this Mullen?" Mike wanted to know.

"I don't know whether it's the same Mullen," Rand explained, "but that's the name of the FBI agent leading the search for Brister."

"Mullen's not that common a name. Sure makes you wonder, doesn't it?"

"Sure does."

"Especially since he's always seemed more interested in Brutkiewicz than in Brister."

Rand added, "But if Brutkiewicz is dead, why would Mullen still be looking for him? Wouldn't you think he has access to that information?"

Mike smiled. "He may have access, but sometimes if you don't know what you're looking for, you don't know what questions to ask. Hard to see a tree when you're standing in the middle of a forest."

"That's true," Rand agreed. "Well, I guess we'll find out as we go along." As an afterthought, he asked, "Mike, did you happen to run across anything else about the No Malice group?"

Mike's brow wrinkled. "Not much. But there was one thing I thought kinda odd."

"Oh yeah?"

"Well, I didn't pay too much attention to it because the fella tellin' me's not always the most reliable source, but maybe you need to check it out just the same."

"Check out what?"

"Well, this fella said that Brister came to him one time and asked if he wanted in on a plan to get outta the war. Like I said, though, I didn't pay too much attention 'cause I think this guy's heard too many shells go off in his head. Know what I mean?"

"I imagine the war left a lot of folks like that. Is this somebody I can talk to?"

"Sure," Mike agreed. "When I get back, I'll call you with the number."

"Where's he live?"

"Some place up in Tennessee. I just don't remember, but I'll call you soon as I get back."

We thanked him for making the long trip to the coast, and his answer was a broadening smile accompanied by an admission. "You just happened to ask me to meet you in my favorite place. As we speak, I've got a date with a blackjack dealer across the way."

"Ah, you like the cards?" I asked.

"A weakness I acquired in the service. Thankfully, it's not much of a habit with me, but I do enjoy testing my skills."

We wished him luck and thanked him again for introducing us to Allan. As we watched Mike drive out of the parking lot, I couldn't help feeling that our luck, too, was about to change.

EIGHTEEN

Dark clouds gathered as we left Biloxi, and by the time we reached Natchez, rain poured from the sky. It came down in heavy sheets, like water out of a pitcher. We had less than an hour of daylight left. With all that rain, we decided our best move would be to return to the motel, call Mullen, and determine what to do next.

The dash from the car into the motel left us drenched, and the room felt like a freezer. I headed for the shower, immersing myself in hot water and then clean clothes. When I returned, Rand was on the phone. I listened as Rand completed the conversation with Mullen and made arrangements for us to meet up with him on the following day.

Rand assured me that we would indeed soon have Brister in custody where he belonged. The pieces were falling into place, but not fast enough to suit me. For three weeks now, I'd been in a time vacuum, and the effects were taking their toll. I'd sent the story in to Katie, but I still hadn't heard. She was either going to love it, or she would no doubt find a way to assure that I never worked again.

And one other thing tugged at my conscience. Since I'd been with Rand, he'd only talked to his daughter a couple of times, but his concern and love for her was apparent. When he talked to her, his voice, his entire demeanor changed. It was as if I was seeing a different person. Not that he was different in a derogatory way, but he was different. And I wasn't a part of that life. Was I taking on more than I could handle there? A grown daughter who was more the age of a sister could resent the hell out of me. And I hadn't even met her yet.

That and dozens of other questions nagged at me, but for the moment I had to squelch them. Rand had put his entire practice on hold to help me find Brister, and find him we would. But we had to find him soon before he had the chance to kill another innocent person.

Local news on television was bringing the public up-to-date on poor Chris Hutchison's condition. He'd gone through several hours of surgery, but the prognosis looked fairly good. Brister's aim was just enough off to spare the man's life, but it would definitely be a different life from that point on. The anchor didn't say, but I wondered if Chris's family had come to Natchez. That would play right into Brister's hands.

We were about to go in search of dinner when the phone stopped us again. This time it was Mike, as promised, with a name and number of the man who knew Brister. Rand looked questioningly at me.

"Go ahead," I urged. "Dinner can wait."

Roy Dalton answered the phone himself. Rand explained who he was and his connection to Mike Fondren, and then he got down to business.

"Mike tells me that Glenn Brister came to you one time with some kind of wild plan that involved getting out of the war. Is that correct?"

"Yep. He sure did."

"Mind telling me about it?" Rand asked, holding the phone away from his ear enough for me to listen in.

"Yep. That man was a wild hare. Know what I mean?"

"I think I do," Rand calmly assured him. "So can you tell me about this plan of his?"

For several seconds, the sound of ice clinking in a glass was all we could hear. Then Dalton's voice resumed, a bit slurred but still understanable. "Well, you see, Brister belonged to Company D, just like I did. You know, we had to stick together, so I wasn't about to rat on him. That's why I never told anybody about this before."

"I understand completely, Mr. Dalton. And I admire your loyalty. But we're really not concerned about why you never told it before. We're just trying to find out what Brister had planned."

Ice cubes clinked again, followed by Dalton's cough. "I getcha," he said. "'Preciate it. So we'd been out on a mission and lost a buncha men. It was pure hell, I'm tellin' ya. Never forgot it. But anyway, we were sittin' around camp that night, when Brister came to me. He said, 'I got a way outta this mess, ya know.' I asked him what he meant, and he started tellin' me all about how we could stage a raid and fake our own capture."

"You mean he wanted you to help fake a raid on your own camp?"

"Exactly."

"You mean he'd fire on his own people?"

Dalton's voice raised a caliber. "He said wouldn't nobody get hurt. Just enough shootin' to get us outta there. Said some locals'd help out with yellin' how we'd been captured and all. I told him that was crazy. Didn't want no part of it."

"Did he ever try to escape?" Rand asked.

"Nope. Somebody squealed, and the captain put a stop to the plan before it ever got off the ground. Brister knew he was in big trouble, so he took off. Word was that he had a woman in a village close by, so I'm guessin' that's where he hid out."

Rand's expression changed from doubt to understanding, and he asked calmly, "And who was this captain?"

"Mullen. Cap'n Mullen."

"How did Mullen put a stop to it?"

"First he put the word out that he knew about some big escape plan. The whole place was talkin' about it. All kinds a rumors. But then before the cap'n could really do anything else, he got shot."

"Vietcong?"

"Maybe. But if it was, it was a solitary sniper. Nobody ever found the shooter, but it sure was strange the way it happened. Air support just made a run, so the area shoulda been clear. Just that one shot, and it took down the cap'n. Nobody else. I always thought that mighty strange."

"Yeah, I do too," Rand said quietly. "Mr. Dalton, do you remember if Harold Brutkiewicz was in the camp when all this happened?"

Dalton snorted. "Remember? Hell yeah, I remember. The best shooter in the entire company, and nobody could find him when we went out lookin' for the captain's shooter. Always thought that kinda funny too."

"I understand," Rand said. "I understand a lot now, thanks to you, Mr. Dalton."

We'd planned to simply go out to dinner and meet with Mullen the following day, as he had requested. But everything had suddenly changed. Was Mullen out to find revenge for a relative possibly murdered by Brutkiewicz, or was he genuinely trying to do his job and stop a murderer from striking again? We didn't have the answers, but for the moment, we decided against revealing what we'd learned to Mullen. If the man was desperate enough, he just might be as dangerous as Brister.

One thing was for sure. We had to find Brister, and we didn't have time to spare. Dinner turned out to be a hamburger on the run, and we headed out to meet Ellen Brutkiewicz. We knew that Mullen had the place watched in case Brister returned, but we doubted that he'd be overly concerned about a wife going to church when her husband was missing.

On the phone, Ellen told us to meet her at St. Joseph's, a pretty little stone church with ivy climbing nearly to the roof. It occupied a prominent perch over the river, not far from the heart of town, and it looked like the safe haven we hoped it was.

We got out of our car around the corner, just in case one of Mullen's men was on the lookout for us, and, in the humid night air coming in off the river, walked up the few steps leading into the church.

A single lit candle wavered tentatively on a table beside the door. From the doorway, the church appeared empty. No more than twenty rows of simple wooden pews with seats covered in wine-colored velvet filled the sanctuary, all empty at that late hour. Flowers before the tabernacle permeated the tiny chapel with fragrance, and outside lights penetrated through the windows' scenes of passion, bathing the church in warm hues.

"Is there something I can do for you folks?" a voice behind us asked.

We turned to face a balding man wearing the collar of a priest. His smile was cautious.

I glanced around the empty church once more, then turned back to him. "Yes. Perhaps you can. We're looking for someone who said she'd meet us here."

"You must be Ms. Wilks."

"Yes, yes, I am."

"I'm Father Boudreaux. If you'll follow me, Ellen is waiting for you."

He turned and led us around a stone path toward a simpler building at the rear of the church, dark except for a light shining somewhere on the bottom floor. We stopped while the priest inserted a key into the ancient lock, then held the door open for us to enter.

Ellen Brutkiewicz waited alone in a small parlor to the right of the foyer. She rose as we entered.

"Thanks for coming," she said and looked past us at the priest remaining in the doorway. "Thanks, Father."

"Glad to help, Ellen," he said quietly. "Let me know if I can do anything."

Rand and I thanked him also, and he slipped from the room and softly closed the door behind him. I looked at Ellen.

"Thanks for coming," she said. "I really need to talk to somebody whom I can trust." Her eyes searched mine for understanding. "Father Boudreaux is a good friend. He won't say anything."

"I'm sure he won't," I answered. Light surrounded her head and cast her features in indistinct shadow. "What is it you need to talk to us about, Ellen? Why the secrecy?"

Her attempt to smile faded quickly into tears. "I couldn't tell you this the other night, but somebody needs to know. And I think I can trust you two."

"Know what, Ellen?" I asked softly.

"Harold may have killed somebody."

"What makes you say that?"

"He told me. At least I think he did. I wasn't sure then, but now I am."

"He told you?"

She nodded. "Yes. But he didn't know he did."

"When was this?" Rand asked.

"We hadn't been married too long, a few months at the most. It was really late one night, and we were out at my brother's place on the river. You remember. I told you about it." She sighed again and continued. "I didn't usually go up there with them, but that time I was tired of staying home, so I went. Anyway, we were sitting out on the porch late that night, and he started talking about a little girl. At first, I thought he was drunk, but the more I listened, the more I felt like screaming. He kept going on about his little girl. How pretty she was and all. But I knew he never had a little girl. At least I didn't think he did."

My skin tingled as her story unfolded, but I didn't want to stop her now. I had to keep her talking. I leaned forward, intent on every word. "Ellen, what exactly did he say about his little girl?"

The fear in her voice was tangible. "He said he punished her for what her mother did."

"Did you ask what that meant?"

"Yes. I asked, but his answer didn't make a whole lot of sense. Until now."

"What did he say?"

Ellen looked from Rand to me. Her eyes lowered, and her voice became almost inaudible. "He said her mother was a traitor, so he punished her. Then he said"—her voice cracked as she struggled, and she repeated—"then he said she didn't even cry when he did it."

Something in my gut wanted out, and I barely squelched the scream. But I had to know more. I had to know what this woman knew. "Ellen, what did he do? Did he tell you?"

"No, only that he punished her." Her eyes sought ours, pleading for forgiveness for her unknown sins. "I was so scared. He'd never said anything like that before. He was never anything but kind to me. All this time, I've wanted to tell somebody, but I didn't know what to say. Then this all came up, and I started to put it together."

I couldn't look at her. I couldn't even think what to say to this woman who'd endured a secret far more terrible than any most people ever have to hear. The only thing I could think to do came perhaps as a shock to me as well as to Ellen and Rand.

"God forgives you," I said. "You've done the right thing by telling us now."

I reached for her hand and took it in my own. "But, Ellen, now's the time to make amends."

"How?" she asked through a new barrage of tears.

"By helping us find your husband. Whatever he may have done in a previous life is not your fault. The man you knew and loved is not the sick person who committed these horrible acts. But what you do now can make a difference. There were actually two little girls, Ellen. One was his own."

The tears stopped suddenly. "He killed his own daughter?"

"We think so," Rand added. "Can you help us find him now?"

"There may be one place," she said. Her chin lifted. "He's talked about it a lot. And it's kinda isolated. I think he may be hiding out there."

"Where is this place?" I asked.

"Out on the trace."

"You mean on the parkway?"

She nodded agreement. "We went there together a couple of times. The last time, he talked to the park rangers for an hour or so about who used to live there, what the house was used for, that kind of thing. Later on, he told me how he figured somebody could hide out in those thick woods and never be found, especially since businesses aren't allowed in the park."

"Does anybody live nearby?" Rand asked.

"The only house I remember belonged to one of the rangers, I think. Why?"

Rand tried to keep his expression noncommittal, but I knew what he thought. Anybody living nearby might be in danger.

He said, "No reason except that a house might provide him with protection."

"I see your point," Ellen admitted. "Harold told me a story about his days in Vietnam, about how he lived in the jungle for ten days once with no food or anything. This'd be easy for him, especially since he'd take supplies with him."

"You may very well be right," Rand said. "But he can't hide out forever. At least it's worth checking out. Does this place have a name?"

"Mount Locust. Do you know it?"

My face must have shown my horror. The place I'd written so much about in my piece could now be harboring Lauren's killer. I answered, "Yes, Ellen, we're familiar with Mount Locust."

"Good. Because that's where I think he is."

For a moment, I couldn't put my finger on what bugged me, but then it came. She told us that Brister had never been anything but kind to her.

I asked, "Ellen, why are you so eager to help us find your husband?"

Her lips pressed together in what could have been a smile, and she answered, "I always knew something wasn't right. It's true he was always kind to me, but especially after that night at the river, I knew. I just knew."

"But you stayed with him anyway?"

"Yes, because I didn't have any real proof. I thought it was just me still grieving over my husband. I thought I was imagining things because Harold was so different from my husband. But now I know. My gut was right the whole time."

"I guess it was," I agreed. "I wish I'd listened to my gut a few times too."

NINETEEN

We made sure that Ellen was safely on her way back home before we left the rectory, and we took the back street to where our own car was parked. With Mullen's men staked out at her house and the Hutchisons in Baton Rouge under strict surveillance, the only thing Brister could do was to outwait everybody until he felt the coast was clear. And that's exactly what we wanted to make sure he didn't have the chance to do again.

Mount Locust is technically only ten or so miles out of Natchez, but aesthetically and emotionally, it's at least a thousand. Merely turning onto the parkway shifts my emotional gears, and this night was no exception.

A full moon was rising over the velvety darkness, luring us forward like a silky siren that obliterated the outside world. Trees formed a nearly perfect arch over the roadway where Mount Locust was supposed to be, and Rand slowed, looking for the sign.

I'd read all about this place, with intentions of spending some real time there when things settled down. I knew that the house itself is set back two, maybe three hundred yards off the parkway and perches on top of a hill, a welcome sight for weary travelers. As such, it offered a splendid vantage point for its owner to keep watch on bandits and, later, Union Soldiers. From its wide front porch, visitors can view the interior rooms, although acrylic partitions prohibit them from actually entering.

Rand doused the headlights, and we turned into the long drive leading to the parking area, but still I suspected that Brister already knew we were there. Deer grazing in the open field lifted their heads momentarily, then returned to grazing. Chances were that if they knew we were there, so did Brister.

To the right of the house and downhill, rangers maintain a small administration building and restroom facilities for tourists, with a sidewalk connecting them to the house; but deep shadows hid them from view at night. If Brister was hiding out in the house, he'd certainly see us long before we saw him.

The night was still hot, but bathed in dark shadows of those monstrous oaks, I felt chilled. A shaking started somewhere in my spine and slowly worked its way outward. In my mind's eye, I could visualize the interior of the house on top of the hill, in daytime, an innocent replica of what life had been like for eighteenth century travelers, but in the dark of midnight, a lure, a trap.

"Ready?" Rand asked as he slipped the .38 he'd brought along into the holster he'd strapped on.

I nodded and followed his lead. The pistol gave me some security, but still I knew that if Brister was watching us, he'd have the upper hand. We kept to the shadows as much as possible, but by the time we neared the house, we had to make a decision. Only two ways led to it. Either we climbed right up the front steps to the porch, or we went around to the back, where we'd have some cover. And the only way around was through an open field, now scattered with huge round bales of hay. In the moonlight, we could be sitting ducks.

Rand motioned me toward the field. I swallowed, forced the fear back into my throat, and ran after him toward the nearest bale. We crouched behind the cover it offered, catching our breath before the next lurch. The moon was directly overhead now, and from bale to bale, we continued until all that remained was a gradual uphill slope that was completely in shadow. Sweat trickled down my back, but still I shook.

"Stay here," Rand whispered, "I'm going up to the house."

I thought he'd lost his mind, but I couldn't argue. I had nothing to fire back should Brister start shooting. Watching Rand creep toward the house, I eased my way uphill and waited in the shadows. The piquancy of pecan bark filled the night air each time I brushed against the trunks, any other time a comforting smell.

Rand had moved to a line directly behind the stairs that led to the back porch. If Brister was inside, Rand was making himself a perfect target. But no shots rang out as he moved ever closer to the house, then climbed the steps, waiting with each one.

I moved out of my safety in the shadows and watched as Rand moved from window to window, then to the door. Nothing. I joined him on the porch, but he quickly motioned me away from the door.

"I don't think he's been here," Rand whispered.

"So what do we do now?"

"Look for him."

I looked at him incredulously. "Where?"

Rand turned toward the rear of the house where a trail led through the woods. "The slave cemetery's back there," he said, indicating the path. "Lots of places to hide out in those woods."

The shaking renewed, and my voice sounded quivery, even to me. "We're going out there now?"

"He'll be gone by tomorrow."

I took a deep breath and tried to stop my rattling, but couldn't. The best I could do was follow down what felt like a chert path. It crossed between a garden area still under cultivation on the left and the family's yard, lined by zinnias and daisies before it disappeared into thick woods.

We followed the path to a slight clearing, marked in front by a large wooden sign. I moved closer and tried to read. It was a list of names of slaves that I assumed were buried in this simple plot. I looked around, expecting to see markers, but there were none. The sign was the only tribute these people would ever have. That and the families they left behind.

Rand and I worked our way carefully around the perimeter of the small cemetery marked off by a rope only a couple of feet off the ground. This area had been kept fairly clear of overhanging limbs, but the woods beyond looked impenetrable.

We followed the roping to the backside of the cemetery. Nothing moved in the woods around us, but I felt something crunch under my foot, and I stopped. At first, I tried shuffling the object with my foot. When I still couldn't see it, I knelt and picked up a cold ember. Rand knelt beside me and picked up a second.

"He was here, all right," he said. "That's pretty gutsy to camp this close to rangers and tourists."

He stood up again and looked toward the darkest part of the woods. "This guy knows his way around at night. He could be watching us as we speak."

"Then why hasn't he shot at us?"

"Don't know. Maybe he wants us to follow him. Maybe he's got some kind of a trap."

"Then maybe we shouldn't go after him," I said, squelching the scream that now broiled in my throat. "Rand, I think we should get outta here. Brister wouldn't think twice about killing both of us. I don't know about you, but I'm way outta my league."

He shook his head and was about to speak when he stopped, and I followed his line of sight toward the deepest part of the woods. My own senses were reeling. Where there had been complete darkness, there was something—somebody—in the woods, and it wasn't Brister.

The figure was small, like a little girl. Moonlight sifted through the trees and glistened about her blond hair, which lifted softly in a nonexistent breeze. My heart fluttered as I strained to see her features. Only the eyes beckoned, alight with fear of their own, and she stood motionless in woods too deep to traverse. I wanted to go to her, suddenly unaware of danger that had only a moment before consumed me.

Rand gripped my arm and pulled me back.

"It's Lauren," I said. "She's trying to show us something."

"Reagan, don't." His grip tightened.

"But you see her too. She's real."

"I see her, but I don't think she's real," he said softly. "At least not like you and I are real."

I looked up at his face, drawn with pain. "We can't turn back now," I pled. "She's been trying to communicate with us for weeks. We should follow her, Rand."

His grip relaxed a bit, and I took off, running toward the spot where Lauren appeared. But as I did, she moved, not like you or I would move, but more like the image of a camera flickering. Then she was gone.

I continued toward the spot where she had been, oblivious to the limbs and briars that scratched and clawed at me from every direction. I stood where Lauren had stood, and the shiver I'd felt before returned with ferocity. I shook uncontrollably until Rand came to me and wrapped his arms around me.

"Why won't she stay?" I asked, trying to make some sense of illusion. "She comes to me, and she disappears. Why?"

"I can't answer that. I don't understand either, but I feel her presence here, just like you do. And, Reagan, I don't think she wants us to continue."

"What makes you say that?"

"I think she's warning us."

"A warning?"

"Yes. Lauren's protecting you now. She knows you'll be killed if you follow Brister. She doesn't want what happened to her to happen to you."

My shivering stopped. What Rand said suddenly made sense. Somehow, some way, this little girl's spirit, so tortured for decades, had chosen me to defend her. And now she defended me.

I reached for Rand's hand and clasped it with both of mine. "You're pretty special, you know that?"

"Why's that?"

"Not everybody can see guardian angels."

We left the grounds, eased our way around the tiny cemetery, and started back toward the house. My nerves had begun to relax, and I was no longer thinking about Brister hiding in the woods behind me. I wanted to get back to the car and back to civilization, in that order. But one thing changed all that in a heartbeat.

The popping sound came from the woods where we'd just been. In the instant, Rand hit the ground. I screamed his name. He grabbed my arm and pulled me down beside him. The popping in the woods continued, but this time I saw the fire behind it and I inched my body to where Rand had taken cover within the rows of okra that someone had thankfully planted in the yard. They wouldn't stop bullets, but they did offer some cover.

Dirt ground between my teeth and sticky leaves brushed against my face, "Is it Brister?" I asked, but the answer was obvious.

Flat on his stomach now, he aimed the .38 toward the woods. Only the outline of the forest was visible, with moonlight filtering scarcely a foot or two through the thick foliage. We wouldn't see our shooter until he fired again.

Rand waited, then fired a shot in the direction we'd seen the last flare, but no shots rang out in return. I strained to hear any shuffling of leaves, any sounds of feet moving toward us. But I heard only my own ragged breath as I waited for what might come next.

We remained prone between the rows of okra for what seemed like hours. Rand's eyes never left the edge of the woods, and his hands remained steady, aimed at an unknown shooter. Eventually, his arms relaxed, and he sat up tentatively behind the rows of piquant-smelling plants and tossed out a small rock in the direction of the cemetery. It landed with a thud, but no other sounds followed. He tried it again and again with no reaction.

When nothing responded, I sat up and inched my way toward him.

"Keep down," he whispered. "I'm gonna take a look around."

He slowly stood up, little by little easing his way toward the woods. Still nothing moved. Satisfied that Brister had given up on killing us for the time being, he turned back to me and motioned with his free hand for me to follow. I crept out of the garden, and using the bushes around the back of the house as cover, I made my way back to the shadows of the pecans where we'd first climbed the hill.

In what little breath I had left, I asked, "Do you think he's gone?"

"Must be, or he'd still be shooting at us," Rand said. "But just in case, let's don't hang around."

"You're not waitin' on me."

Thinking that the matter was closed for the moment, I easily kept up with Rand as we hurried back toward our car. This time, we took the direct route down the sidewalk. The car was parked at the end of it, and we were nearly there when something splintered from the tree overhanging the end of the sidewalk. Before I could see where it had come from, I hit the pavement beside the car. Rand ran to the other side of the car and crouched behind its cover. He returned fire in the direction of the woods behind the ranger station.

"Get in!" he ordered.

I'd never been in a situation like that before, but instinct told me what to do. Oblivious to the gravel and grime of the parking lot, I found myself beneath the car. I scooted on my belly, using my hands as sort of flappers, until I'd reached the place where Rand crouched. He opened the door with one hand, while getting off another round in the direction the shots were coming.

I slid across the seat, cowering half on the floor, while Rand slid in beside me and started the car. He didn't bother to back up and turn down the lane, which we'd come in on. Instead, he took the car in a straight line across the open field. Shots still pelted the parking lot behind us while deer scattered in every direction. And our car pummeled toward the safety of the parkway.

Even though Brister had to be on foot, Rand didn't slow the car until we'd made it safely back to the highway that connected us with Natchez. Brister might have given up on killing us for the moment, but it was now obvious that he knew we were after him. And Brister wanted us dead.

TWENTY

We had a decision to make. If Brister knew who we were, he'd probably come looking for us. The question was whether or not we'd continue looking for him or leave that to the authorities. We'd come that far, and we knew more about Brister now than anybody else did. But was it worth risking our lives over? Somehow, in Brister's convoluted thinking, we'd become the next target; and I didn't like that at all.

Another question had to do with Mullen himself. Now that we knew he was looking for Brutkiewicz for some personal vendetta, most probably the death of his father, Mullen's part in the search had become questionable. If a showdown with Brister came about, would Mullen do something that would ruin his career forever and perhaps silence Brister before we had a chance to get him to talk?

All in all, we decided that there was far too much at stake to leave Brister out there in the woods evading capture. Even though Mullen's motives might be suspicious to us, there was no doubt he wanted to stop the killing. That said, Rand called Mullen's cell as we were driving back into Natchez.

I could tell from Rand's end of the conversation that Agent Mullen was none too pleased that we'd taken on the job of going out to Mount Locust alone, but Rand reminded him that we knew nothing for sure. We had simply gone out looking and got lucky. In more ways than one, Mullen had retorted.

While we headed back to our weather-beaten little motel in Natchez, we had no doubt that Mullen had already summoned as many people as he could muster on their way to Mount Locust. We also had no doubt that all they'd find would be evidence that someone, probably Brister, had been there. He was too smart to stay put now that we knew about him. Brister's next move seemed to be the biggest question, and that might be anybody's guess.

It was nearly three o'clock when we finally returned to the room, and within minutes, I was in another world. When my cell phone intruded, I had a hard time shaking off the stupor. But Katie's insistent voice wouldn't be denied.

Her greeting was crisp, as usual. Wondering what she was doing calling in the middle of the night, I glanced toward the window where light streamed through the slit in the drapes.

"Fine, Katie," I finally mumbled.

She was saying something that hadn't quite registered yet, but the tone sounded positive.

"I absolutely love it," she repeated.

"You do?" I felt like doing one of the double takes that they do in comedies and repeat the words without the question mark at the end, but it was too late. So I did my best to cover by adding, "Thanks. I'm glad you like it."

"In fact," she continued, "I think it's extraordinary. But I've got to know. How did you ever come up with that angle about the missing family?"

By that time, I had sat up in bed while Rand watched me through droopy eyes. He slid out the other side of the bed and headed toward the bathroom.

"Kind of an accident, Katie," I confessed. "I guess sometimes you get lucky."

"Well, whatever works." Whenever Katie crooned, I was suspicious. Unfortunately, I knew her mood wouldn't last, and I waited for the other shoe to fall.

And it fell. "Look, Reagan, I've got a message here from Jake. He wants you over in Alabama right away."

"Alabama? Where in Alabama?"

I heard the rustle of paper, and she said, "A state park called DeSoto. I think it's in the northeast corner of the state."

"What does he want me over there for?"

Her voice never skipped a beat. "There's a family missing in the wilderness up there, and Jake wants you to cover it right away. Apparently, some witnesses saw a single man holding a family hostage, and they think it might be your killer from Mississippi. Think of the story you've uncovered, Reagan."

"What? How could he be in Alabama?" I didn't even bother to tell her how improbable that was since we'd spent the night before serving as his target practice. But I did think to ask, "When did this happen, Katie?"

"Only hours ago. That's why it's so imperative for you to get there. By dark, all the newspapers in the country will have people on it, but we'd be the first magazine on the scene, and certainly the only one with a writer who has personal knowledge of the killer."

"Katie, have you thought about the possibility that this is a copycat?"

"Yes, I've thought about that. All the better. You do your travel scenario about this park, and then you draw the connection. Believe me, people will be following your next move."

"Katie, I'll have to think about it."

"There's no time to think, Reagan. Just get there. If they find this family alive, great. You interview and write their story, backed up by local scenery and characters. If not, then you've still got a hell of a story, not to mention follow-up."

I didn't know whether to throw up or throw the phone against the wall. Just like that. A family's survival amounts to little more than the slant a story takes.

"I'll let you know," I finally said.

"You can't do that," Katie insisted. "Your story in Mississippi's finished, and Alabama's right next door. How far can it be?"

I gripped the tiny cell phone while she continued with the orders. Then I pushed the button that silenced Katie and her world for the moment. My search for Lauren's killer wasn't nearly finished yet. Katie couldn't know it, but that was her problem. Some things never change, and neither do some people. The media would always be around for the kill, but now I wasn't so sure I wanted to be part of it.

Rand's call to Mullen produced the expected results. No fewer than forty local and state police, along with FBI, were currently combing the woods around Mount Locust. So far all they'd turned up were some cigarette butts and trampled vegetation, plus, of course, the remains of our gunfights near the cemetery and again on the parking lot. Brister was too smart to stay in the area after our encounter, so a move across state lines was certainly a possibility that we couldn't ignore. But for the moment, I was more concerned with having an honest talk with Agent Mullen.

He agreed to meet us at Mount Locust, and we were there by midmorning. He'd made arrangements with police blocking the highway to allow us to enter, and we turned from the highway onto the grounds of the old plantation. A quartet of police officers, one of them a young woman, worked within the confines of an area of the parking lot, roped off with yellow tape.

A tall lanky ranger watched us approach and sauntered toward us where we stopped near the roped off area. His glasses reflected bits of sunlight that filtered through the covering of oaks, and our own image grew larger as he approached.

"Morning," he said and bent down beside my lowered window. The corners of his mouth turned up, and the heavy mustache lifted into a smile.

"Good morning," I answered. "Agent Mullen said we could meet him here. Do you know where we might find him?"

A flicker of disappointment crossed his face, but he quickly recovered. "He's up at the house. You can park over there, and I'll take you to him."

When we got out of the car, Rand asked innocently, "What's all the hubbub about?"

Ethan Clarke stopped at the end of the sidewalk and looked back incredulously. "You haven't heard?"

"Not really," Rand said. "We just came out here to talk to Agent Mullen about another matter. What's going on?"

Ethan studied the house on top of the hill, then turned back to us, speaking confidentially. "Well, I guess it's no secret. Seems that some murderer's been hiding out back there in the woods behind the house."

"A murderer?" I asked.

His eyes narrowed as he took me into his confidence too. "But I'm sure he's gone by now."

"I certainly hope so. Who did this person kill?"

"I don't know the whole story, but they say he killed a buncha folks a long time ago, then just yesterday shot that fella in the casino over in Natchez."

"We heard about that," Rand said. "Is that man going to be okay?"

"Last I heard." Ethan shook his head. "There's all kinds of nuts out there." He turned back toward the house and led us briskly up the sidewalk. "You never can tell what's in somebody else's head."

"That's the truth," I agreed and fell into step behind him.

Mullen waited on the front porch of the old house, watching us as we approached. I couldn't help looking off to the right, where the innocent field now lay bathed in sunlight, where its dappled bales of hay still awaited pickup. I had to shake my head to dispel images from the night before. Our close call had probably been a lot closer than either of us was willing to admit.

Without a word of greeting, Mullen turned and led us through the house and onto the back porch where two tables of communication equipment had been set up. Pictures of Brister were spread out on the larger one.

"Care to sit?" he asked, pointing to some folding chairs.

"No, thanks," Rand answered for both of us. "We just need to talk for a few minutes."

Mullen finally removed the dark glasses and laid them on the table. "That's fine. What about?"

Rand's eyes met Mullen's. "About Harold Brutkiewicz. The real one."

"What about him?"

"Why are you so interested in him? The person who's committed all the crimes in this state is Glenn Brister, yet you keep looking for Brutkiewicz. Maybe you'd like to explain why that is."

Mullen's arms crossed over his chest, and he leaned back on his heels, but his eyes never wavered. "You're wrong about that. Of course, I'm looking for Brister, but that's because he's been using Brutkiewicz's name. It's that simple."

"We don't think so," Rand continued. "Our source tells us that there was a Captain Mullen in Vietnam. A Captain Mullen who just happened to be in the same unit with Brister and his namesake."

Mullen's eyes flickered for a moment; then the steely resolve returned. "So. Coincidences happen."

"It gets stranger," Rand added, smiling slightly. "This captain was shot under some very mysterious circumstances."

"Thousands of people get shot in a war. What's strange about that?"

Rand took a folded sheet of paper from his pocket, pressed it open, and laid it on the table in front of Mullen. "That's true, but none of them had the same name and social security number as your father."

Mullen's arms fell to his sides. He turned away from us and walked to the edge of the porch. A radio on the table called his name, but the agent ignored it. He gazed out over the yard and the garden where Rand and I had taken cover a few hours before. When he turned back, his face had lost the arrogance, although his voice remained impassive.

"How'd you find out?"

"I have friends too," Rand said softly. "Is this why you're looking for Brutkiewicz?"

He neither agreed nor disagreed. Resignation tinged his voice. "You're right, McArdle. Brutkiewicz killed my father. But do you know why?"

Rand nodded. "Your father found out about their plan to get out of the war. And they silenced him."

For a second, Mullen's surprise was apparent. "So. You're right about me looking for Brutkiewicz. But this man's not him. I'm sure of that now."

I sighed my own relief at knowing that Mullen was no psycho himself, using his office to exact revenge. Although he may have started out with that intent, he now knew that the person he was looking for was somebody else.

"Agent Mullen," I said, "how long have you known for sure?"

"Not long. Actually, not until this morning when I got the blood results in from the lab. Their blood types don't match."

"How'd you get a blood type?" Rand asked.

It was Mullen's turn to smile. "Easy. His wife was glad to supply medical records."

Ellen Brutkiewicz again. When this was all over, I was going to take this woman to dinner.

Little by little, the pieces began to fit, and I knew that Mullen and his agents were far better equipped to handle Brister when they eventually found him than I was. With that in mind, I also knew something else. As much as I hated to admit it, Katie was probably right about my need to get to Alabama.

If I ever wanted to be a part of the inner circle, I'd have to follow up on the story she'd sent my way. But that brought on another problem I hadn't counted on. Over the past weeks, Rand and I had formed a relationship that I very much wanted to develop to its fullest, and that's always harder to do long distance. Be that as it may, I also knew that I needed time apart to think. The questions I'd allowed myself to verbalize about our future could be better thought out with some distance between us.

"Agent Mullen," I asked, "have you heard anything about a family's disappearance in Alabama?"

My words finally hit home, and he admitted, "A bit. Why?"

"My editor's sending me to cover it."

His whole face pursed into a scowl. "Not my assignment. Our job here's not finished. Not until Brister's in custody. Or dead." Then his expression changed. "You don't think Brister's in Alabama, do you?"

"Couldn't he be?"

"I don't know. Where is this place?"

"Northeast corner," I told him. "It's a state park with a lot of wilderness area."

"When did this happen?"

"A few hours ago. If Brister drove all night, he could be there, couldn't he?"

As Mullen processed this information, he reached for the cell phone and punched in numbers. He turned away from us, but we could still hear the gist of the conversation. He asked about events that had taken place in north Alabama. Judging from his tone, he was none too happy about being excluded from the initial investigation. Mullen made it clear that he was moving his base of operation to Alabama, and Rand's expression showed his concern.

I eased closer to him. "Rand, forget it. You need to go home."

When he didn't answer, I tried again. "You've got a business to run. There's no telling how long this thing in Alabama might last. Go on. I'll be fine."

Rand still didn't answer me, but when Mullen turned back to us, he asked, "It's our man, isn't it?"

"Sounds that way."

Rand's expression displayed all the frustration I felt. We'd spent the last week following Brister, and now he'd slipped through the net. For whatever reasons I'd started looking for him, now I had even more. Little Lauren and her parents had finally been found. Everette Suttle knew what happened to his family. But we had a chance to take that one step further. If that family in Alabama could be saved, I wanted to be part of the rescue. Katie or no Katie, I was going.

Lines across Rand's forehead that weren't there days before told me how much this had worn on him, and I knew he needed to go home to Jackson. "Rand, go. Your work's been on hold too long."

"But you don't need to go alone."

"I won't be," I admitted, glancing toward Mullen, who now barked orders into the cell phone. "I'll be more than safe. But if I'm going to write this story, I've got to be there."

I could tell that the decision was a tough one for him, but I held fast. "Come on. We'll drive to Jackson, I'll pick up my car, and I'll call as soon as I get there."

His shoulders sagged, and he said, "I guess that makes sense. I really do need to catch up."

The agreement made, we were in Jackson within two hours. I had to admit that as I switched my belongings into my own car, the pit of my stomach bottomed out, and I had more than a few second thoughts. How could someone as independent as I feel this way? I was only going a few hundred miles to the east, but for some reason, I felt as if I could be leaving a whole life behind.

I put the last of the things in my rental car and stood up to face Rand. He gave me that slightly injured grin, but he held his arms out to me, and I slid comfortably into his embrace. We stood there in his driveway, rocking back and forth, enjoying the feel and smell that we'd both become so accustomed to over the past days.

"How did I get so lucky to meet you?" he asked.

"Same way I got lucky to find you," I said in our now customary exchange. I looked up at him and tried to swallow the enormous lump in my throat. "I'll be through with this story in no time. Then we can talk. And figure out which way to go from here."

He smiled, but his eyes at first didn't meet mine. When he did look at me, the smile was gone, and in its place was seriousness I hadn't seen. "Reagan, I haven't felt like this in so many years. And I don't want to lose it."

"Me either. Count on it."

He kissed me once more, and I turned to get into the car. "Okay, guess I'd better hit the road."

"Yeah, you'll never get there at this rate."

I slid into the driver's seat. "I'll be back in a few days," I said, more to assure myself than him. "Get caught up on your work, and I'll call you tonight."

As I crossed the state line just beyond Meridian, I could still hear his voice calmly tell me to be careful. All doubts I might have harbored over the past few days were vanishing rapidly. If Noelle was anything at all like her dad, we'd get along just fine. We'd work out the rest. What I felt for Rand was something I had thought long gone from my life, and I wasn't about to let it slip away.

TWENTY-ONE

Katie's idea of a few hours turned into a marathon. As the old adage says, nothing's impossible as long as it's somebody else's job. By the time I finally entered the town of Fort Payne, all vestiges of sunlight had disappeared behind what I would soon come to know as Lookout Mountain.

Five hundred miles, added onto the scene in Rand's driveway, left me feeling like a cornstalk after a hail storm. I shook from sheer exhaustion, and I wanted nothing more than to peel the contacts off my eyeballs and stand under a hot shower until sleep overcame me. Whatever was going on in DeSoto State Park would just have to wait a while, at least long enough for me to regroup.

The highway took me down the main street. All the while, I kept my eyes open for anything that looked like suitable accommodations, but the town was closed up for the night. I was about to give up when I spotted a well-known sign off in the distance, and I headed off in its general direction.

Katie was right about one thing. It appeared that the entire nation of reporters had convened in that tiny town, and from the looks of the parking lot, I'd be lucky to get a room. But I remembered that I was there to find Brister, and that's exactly what I intended to do, room or no room. I crossed my fingers and entered the lobby.

To my surprise, there were very few people milling about. Everybody else must already be on the scene. But then I spotted a pair of reporter-looking types standing near the back of the lobby, engaged in conversation. From the back, I couldn't be sure, but when the man facing my direction smiled and nodded politely, the other, taller and better-looking one, turned to follow his partner's gaze. Recognition spread across his face as a sickening wave rose in my throat. Ray immediately stopped talking, excused himself, and headed straight for me.

I felt as if I'd been punched in the gut. There was nowhere to run, and Ray wouldn't have it anyway. I couldn't exactly call it a smile, but no doubt his expression was more pleasant than my own.

He towered over me, as he'd always done, intimidating in the way only he could be.

"Reagan! What in the world brings you here?" he asked confidently.

"Haven't you heard? There's a huge story going on nearby." I turned my head as he leaned to kiss me on the cheek. "I'm a writer, Ray. Or did you forget?"

He drew back, pretending affront. "And a darn good one too. I'm just surprised since this isn't your usual gig."

"Times change," I quipped. "And so do people."

A shock of straight dark hair fell over his forehead, and he managed to look hurt. "Yes, yes, they do." A hint of seriousness flickered in his eyes. "I'm just surprised."

His sharply defined, handsome features had only grown more so in our absence, but still there was something around him as cold as an Arctic winter. How could I have ever been so enamoured?

He glanced back at the man who'd watched our encounter and now smiled uneasily.

"Your reputation in danger?" I asked.

His features relaxed into his signature smile. "What reputation is that?"

"Never mind. Well, good to see you, Ray."

"Reagan, this is a most pleasant surprise. I don't suppose you'd have a drink with us," he asked more softly.

"You suppose right. Well, nice seeing you, Ray," I added and brushed past him as I hurried to the desk. For once, he was the one left to cope.

A young woman with mousy brown hair had watched the encounter with wide eyes.

"Is it possible for me to get a room?" I asked her.

I could still feel eyes on me as he rejoined his partner. The other man laughed a bit uneasily, and they sauntered through the lobby and went outside.

The girl lowered her eyes and studied the computer screen on the desk. She shook her head slowly, still studying the screen. "I wish I could help you, but we're full up." She looked at me sadly. "It's all these reporters. Biggest story around here since that man from California showed up with a dead woman in his trunk."

I didn't even want to know about the dead woman. I already knew what her answer would be. Still, I had to have some rest, or I'd soon be a melted Popsicle.

"Are there any other motels close by?"

Again she shook her head, but then she stopped, and her eyes lit up. "Wait a minute. I've got an idea. It's a long shot, but what with all the goin's-on up at the park, I bet nobody's staying in the cabins. Want me to check?"

"There are cabins up where the manhunt's going on?"

"Yep. And I'll just bet they'll let you stay there since nothin's available in town. I can call and find out if you want."

"That'd be nice," I agreed. Then another thought occurred. "These cabins do have electricity, don't they?"

She laughed. "Sure. They got air-conditioning and cable TV too."

As I laughed at my own foible, she picked up the phone. Within a minute or so, I was safely booked into what she referred to as a rustic cabin at DeSoto State Park. However, her reservation came with a warning attached.

"Now they'll have the road blocked 'bout halfway up the mountain, but I'm gonna give you a number showin' that you've got a reservation, and they'll let you through." She leaned over the desk and whispered, "I told 'em you're a writer, so they'll let you in."

I thanked her, got directions up the mountain and to the park, and headed back to my car, somewhat invigorated by the night air. The sky was as clear as I'd ever seen it, partly because the nearest city lights didn't offer much in the way of interference. With the change in altitude as well as latitude, I even felt a little chilled. Maybe I could stay awake long enough to get to the cabins after all.

Before I could muse about the possibility too much, though, I pulled into the drive-through lane of the fast-food place next door, ordered, and once again headed out. The snaky road couldn't be the best under normal circumstances, but in the dark, gripping a greasy hamburger with one hand and trying to navigate with the other, I felt as if I'd relapsed into one of my crazy dreams where I couldn't see but still barreled ahead. I was actually thankful when I spotted the blue lights on the roadway ahead at the apex of a hill.

I eased the car off the road amid a flurry of lights flashing me to turn around and waited while an officer came to my window.

"Ma'am, you'll have to turn around," he instructed.

"I'm here to see Agent Mullen," I said. "I'm working on this case with him."

"You FBI?"

"No. I'm a writer, but I've been on this case since the beginning. Can you direct me to him?"

He stood upright and looked off toward the spot where a small group was huddled in conference beneath flashing lights. Then he aimed the light in their direction.

"He's over there. Does he know you're coming?"

"I'm not sure. But if I could speak to him for a minute, I'd appreciate it."

He hesitated for a second, then answered, "You can leave your car here and walk over."

I thanked him again and walked toward the group. The hill offered a panorama of the valley below, but I doubted Mullen or any of the others huddled at this crest had noticed. I would have recognized Mullen's stature anywhere, but in the dark, he somehow looked more impressive. And more amazingly, I was glad to see him.

"Agent Mullen. It's me, Reagan Wilks."

"I saw you coming," he said flatly.

"Any breaks?" I asked.

"If you mean have we spotted him, no. But as far as we know, the family's still alive."

"Where are they?"

He motioned with his head toward a spot farther up the mountain. "We don't know for sure. We've got so many sightings, he'd have to be Superman to be in all those places."

"Anything about the family?"

"Nope. At least that part's good. If he'd killed them, we'd probably have evidence of that by now."

I agreed with him, and he asked, "Where's your partner?"

"In Jackson. He had to catch up on work."

"Understandable. So you're here to write about it all?"

"I'm here to help you find Brister," I corrected. "Sure, I'll write a story, but more than anything, I want to see Brister stopped."

He didn't answer immediately. When he did, the sarcasm surprised me. "Do you think taking him in will bring back that family?"

"No," I said flatly. "No, I don't." I thought about Lauren and how she'd first led us to Brister, then how she'd shielded us from his latest attack. I didn't know how to explain all that to this man, so I didn't even try. I simply added, "But I may be able to keep him from doing it again."

In more of a statement than a question, he said, "You know what he looks like, don't you?"

"I've seen pictures of him at his mother's house. Of course, he was much younger, but I know what his build looks like. And I'd never forget that face. I don't think it's possible for him to have changed that much."

"Well then, you just may be able to help. We've got some witnesses around here who said they saw him. But when we showed them pictures, two said it was the same person, but the other wasn't sure. One thought our man here was too tall, the others thought he was older."

"So you're thinking that maybe if I talked to them, we'd get a better picture of who we're dealing with here?"

"The witnesses just got quick looks at him from a distance. You know how it is. Ten people see an accident, and you'll get ten different versions. I'd just like to know what we're up against. We can't use personal information if he's not our man."

"I'd be more than happy to do that," I agreed. "But do you think it can wait a few hours?"

His look asked why.

"I'm dead on my feet. If I can get a few hours, I'll be a lot more help to you."

Mullen looked even more puzzled, and he asked, "Where?"

"Where am I staying?"

"Yeah." He looked around at the empty wilderness. "Not too many hotel rooms up here. There's a buncha houses that rent out, but they're empty now. Only folks left are the ones that live here and refused to move when we asked them to. Nothing we can do if they refuse to leave."

"I'm staying in a cabin at the park."

"What?" He looked as if I'd taken a swing at him. "Nobody's in those cabins."

Suddenly the cold fingers wrapped around my throat again. "Well, I've got news for you. The lady in the motel down in Fort Payne called somebody and made me a reservation for a cabin in the park. She called it a rustic cabin."

He sighed heavily and rubbed the bridge of his nose. "Okay, okay. My men are all camped out there. I guess you'll be safe."

Now it was my turn to be surprised. "You mean the only people up there are law enforcement?"

"That's about the size of it. The park's running a skeleton staff so we have food, but I wouldn't count on much."

Suddenly I felt ill. "Why didn't she tell me?" I asked futilely.

"Ms. Wilks," he began, then stopped.

I guess he didn't know what to say either, so I filled in the gap. "Look, Mullen. I'll manage."

A humming sound made him pick up the phone attached to his belt. "Mullen," he answered then and held his watch up to the light. "Be there in five minutes."

"Gotta go," he said to me. "We may have something this time."

"In the park?"

"Yep."

"May I follow?"

He looked across the street, where my car waited, then instructed, "Stay behind me. And don't leave your car until I tell you. Clear?"

"I understand," I told him, already running toward the car. "I'll be right behind you." I knew this could be the chance I'd waited for, and I wasn't about to let it slip by.

Mullen was in his car and headed up the mountain, followed by a second unmarked that I assumed was also FBI and two state police. I had no idea where we were headed or what might happen when we caught up with Brister, but I planned to be there when it happened.

I followed the taillights as they spiraled up the mountain, one dizzy turn following the other, and I barely had time to glimpse a wooden sign on the side of the road before the cars ahead of me turned sharply to the right and proceeded downhill. We sped downward through a soundless blanket of forest on either side. The only light came from what filtered through the trees, then dissipated before it reached the ground. Finally, we stopped near a large rustic building made of gray-colored slats. It looked like the hub of the park's activities, and lights streamed through the long slits of windows that covered the front of the building. I could clearly see Mullen's figure as he jumped from his car, weapon drawn ahead of him, and disappeared into the thickness of the forest behind the building.

Others followed. At least two of them were women, but I had no idea which ones were local law enforcement and which ones were FBI. From my station in the car, I saw nothing more than an occasional beam of light flickering through the dense woods, and I heard no more than a few words spoken in staccato as they disappeared into the forest behind the building.

The night was only slightly cool, but again I shook. True to my word, I remained in the car; but the more my insides turned to jelly, the more I wanted to leave this place. Then I remembered the sight of little Lauren on the side of the road, and I remembered how she'd saved us from being shot by Brister. The least I could do was to wait, to make sure he couldn't hurt anybody else. That I owed to Lauren.

How long I remained like that in the car, shivering and wondering, I don't really know. But eventually, the two I'd first seen follow Mullen into the woods emerged, talking easily to each other as they returned to their cars. Then Mullen himself returned. He started toward his car, then looked my way and changed direction.

I got out as he approached. "Find anything?"

He made no comment to my question, but instead, said, "Follow me. I'll take you to a cabin where you can stay. You'll be safe there."

When he turned off the main road, I thought he'd made a mistake, but I followed anyway. We inched down a driveway for perhaps a hundred yards, through darkness deep enough to be a black hole, and I stopped beside Mullen's car. We'd only taken a few steps when a motion light at the top of the building came to life, revealing a tiny cabin, the sort built back in the 1940s as part of a government program to give work to the masses of unemployed.

You must be kidding, I thought. But before I could express that sentiment openly, he took off toward the cabin, and I had to follow or be left outside alone.

A screened porch fronted the side of the cabin that apparently perched on the edge of a cliff overlooking Little River. This popular vacation spot billed itself as the Grand Canyon of the South, but for all I could tell in the dark, the land simply ceased to exist beyond the light's edge. I'd never seen a more complete dark.

Thankfully, there was a light on the porch, too, and Mullen left me there while he entered the cabin and turned on lights as he went from room to room. His footsteps sounded heavily across the floors, and that musty smell of old wood filled my nostrils.

When he returned to the door, he told me, "It's safe. Come on in."

I entered and stood there transfixed, unable to think beyond the moment. Mullen fidgeted with a window air conditioner, and it hummed to life.

"Is anybody else staying here?" I finally asked as I looked past him to the minute bedroom and its single bed squeezed between two walls. Windows filled both outer walls, and I visualized trying to sleep within arm's reach of whatever might be outside.

He followed my gaze. "Somebody'll be in and out of here all night. You won't be alone, if that's what you're thinking."

I didn't know what I thought, but before I could respond, another car crunched its way down the gravel drive and came to a stop beside ours. Two of the uniformed officers I'd seen following Mullen into the woods now entered the cabin.

The young dark-haired woman who entered first smiled at me and extended her hand. "Hi. I'm Janet Dowdy," she drawled. "I'm gonna stay here for a couple a hours, if you don't mind."

"No, I don't mind," I readily admitted, and I held my hand out to take hers. "Glad to meet you. Reagan Wilks."

"I know."

The second uniform was slightly older and definitely tall enough to qualify for somebody's basketball team. "Howdy, ma'am," he said, nodding his blond head at me. "Mind if we take a look around?"

"Be my guest."

I stood aside as these two made their way through the cabin. They opened each tiny closet, even the cabinets beneath the sink, then proceeded to the miniscule bedroom where they peeked into the darkness outside, then drew the blinds on each window. Mullen had stepped back onto the porch where he conversed on his two-way.

When the two officers were satisfied that there was no one else in the cabin, they returned to the living room. Its entire furnishings consisted of a seventies-style sofa covered in a rough plaid fabric, a small table where the twelve-inch television sat, and another small round oak table accompanied by four captain's chairs positioned between the common area and the kitchen.

Janet looped her thumbs through belt loops at her sides and smiled casually for my benefit.

"Everything looks okay here. Like I said, I'm gonna stay for a while. Then Marty here'll be back around two to stay the rest of the night. Sound okay?"

I only nodded. What more could I say? These people were risking life and limb for me, and I wasn't about to complain. But I knew that as soon as daylight etched its way through the woods, I'd be out there again, looking for Brister.

Knowing that my new friend Janet was in the next room, I finally managed to relax enough to strip off my tired clothes and step tentatively into the square box that served as a shower stall. Hot water rushed over my aching body, and I tried to remember how long it had been since my last shower. And I tried to remember how long it had been since the peaceful nostalgia of the trace before all this nightmare began.

Satisfied that I was secure for the moment, I dried off and put on a fresh tee shirt over pajama bottoms, then slipped between surprisingly crisp, clean white sheets. I propped both pillows up behind me until I was comfortable and sat there wondering what next to do. I'd begged for sleep for hours, but now that I had the chance, my brain raced uncontrollably.

At first, I thought the sound might be coming from the television going in the next room, and I tried to ignore it. But then the more I listened, the more I was mystified. An uneven high-pitched cacophony reverberated through the woods around me. In those rare years, I'd heard the racket made by cicadas, but this sounded like something else entirely. It was as if millions of tiny violins unsuccessfully tuned up in the woods.

I tried to shrug it off because I knew that it had to be some local phenomenon, nothing to be afraid of. Still, talking to Rand might make it better. I held the cell phone under the lamp next to the bed and turned it so I could see the signal strength. The sound outside grew louder, but my signal didn't.

I tried again this time and, in spite of my better judgement, moved toward the outer wall of windows. Still nothing. No matter how I turned it, the results were the same. We were too far from a tower to get a signal through these thick woods, and making a call out would be impossible.

I knew there was no other phone in the cabin. *Calm down*, I told myself. *It's only a phone call. Rand will still be there in the morning.* Still, I couldn't shake the feeling of being trapped with a strange noise that had grown beyond mere levels of irritation.

I'd left the bedroom door open and could see Janet propped casually on the sofa opposite the television. No more than five feet separated her from the set, but the volume reached me easily in the bedroom. On the screen, black-and-white photos of mutilated bodies flickered across, one gruesome scene after the other.

Janet appeared totally engrossed. Her hand rested calmly on the holster bulging at her hip, but her attention was on the screen.

"Hey," I said as I flopped down beside her on the sofa. "Mind if I join you?"

"Of course not. Can't sleep?"

"No, not yet." I tried to focus on the screen, but with the door to the porch open, the noise was even louder in the living room. I couldn't concentrate.

"What's that noise?" I finally asked.

She looked at me at first uncomprehending, then grinned. "Oh. You mean the noise outside?"

"Yeah. What in the world is that?"

"Tree frogs. You never heard 'em?"

"I guess not. Are they always like that?"

"No, not always. Mostly in the summer."

"I see." I thought about that for a minute. While I'd spent most of my life in the South, admittedly I'd spent it in the city, and I was on new territory here. "How big are these tree frogs?"

"Oh, they're little bitty. About the size of a grasshopper."

"Oh." I turned my attention back to the screen and tried to remember how big a grasshopper was. The episode was concluding, with a stern warning from the moderator that this particular serial killer had never been caught and was believed to be still at large.

"Janet, do you think there's anything else on?"

She looked at me for a second; then her eyes darted back to the TV. "Oh, you mean that," she laughed and aimed the controller at the set. "I'm sorry," she said as she raced through the channels. "I wasn't thinking."

"Ordinarily it wouldn't be a problem," I confessed. "I guess I'm just a little edgy tonight."

Although I was still a bit chilled, the roughness of the sofa's fabric made me itchy and hot. I stayed there for a few minutes, aware of faces and voices filling the room, but unable to focus on any of them.

"You know," I said, "I tried to get a signal on my phone in the bedroom, but I couldn't get a thing. Is that usual?"

"I'm afraid so," she said consolingly and hit the Mute button on the TV again. "But sometimes, you can get a signal outside."

I thought about the envelope of darkness that surrounded the cabin and cringed. I didn't know if tree frogs leapt from their branches onto unsuspecting passers-by, but the look on my face must have signaled something. She volunteered, "If you wanna go outside to try calling, I'll go with you."

"Bless you," I said and followed her onto the porch with its light.

"You go on a bit, out toward the car," she instructed. "I'll stay here and keep an eye out."

It hadn't occurred to me that we might be leaving ourselves open with the cabin unattended, so what she said made sense. I agreed and turned to leave.

"Here, take the flash," she added.

The motion light covered the first fifty or so feet where the picnic table and benches were. Then I stepped up over the low rock wall that separated the driveway and parking area from the yard and turned on the flash. My car was only a few feet farther. I held the phone under the light and prayed for a signal. There wasn't much of one, but still it was better than it had been in the cabin. My desire to talk to Rand now overrode my fear, and when I reached the car, I set the light on top of the roof and punched in familiar numbers. To my relief, a sporadic dial tone finally sounded.

I let go of the breath I'd held forever but, in the next instant, drew it back with greater force. Someone or something was out there. A definite crunch on the gravel riveted my attention down the lane toward the road that ran through the park. I sensed movement, and the flashlight's beam confirmed my suspicions. Silhouetted in the lane stood a solitary male figure less than fifty yards away.

I ran for the cabin, but in my haste, I'd forgotten about the rock wall; and when my foot reached out for the next step, it met with only air. I tumbled down with a thud. My knees ground into the rocky earth, and my hands scraped across grainy soil. I scrambled to get up, knowing that the intruder must be nearly on me.

"What is it?" Janet called from the steps.

I lifted myself from the ground like a dream in slow motion. "Somebody's out there!"

She met me and took the flashlight from my hand, then aimed it down the lane into the darkness. A slow smile emerged. "Hey, Arthur! You scared us."

"You know him?"

She nodded and called out to him again. "It's Janet Dowdy. What you doin' out there?"

As she spoke, the tall lanky figure emerged from the shadows and entered the lighted area on the front of the cabin. His weathered face squinted into her spotlight, and she lowered the flash as she moved her hand away from the holster.

His nearly toothless smile and humorous eyes focused on Janet, ignoring me as I rubbed debris from my knees and palms. His gravelly voice lingered over each syllable, which he caressed with slow emphasis. "What you two girls doin' up here all alone at night?"

"Arthur, you know perfectly well I'm a trained police officer. We're here on business—probably the same business that has you out here."

He grinned wider. "And what business would that be, Ms. Janet?"

"Come on, Arthur. You're not foolin' me. You're out here lookin' for that kidnapper, aren't you?"

"Just doin' my rounds," he said, shaking his head. "Don't know 'bout no kidnappers."

"I'll bet." Janet grinned. Then she remembered me. "Reagan, meet Arthur." He's a fixture in this park. Looks out after every one of us."

"Glad to meet you, Arthur," I said, still not sure whether to shake his hand or tell him what for.

"Same here." He nodded. "Hope I didn't scare you too much, miss."

"I'll survive. I guess you could tell I was a little frightened."

He nodded again, but his words were aimed at Janet. "They tole me to leave till they captured that guy, but you know how it is." He patted a bulging pocket at his thigh. "Nobody's gonna mess with Old Arthur so long as he's got this here snake charmer."

"Well, you be careful anyway," Janet reminded.

"Count on that," he assured. "Well, guess I'll be getting on my way now." He took a few steps before he stopped and turned back. "You ladies be careful now. Just call out if you need me."

"Thanks, Arthur," she said warmly.

Janet's familiarity with this strange man still didn't make me feel a whole lot better, but we remained there for a moment at the foot of the lane, watching Arthur walk out of our light and back into the darkness beyond its perimeter.

I asked, "Is he really a park employee?"

"No. Not really an employee. He's just a harmless old guy who thinks he takes care of the park. He lives in a shack he made down by the river years ago. Arthur stays out of the way, and he doesn't bother anybody, so the park folks just look the other way." She opened the screened door to the porch. "It's prime real estate, but I don't think he has anywhere else to go."

TWENTY-TWO

I spent what little remained of the night doing what I'd gone to the cabin to do in the first place. For some reason, the encounter with Arthur made my fears seem all the more unfounded, and I drifted off to sleep in only minutes.

Shortly after dawn, however, the sound of male voices in the next room broke the trance, and I was instantly awake. Surprised that I'd been out of it so completely, I awoke with a clear head and went to find out what was going on.

Mullen and Janet's male counterpart stopped talking when I opened the door.

"Has something happened?" I asked.

"Yeah. We've got him cornered in town. I'm on my way there now, but I stopped by here because I thought you might want to be in on it."

"Yes, yes, I would. Thanks, Mullen." I turned back to the bedroom, then stopped to ask, "By town, do you mean in Fort Payne?"

"No. A little place called Mentone, a short distance on the other side of the mountain. Nobody much lives there, but he's holed up in an old hotel. Some local guy spotted the family down by Little River, in a remote part of the canyon."

"Are they alive?"

"Not only alive, but apparently unharmed. Of course, they're tired and scratched up a bit, but otherwise okay."

"Thank God," I breathed. Then it occurred to me to ask, "You said some local guy?"

"Yeah. Apparently it's an old guy who lives on the river. He spotted them before daybreak this morning."

I smiled at the memory of my encounter with Arthur, but for the moment kept that to myself. "So Brister just left them out there and took off?"

"Yep. It's kinda hard to figure, but right now, we're more concerned with taking Brister in. He's got a lot of answering to do."

"You can say that again."

"Anyway, if you want to come along, you can. You'll have to stay out of the way, but you can watch."

"You bet I want to go."

I was out of the cabin in less than five minutes, again following Mullen's car in my own. In the daylight, I could tell why this place had become so popular. An amazingly thick forest blanketed the mountain, covered with early morning's crystal dew. Three deer scampered across the road ahead of us on a curve, and birds flitted back and forth over the roadway.

Scattered all over the mountain, there were homes tucked beneath trees, but near the rim they morphed into a different sort. There, where people from Birmingham and Atlanta had taken refuge, bigger and more impressive rows of eye-catching homes paid tribute to the landscape, but more so to the power of the dollar. Lured there by the mountain's sheer beauty and isolation, these refugees would repeat a familiar pattern. Real estate prices would skyrocket, and the less fortunate would have to look for dwellings elsewhere, priced out of the place they'd owned since a time when nobody else wanted it.

I followed Mullen across the top of the mountain and down to a quaint little town dotted by a few buildings that housed antique shops and several stately old homes that had seen better times. I had no trouble telling where they'd cornered Brister since official cars of every description surrounded the graceful hotel that perched on the side of a hill overlooking the town.

The hotel, a white wooden structure with traditional green shutters, was built long and low, no more than three stories high. Although obviously some work had been done to bring it up to par, the building still yearned for additional restoration. It reminded me of a beauty queen, though still lovely, past her prime.

A decorative wrought-iron fence corralled the entire grounds from the street to the hotel, and in the space between, someone had planted an English-type garden where snapdragons of every color competed for space with Queen Anne's lace and showy purple verbena. The stone pathway led to a tall porch that encompassed the entire front of the building, complete with white rocking chairs and ceiling fans that spun idly in the morning's breeze.

Mullen parked on a side street perpendicular to the hotel and met me as I was getting out of the car. "You'll have to stay back here. Can't afford to let you get any closer."

"What's going on? I mean, do they know for sure he's in there?"

He nodded. "One of the owners of the hotel called the local police when he took over." He looked across the street where three men waited behind a van. Each of them wore light jackets emblazoned across the back with the familiar three letters, FBI.

"How long has he been in there?"

"Not long. I was on my way down here when I stopped by your cabin." For a moment, I thought he might actually smile, but the stony face returned. "I figured since you'd come this far, you had a right to be there when we took him down."

"I appreciate that." Before I could ask anything else, Mullen returned to his car where he reached in to pick up the two-way that called his name. He listened for a moment, then spoke briefly, still holding the mic as he glanced at me.

"He's got somebody in there with him." And with that, he was gone.

He crossed the street and joined the three men hidden from view behind the van. He gestured to them, and they scattered to different positions around the hotel.

In movielike fashion, people scurried in every direction. Then I heard Mullen's voice. Loud and clear, he called to Brister in some form of amplification, identifying himself and ordering Brister to give himself up.

"We know somebody else is in there with you," he concluded. "Don't make this any worse on yourself than it already is."

From every angle, sharpshooters positioned themselves, poised to take out the man responsible for at least three deaths. Mullen repeated his orders, and everybody waited.

When nothing happened, Mullen's orders took on a slightly different approach.

"Brister, come on out. The game's over. Start by sending out your hostage. We'll take that as a sign that you're willing to talk."

Again, uniforms and plain clothes alike waited. Rifles all pointed toward the front door, but no one came out of the hotel. For all appearances, it was an ordinary day in the little village, and Mullen shouted to an empty building. I began to feel as if the whole thing was wasted motion when I spotted movement at the main entrance.

The wide double doors that served as a main entrance were already open, but something had changed. At first it was only a shadow; then the outline of two people appeared. As they came through the doorway, I could see that one man walked slightly behind the other and held an object pointed at the head of the first. They took several tentative steps forward, out of the shadows on the porch and into the bright morning's sunlight.

Icy fingers laced around my throat as I gasped for air. I knew one of those men, all right, and it wasn't Brister. I should know. I'd chased him over two states now, and the man I'd come to know was nowhere around. Instead, Everette Suttle held a stranger hostage and pointed a gun at his head.

At Everette's urging, the men walked forward to the edge of the porch. Sunlight glinted off the barrel pointed at the stranger's head, and Everette held it fixed against the temple. The man's arms draped uselessly at his sides.

"Put it down," Mullen called. "You don't want your life to end this way."

I rushed from my safety and headed for Mullen.

"Wait! That's not Brister," I shouted as I ran across the street to where Mullen waited behind the van.

As I approached, he turned to look at me, his eyes narrowed into a scowl. "Get out of here," he ordered.

I continued toward him. "That's the wrong man," I repeated.

Comprehension finally registered, and I leaned against the van and tried to catch my breath. "That's not Glenn Brister," I said once again.

"Not Brister?"

I shook my head, gasping for air.

"Well, who the hell is it then?"

"I don't have any idea who the hostage is. But the shooter is Everette Suttle."

"You mean the grandfather of the little girl?"

"Look, I don't understand this either, but you've gotta stop Everette from making the biggest mistake of his life."

Mullen turned back toward the hotel and picked up the megaphone. "Everette Suttle, put down the gun."

From my position behind the van, I couldn't see what was going on, so I slipped away while Mullen talked to Everette. He continued trying to convince him to lay down the weapon and thus save his own life. I inched my way from car to car until I was nearer the hotel, near enough for Everette to hear me.

"Everette, this is Reagan Wilks. Remember me?"

He looked around, trying to find the source of the voice. I stood up slowly, leaving the cover of the police car. "Everette, I know you think you're doing the right thing, but that man's not Brister. I swear to you it's not the man who killed your family."

Everette held his position for what seemed like eternity, then called back. "Are you sure, Ms. Wilks?"

"You know me, Everette. I wouldn't lie to you. You know that. Put the gun down, Everette. It's not too late, but if you do anything stupid, everybody loses. You, Danny, Stephanie, Lauren. They lose again. Do it now, Everette."

The hand slowly fell away from the man's temple, and Everette's grip on the hostage relaxed. Before agents could reach the top of the stairs, the kidnapper, now hostage, had run right into the hands he'd avoided for days, and Everette stood still as officers surrounded him too. The gun was lifted from his hand, and cuffs glinted in its place.

Everette shook his head, as if by doing so he might make it all go away. He cast one last look my way before they ushered him toward a waiting automobile and tucked him inside. But his face said it all. This man had been fully prepared to give his life in order to kill the man who'd taken his family from him. Everette had played his hand and lost.

I only thought I'd been haunted by looks before, but that face would haunt me for the rest of my life. Surely this man had known more torturous nights than most of us can imagine, and now he would suffer the ordeals of a trial. I'd do what I could, but the system doesn't seem to understand compassion.

The car containing Everette Suttle drove past me, but the man himself looked straight ahead into an unknown future. The man had aged tremendously since I'd last seen him, and I wanted to reach out to him, to tell him how very sorry I was for every injustice he'd been dealt. But all I could do was to stand and watch idly as police drove him to some ratty jail to be processed like a common criminal.

There was nothing common at all in what had happened to Everette Suttle. And there was nothing common in what was going on in DeSoto State Park either. If this man who'd held a family hostage wasn't Glenn Brister, then who was he?

Before I could process that line of reasoning any further, I heard Mullen call my name as he stomped across the road. His normal placid complexion had turned a boiling red, and his usual quiet tone erupted into a rage.

"I thought I told you to stay back where I left you. What the hell was that heroic act?"

"It wasn't heroic. I was scared to death. But I was more scared that you'd shoot an innocent man."

"He's not so innocent." He swabbed at his beaded face with a handkerchief. "He held somebody hostage, and he wouldn't have thought twice about shooting him. That's not innocent."

"You don't understand."

"Hell, right. I don't understand. You could've gone down in a second."

I drew a deep breath and relished the softness of the air. "But I didn't, did I?"

Mullen had no answer, and he visibly relaxed too, leaning against the police car I'd used as a shield. When he spoke, his words had lost the edge of anger.

"I hate hostage situations. You never know what's gonna go down. I could see you getting wiped out by this crazy. And what would I tell your friend McArdle then?"

For the first time, I spotted the hint of a smile on his face, and I thought about Rand. "I guess you'd just have to tell him that I couldn't let you shoot somebody who's already been through hell through no fault of his own."

"Yeah, well, that's fine and good now. But believe me, you scared the crap out of me."

"Sorry. I did what I had to do."

We stood there leaning against the car, enjoying the peace of the moment.

"Well since that's not Brister, who is it?" I asked.

Mullen shook his head and allowed himself a full smile. "Darned if I know. My best guess is it's some copycat, out for his fifteen minutes of fame."

"Wouldn't you think he could think of some better way to be famous?"

"You'd think. But believe me, there's no accounting for what people will do."

By that time, others milled around the car, and two of the FBI jackets approached Mullen.

He anticipated their questions and told them, "We'll be headed back to Mississippi. You go on back up to the camp, and I'll be right behind you."

As they walked off, I asked, "So you're going back to Mississippi?"

"I guess so. That's the last place he was seen for sure, so that's probably where he still is. He knows we've got the Hutchisons staked out. My guess is he's still right under our noses. We'll just have to be smarter than he is this time."

Mullen mumbled a hasty exit and headed back to his car. My scraped knees stung in the heat of midday, and I was good and tired of Brister outsmarting us. There had to be a way to find him, and I was going back to Mississippi to give it one more try.

TWENTY-THREE

As soon as I got off the mountain, I called Rand and filled him in on what had happened. He was as sorry as I that Everette had chosen to take a less than wise, although understandable, course of action; and he advised me to meet him at his house as soon as I could make the trek back across two states. We planned to continue our search for Brister, but we'd start by regrouping in Jackson. At some point, the chase had to end, and for us, the sooner the better.

I planned to spend the night at Rand's house; then together, we'd journey back to Natchez, the last known hangout of Glenn Brister. Somewhere along the way, I remembered that I'd purportedly gone to DeSoto to get a story, so I took out my tape recorder and began composing as I drove south across Alabama. Although I had no pictures, I sure as hell had the story. Pictures we could buy. Later on, I'd do some research on copycat criminals, adding that as a sidebar. But for the moment, if Katie wanted a story, she'd get one. It might not be what she had in mind, but I could guarantee that readers would never forget the story of Everette Suttle, who took on the establishment and lost.

Lights from Rand's house beckoned to me from the top of the hill when I turned onto his street. His house looked like a beacon in the growing darkness. I didn't even have to use the key he'd given me because the side door opened before I could get out of the car, and Rand met me in the driveway.

We embraced for what seemed like a long time, standing where we'd stood only a few hours before. When he finally let go, he said, "I missed you. Missed you more than I thought possible."

"Me too. How many months was I gone?"

"Oh, I can't count that high. I guess we'll have to make up for lost time."

We entered the house, arm in arm, through the kitchen doorway that opened onto the patio. I hadn't really laughed since I'd left him, and it felt good. But as we entered the kitchen, I stopped. There, perched on a stool at the bar, was a lovely, female version of Rand. I knew her from the pictures, but I was totally unprepared for her beauty in real life.

Her dark eyes smiled at me, although a bit tentatively, as if waiting to see what I might do next. I turned to Rand for a clue, but he stood there between us, his hands on his hips. He lifted his shoulders in a tiny shrug.

"Reagan, meet Noelle. Noelle, this is my friend Reagan."

To my relief, her smile widened. She slipped gracefully off the stool and met me with slender arms outreached. "Hello, Reagan. Glad to finally meet you."

She and I hugged for a moment like old friends. "Finally?" I asked, turning to Rand.

Again he shrugged, as if he didn't know what was going on. "She surprised me too. Noelle's like that. Full of surprises."

"Well, surprise or not, I'm so glad to meet you," I admitted. "When did you get in?"

"Just a little while ago. I've only got tomorrow, and then I have to get back to school, but I couldn't stand being away from my dad another weekend." A gorgeous smile focused on her dad, but her words were to me. "He's told me so much about you. Dad says you're a writer."

"Guilty," I said.

"I've always admired writers. In fact, if I didn't have this love affair with cooking, that's what I'd pursue myself."

"Is that right?" I felt the flush spread from my neck up to my ears. Of all the things, I hadn't expected to happen when I finally met Rand's daughter, I surely hadn't expected her to be the presence that she was. Jealousy, maybe, but I hadn't expected this composed, mature young woman who had suddenly taken charge.

"She means it," Rand said. "And she won't be happy until she's gotten your life story out of you, so you may as well get started."

"Dad," she chided, "don't give away all my secrets." She slipped her arm around his waist. "Tell you what I'll do," she said looking up at him.

"Cook?" he asked eagerly.

She shook her head in mock disgust, making the glossy dark hair shimmer in the kitchen lights. "No, not exactly. Reagan and I will make the salad and a special little dessert I've invented at school, but you, my dear father, are designated for grill duty tonight. Steaks. The juicy kind you do with the crispy outsides."

Their shared smile told me they'd done this before.

"Deal," he said.

Noelle took over the kitchen like the pro she was rapidly becoming, and by the time Rand brought the steaks inside, she had created a raspberry and chocolate affair that looked as if it had taken all day, and I had proudly assembled a salad worthy of our efforts.

Little by little, my fears faded away. Noelle was delightful, and I think she actually liked me. For all my preconceived notions about jealous daughters with too little in the way of age difference, I couldn't have asked for more.

By the time we finished dinner and shared our glasses of wine on the patio, Noelle had become a friend. Shortly after that, however, she declared that she was pooped from her flight and that she wanted to retire. Leaving us downstairs, she retreated to what had been her bedroom since early childhood. I could only imagine what she must have felt, leaving her father downstairs with the woman who could potentially replace her mother. Whatever she felt, she covered nicely. Rand was right. This girl was special.

As Rand and I talked, I realized that, although I'd filled him in on the events of the past two days, I hadn't spent much time on the emotional part of the story.

"I wish you could have seen Everette," I said. "He was so sad. All these years, and he thought he was finally going to get even with Brister. Now he's looking at a jail sentence himself. I can't bear to think of the degradation he'll have to go through. I wish there was something we could do."

"I know. Me too." Rand's sadness was apparent. "But we can't do anything about that now. All we can do is help find Brister." He reached for my hand and interlaced our fingers. "And these fingers can do the rest," he concluded.

"What?"

"These fingers can do what nobody else on earth can do for Everette Suttle now. And for Lauren."

Slowly the understanding inched its way into my brain. "You mean write about it, don't you?"

"Exactly. You write this story like you did the first part, and not a court in the country could inflict much damage on that poor man."

Little by little, the idea blossomed. "You're right. I agree. That's the one thing I can do. By the time I get through with this story, Everette Suttle might be a free man."

"That's the spirit. Show the world what really happened. This man waited twenty-three years for the system to do its job, and when it failed him again, he did what he thought he had to do. It's your job now, Reagan, to present the man behind the actions."

We sat there for a few minutes, enjoying the glow of our future accomplishment, and then the sobriety of the moment returned.

"So what's our plan for now? I mean, do we go back to Natchez?"

I'd already learned that whenever Rand hedges about something, he turns his head sideways and tugs on his earlobe, so it came as no surprise when he started to do just that.

"I'm not sure," he admitted. "The last place we saw Brister was at Mount Locust. Nobody's seen him around Baton Rouge, so my guess is he's still close by. Wouldn't you think?"

"My gut tells me you're right."

"Do you think he'll try to get to the Hutchisons in the hospital?"

"No. I think that's too obvious. He won't take that chance, but I do think he's close by."

"Then that's where we need to be."

"I agree. But one thing's for sure."

"What's that?"

"We're not leaving till Noelle's back on the plane."

He grinned and kissed me lightly. "I knew you'd like her."

TWENTY-FOUR

Jackson's airport was crowded on Sunday afternoon when we watched her go through security and waved our final good-byes. I, too, felt more than a tinge of sadness as she left us and headed back to her world of school and friends. Not sure how I'd become so attached to her in less than twenty-four hours, I had to assume it was by transference. Love the father, love the daughter, I guessed.

Noelle's plane left close to four, and we were headed out of the city as it lifted into a sky rapidly filling with dark thunderheads. Humidity clung to me like worries, and when I took out the map that Ethan Clarke at Mount Locust had given me, my fingers stuck to the glossy surface. Finally, I laid it out across my lap and drew an imaginary circle around the old house. Brister had to be hiding some place nearby.

I looked for landmarks, anything that might offer a place of concealment. The terrain all seemed too much the same. Flat land filled with hardwoods and pines. As I studied the map, Rand asked, "Is there any place he might dig a tunnel?"

"How would I know?" I asked in frustration. "Can't you dig a tunnel anywhere?"

"Afraid not. This close to the river, you've gotta have some sort of rise in the ground, or you'll wind up with a cave full of water. See anything that's above the rest of the terrain?"

Once again I studied the map. It was nearly dark, and when a green symbol caught my eye, I turned on the overhead light and brought the map closer to my face to read the tiny lettering. "What's Emerald Mound?"

"I've heard of it, but I've never seen it. I think it's some kind of ceremonial mound built by the ancestors of the Natchez Indians." He leaned across to sneak a look at the map, all the while keeping one eye on the road. "Is it close to Mount Locust?"

"Yes. Really close. Do you think he could be there?"

"Might be. But I'd be kinda surprised if he's holed up there because there are too many tourists. Too many people could stumble on his hideout."

I turned back to the map. "Then I don't have a clue. There's nothing else here that looks as if it's higher ground."

"It doesn't necessarily have to be higher ground. It was just an idea. I remember one place, I think they call it the Sunken Trace, where the actual trail has eroded a deep path into the earth through the years. If he's found a place like that, he could have dug into the side of the trail and made himself a hideaway. I guess we'll just have to get out and do some looking, won't we?"

Visions of tromping through sweltering woods filled with chiggers, fist-sized mosquitoes, and who knew what else could dampen my enthusiasm. My own ideas, though, were in short supply. I asked, "Do you think we've got a chance to find him?"

"Of course we do, Reagan. Besides, Mullen's not going to quit. And neither are we."

It was nighttime as we approached Mount Locust again, this time from the north. The only lights came from the ranger's house, situated a couple of hundred yards to the north and east of Mount Locust itself. Only darkness emanated from the house on top of the hill, but my mind's eye could still see it quite clearly.

Deer grazed quietly over the grounds as they had before, and they barely turned their heads when we came to a stop at the foot of the drive. Lights from the ranger's house presented a picture of peaceful domesticity.

"Think we should alert him?" I asked.

"I don't see why, do you?"

"No. Probably the fewer people who know what we're doing the better."

I held my breath. I didn't want to ask, but I had to. "Are we going out there tonight?"

"No. We don't want to do anything that gives Brister the upper hand."

I breathed a sigh of relief. "Are we going to call in Mullen before we go looking?"

"I don't think so on that either. Not at first anyway. We can do some looking around, then if we get onto something, we'll call him in. I just don't see where we'd get much accomplished by letting the entire countryside know what we're doing, do you?"

I agreed in theory, but I kept thinking about all those people I'd seen looking for a single man in DeSoto. If all of them couldn't find a kidnapper, what did we think we could accomplish alone here? We could use help. The man in

DeSoto was a mimic, a copycat, not even the real criminal. I asked, "Couldn't we use the help?"

I hadn't even noticed that my left thumb and index finger twitched fast-paced across each other until Rand reached across and laid his hand on top of mine to stop them.

"Honey, relax. We're not taking on the whole army by ourselves. Tomorrow, in the daylight, everything will look better. I just wanted to stop by here on the way into town." He added with a shrug, "Thought we might get lucky and pick up a clue."

"You're right. I'm tired. And I'm worried we won't ever find the bastard."

"Oh, we'll find him all right," Rand assured me. "But we don't want him to find us again. The last time was a little too close. He doesn't need any advantages." He turned the car around in the drive. "Let's head back into town for now. Tomorrow's another day."

We checked into the same motel, but we'd been moved to another room down the hallway from the last. In all the excitement of the day, I'd forgotten about the view from this perch. Lights from Vidalia, across in Louisiana, twinkled on the river's fast-moving water. Above it, on the high-arched steel bridge, a steady stream of cars crossed in constant exchange between the two states.

I finally began to let go. Some day, when this was all over, we'd have to come back to this town and do some touristy stuff of our own, but for the moment, all I wanted was sleep.

I awoke at dawn, feeling as if I'd spent the night on a bed of nails. Every corner of my body ached from tension, and I figured it better to be up and doing something than to sleep any longer. Brister was still out there. I thought I'd slip out of bed, but the minute I moved, Rand got up too. Brister was still out there, and he couldn't rest either.

The difference in climate after DeSoto was more noticeable in the morning's rapidly growing heat. Although the sun was still new in the sky when we left the motel, heat had already gathered momentum. I'd put on the only pair of shorts I'd brought, but even those wouldn't help much.

Rand drove back toward the entrance to the parkway while I studied the map we'd picked up from the ranger station. On its neatly folded sections, the entire trail, from Nashville to Natchez, was presented in compact form, with each marker and special point of interest between the two cities. I stared at the map, but couldn't focus on any single point. For now, they were no more than names on a map. What I needed was a clue.

I absently turned over the map where pictures and brief descriptions filled the long page. In the very top sections, the one last unfolded, one picture made me stop. The night before, Rand had mentioned something referred to as the Sunken Trace, but I had no mental picture to go along with it. Now I did.

The photo did what Rand's words had not. I stared at the pathway made by pioneers on foot nearly two hundred years before, and I could visualize a band of ruffians who fought each other as well as the elements as they struggled to make their way back to Nashville. On cliffs banking either side of the trail, huge tree roots clung to remaining soil, leaning ever closer toward each other. They formed an archway that nearly blocked out light to the pathway below. The path itself was probably fifteen to twenty feet below the banks on either side.

Human feet had created a canyon of sorts from the very countryside. Hundreds, perhaps thousands, of people trod this very path, now only a hundred feet off the paved parkway, a stark testament to the fact that life hasn't always been as easy as it is today.

What if Brister used this path himself to take cover? "Rand, look at this." I passed the folded map over to him, displaying the picture of the Sunken Trace. "Is this what you were talking about last night?"

He held it over the steering wheel, moving his eyes from the map to the road, then back again. "That's it. See how deep the path is? It'd make a great hiding place. All he'd have to do is dig out a little cave, and nobody would ever see him."

I took back the map and stared at it again. I half-expected to see Brister's face poking out from beneath the tree roots. "It's perfect." But my excitement abated as another idea registered. "There's no way we can explore the whole trail. That's several hundred miles."

"But we don't have to worry about the whole trail. Only the part around here. Remember that, Reagan. He's some place close. We know that for sure."

True enough, Brister had to be close by. "If we hadn't all gone off chasing him in DeSoto, we may have caught him by now," I mused openly.

"Yeah, but nobody knew that. Mullen went too, remember?"

"Yes, I remember." The next thought came harder. "But if it hadn't been for Katie's insistence, I probably wouldn't have gone."

"So what are you thinking? That doing your job is wrong?"

"No, not doing my job. But I do question why I went up there. Was it to catch Brister, or was it to get the big story Katie promised?"

"You know better than to ask that. Your motives couldn't ever be suspect. Besides, does it matter whether you went to write the story or whether you went to see him taken in? I don't see a whole lot of difference."

"It matters. That's all I can tell you." Watching the canopy of huge oaks glide silently by, I admitted, "It matters because I don't ever want to be an ambulance-chaser, or whatever the writers' equivalent of that is."

His frown softened, along with his voice. "Reagan, judging by the questions you're asking yourself, I really don't think that's ever going to be a problem for you. An old softie like you couldn't become an ambulance-chaser."

"I hope not. I really hope not."

We slowed as we passed Mount Locust again, but there was no reason to stop this time. Brister may have ambushed us there once, but he wasn't stupid enough to come back to the scene. Wherever he was now, it probably wasn't at Mount Locust.

Several miles clicked by, and we passed a sign stating Port Gibson to be thirty miles farther up the trace. I unfolded my map again. My one and only visit to this town had been only a couple of weeks before, but it now seemed like eons. I knew I'd taken pictures of the Catholic Church and its blue interior, created by light streaming through its blue stained-glass windows. I knew I'd taken pictures of the golden hand atop the Presbyterian Church, but for the life of me, I couldn't remember anything else.

I looked back at the map. The Sunken Trace couldn't be more than three or four miles north of town.

Finally, I said, "Rand, let's go on up to Port Gibson. I've got a feeling about it."

"You think he's traveled that far north?"

"It's only thirty miles, and he's bound to have a car. Besides, the Sunken Trace is just outside town. I want to see it."

"Okay by me. I trust your intuitions. We'll go to Port Gibson."

Bits of recollected information resurfaced as we entered the town, but still I had that feeling of being off kilter, out of sync. What was it in the back of my mind that stayed just beyond recognition?

Rand interrupted my thoughts with a question. "Have you still got that picture?"

I turned to retrieve the folder I'd laid on the back seat as we left the motel. "Yep. It's here. Why?"

"It's a hunch, but I thought that since you've got a feeling about Port Gibson, maybe we should show his picture around. Ask if anybody's seen him."

I agreed that sounded like a good idea. We turned off the parkway and onto Highway 61, which led through the little town. We stopped at the information center, an old two-story brick home currently doing double duty as the Chamber of Commerce. Inside, a lovely gray-haired woman behind a glass counter welcomed us.

"Hello there! Welcome to Port Gibson. May I help you?" Her silvery smooth voice held no trace of Mississippi.

"Yes, you can," I answered and set my folder on the counter. "Actually, we're looking for somebody, and we thought maybe you'd seen him."

Her brows raised. "Who are you looking for?"

I opened the folder and turned the picture around to her. "This man. Have you by any chance seen him recently?"

She lowered the glasses from atop her head and bent over to get a better look. "Hmm. I don't recognize him." She looked curiously up at me. "Is he a friend of yours?"

"No, not a friend. We're looking for him because of something he's done."

"Oh, I see." She smiled tentatively. "May I ask what he's done?"

"I don't mind at all if you ask. This man killed a family of three more than twenty years ago and most recently shot an innocent relative in Natchez. He's gotten by with murder all these years, so if you do see him, we'd appreciate it if you let us know."

I handed her a card bearing my identification and cell number, and she studied it momentarily, then asked, "You're a writer?"

"Yes, I'm a writer. Suffice it to say that we're helping with the investigation. If you don't feel comfortable calling me, let me give you another number."

I reached for the card, turned it over, and wrote Mullen's name and number on the back. "This man is an agent with the FBI," I told her and handed the card back to her. "If you'd feel more comfortable calling him, that's fine too."

Her wide eyes were alight with curiosity. "I'd be happy to call you, Ms. Wilks. But who were the people this man murdered? Were they residents of Port Gibson?"

"No. They were just an innocent family on vacation, on their way to see Grandpa in Natchez. It happened up around Kosciusko. You might remember reading about it."

She shook her head sadly. "No. You see, my husband and I moved here a little over ten years ago from Pennsylvania. We weren't here then."

"I see. Well, if you do see him, would you give us a call?"

She promised that she would, and we returned to the car and turned back onto the thoroughfare, aptly called Church Street. We followed it through the rows of old homes and churches, even a synagogue dating from the nineteenth century, to the north part of town where we turned to get back on the parkway.

As I'd surmised, the sign directing us to the Sunken Trace appeared almost as soon as we were back on the trace, and we promptly turned off. The parking lot was empty, save for a motorcycle and a middle-aged couple with red faces and tousled hair standing beside it.

"How's the view?" Rand asked when we got out of the car.

"Impressive," the sandy-haired man said with a grin. "But hot as the devil."

"I can imagine," Rand said.

I joined them beside the bike. "Are you folks from around here?"

"Oh, no," the woman answered. "We're from Indianapolis, but we got on the trace in Nashville. We've almost gone the whole length now. When we get to Natchez, we'll be done."

"Wow! That's some feat," I told them.

Rand asked, "How long has it taken you?"

"We left home over a week ago, but we've only been on the trace for four days," the man explained. "When we get to Natchez, we're renting a truck for the trip back."

The woman laughed, "I think we've had enough."

"I certainly would have," I agreed. Then I took the picture from the folder once again and handed it to the woman. "By the way, since you've been on the trace for several days, have you by any chance seen this man?"

She studied it briefly, shook her head, and handed it to her husband. "I haven't, have you, Fred?"

He studied the picture and shook his head too. "Has he done something?"

"He's a murderer," I said simply. "It happened twenty-three years ago. Up the trace from here."

They glanced at each other, but remained firm in their position. Neither had seen the man.

"Well, thanks anyway," I added. "I hope you enjoy the rest of your trip. And if you see this man, will you give us a call?"

They agreed and took the card I offered them.

Rand added, "And don't pass by Mount Locust without stopping. It's definitely worth the effort."

They asked a few questions about Mount Locust and then got back on the bike and started the noisy engine. But before they took off, the man called out, "Is this guy you're looking for still around here?"

"We don't know for sure," Rand admitted. "Just be careful."

"Will do." He gave us a thumbs-up as he turned the bike onto the parkway and headed toward Natchez.

We followed the sign directing us to an asphalt walkway that led through dense woods. After a few yards, we could see why this place deserved its name. We left the asphalt and followed a dirt path down the steep slope until we reached the floor of what had once been the trace. Millions of leaves that had deposited their remains on the path softened our footsteps, but the imprints of pioneers were still there. Their very presence had left a mark on the land in so many ways.

Deep woods created a blanket of silence so complete that the buzzing of a mosquito at my ear sounded more like the drone of an airplane. I brushed it away, and the stillness returned. Scattered leaves drifted downward in airy paths of random flight.

We stood in the middle of a pathway about eight feet wide. Ahead of us and behind us, the overhead canopy closed in after a while and seemed to smother what remained of the pathway. I closed my eyes to drink in the aroma of loam saturated with layers of leaves. Somewhere an animal skittered across the forest floor, and again a mosquito buzzed nearby.

I opened my eyes, half-expecting to see the early travelers, but not entirely disappointed when they didn't appear. After all, I'd had one ghost make her presence known to me. And that was the only one that mattered. Had there been more of a breeze, I might have been tempted to spend the remainder of the day in that lovely spot, but high banks on either side kept it out, smothering us in heat. And the mosquitoes buzzed closer and closer.

"Seen enough?" Rand asked.

"I think so." I turned back toward the path that led out of the Sunken Trace. Fierce roots grabbed at the last grains of soil that kept them from tumbling into the ravine. "At least we know he's not here."

Rand looked inquisitively at me. "We do?"

My head spun back toward the trace. "We'd have seen him, wouldn't we?"

"I don't know. That's my point. We could stand right here, and we might not see him if he was twenty feet away. So how could we possibly see him if he's hidden far back in the woods?"

I didn't know whether to cry or shout. I did see his point. And I didn't like it one bit. With so much pristine forest around us, this man could hide anywhere, and we may or may not find him. The best we could do was to keep asking and keep looking.

As we entered Port Gibson the second time, my stomach had alerted me to the fact that it was well after noon, and we hadn't eaten in a very long time. So accustomed to a country where every hamlet offers fast-food, we gradually came to the realization that we'd found one that didn't. We even turned off Church Street and made several blocks running parallel with it, but found nothing in the way of restaurants. Either the people of Port Gibson don't eat out, or they know something we didn't.

We were about to give up and drive back south when I caught sight of a place tucked behind a convenience store, nearly out of sight. The tiny trailer had been painted bright pink, and the sign, Slow Mo's, was hand-lettered. But the aroma that came from the smokestack smelled unmistakably like good barbecue, and we agreed to check it out.

We parked next to two pickups and got out into the stifling heat. A sign on the bank in town had read ninety-eight degrees, which to me seemed conservative, and I'd kidded about frying some eggs for lunch.

An air conditioner poking out the side of the trailer churned away, but once we opened the door, we knew its efforts were futile. The inside was only a few degrees cooler.

The inside also offered no place for seating, only a glass case and two or three feet of counter space, enough to hold a small cash register. Behind the glass counter, a young African American man watched us a bit defensively as he handed over an order to two older customers. They gave us proper smiles and a greeting, but promptly left, leaving us alone with the young man.

"May I help you?" He glanced toward the door as the two men closed it behind them.

I peered into the glass case where chunks of pork tips simmered in a rich-looking sauce, the color of paprika, and beside them a dark beef brisket sweltered under the light. Next to them were thick strips of browned potatoes, several short ears of yellow corn, and a mound of okra fried in batter.

He perfunctorily took our orders to an even smaller back room, then returned. "Anything else?"

Rand and I both had taken soft drinks from a glass case behind us and laid them on the counter. "I think this'll do it," I said and took out my picture once again. "But we did want to ask you if you've seen this man."

He studied the picture hastily and was about to say something when an older, much larger man came out of the back room. He smiled, towering over the boy, and placed a hand on his shoulder. "Can I help you, folks?"

"Yes," Rand answered. "We're looking for this man and wondering if you'd seen him."

The boy moved aside, and the older man picked up the picture. His lips pursed as he studied the picture, but he handed it back to Rand with a shake of his head. "No. Don't think I've ever seen that fella. Is he missing?"

"In a sense," Rand answered. "But that's not why we're looking for him."

"If he ain't missing, then he's done somethin' wrong."

I smiled at this man's wisdom. "Yes, he's definitely done something wrong."

"How wrong?" the man asked pointedly.

"Wrong enough to kill three innocent people," Rand answered.

The man looked back at the picture, but again shook his head. "Nope. Wish I could help you, but I haven't seen anybody around here that looks like that. Sorry."

Rand thanked him for his trouble, and the man disappeared again into the back room. Shortly, the boy returned with our order, which we took outside to a makeshift porch, where a rough wooden table and a bench had been set up. Even in the shade of the overhang, the heat was powerful, but my hunger overrode even that. I gladly plunked down beside Rand on the bench.

We'd taken only a couple of bites out of the huge sandwiches when the young man came out, nodded briefly as he passed, and got into the remaining truck. When he'd eased his truck into passing traffic on the street, the door opened again, and the older man came out. He first glanced toward the street, then stopped beside our table.

Rand looked up inquisitively.

"Hate to bother you, folks," the man began, "but I couldn't say nothin' with my boy in there."

We both had stopped eating and waited for him to finish. "That picture ya'll showed me?"

"Yes?" Rand asked.

"Well, I think I might know where that fella is."

My heart now raced from something other than the heat.

"Yep." With each sentence, the man glanced back toward the street, as if by his admission, some force might arrive to whisk him off the porch. He took a deep breath and continued. "I'm pretty sure it's your man. There's a place outside town, down south a bit on 553, called Springwood Plantation. They got a workin' farm down there, and they hire just about anybody willin' to kill himself in this heat for minimum wage."

Again he looked out to the road. "My boy worked down there for a couple a weeks, and he told me 'bout this man who was hidin' out on the plantation, in an outbuilding they don't use any more. Lo and behold, the man in that picture came in here just yesterday. My boy told me all about it after he left."

"So your son knows where he's hiding?"

The big man's smile had vanished, and his expression turned serious. "That he does. But my boy won't be goin' back. It's too dangerous. We don't need the money that bad."

"Good idea," Rand admitted.

The man asked quietly, "You said this guy's a murderer?"

"Killed three people," Rand said flatly. "It was over twenty years ago, but we're closing in on him now."

Shock on the man's face turned to quiet resignation. "About time," he said quietly. "About time he got his."

TWENTY-FIVE

Mullen called before we could get out of Port Gibson to let us know that he and his people had Mount Locust staked out, along with the Hutchison's house in Baton Rouge and the hospital in Natchez. He also wanted to know where we were. I think he suspected that we weren't going to sit around while he solved the case, but he never said as much.

Since I'd taken the call, it was up to me. I watched Rand, who was doing a good job of staying out of it, right down to staring straight ahead. If I told Mullen what we knew, he and scores of law enforcement would beat us to the plantation, alerting Brister. With miles of uninhabited land surrounding this plantation, he could easily slip through the noose again, and that was the last thing we needed.

"We're up near Port Gibson," I admitted truthfully, also adding truthfully that we'd shown Brister's picture around. That's where I deviated.

"But we didn't really come up with anything. We're headed back south now, so I guess we'll wait around Natchez to see what your people turn up."

"Good idea," he said. "That'd be a big load off my shoulders. You two stay put, and I promise to call if there's any change."

I hung up and watched as Rand's lips curled into a grin. "Good job," he said. "We haven't found a thing—yet."

I knew I'd lied about what we knew, but at the same time, I wasn't willing to risk losing him again. Rand and I would take a look. No harm in that. And if we found enough evidence to support our theory, then we'd call in the troops.

Afternoon had worn fast away, but the heat gave no promise of surrender. It surrounded us in its grip as it hovered over the state highway, like a never-ending mirage. By the time we saw the sign leading to Springwood Plantation, parts of the sky had turned to India ink, but the edges still flared out in orange flames.

Highway 553 twisted and turned through the forests of lower Mississippi like the river it paralleled. One of my original stops in my writing tour was to have been at Windsor Ruins, just a pebble's throw from where we were then. And I kept thinking how everything had changed since I first started out on this journey. I started out to write about antebellum mansions and cotton plantations now defunct. Not only had my purpose changed, but my entire life now was apparently changed. My feelings for Rand made sure of that.

I watched him in the sun's waning rays, watched the set of his jaw and the easy way he moved. I'd come to Mississippi to write a simple story. And I would leave soon. But that's where the simplicity ended.

Rand slowed the car. "Springwood's five miles down this road. Are you ready?"

"More than ready." My heart raced at what might lie ahead. I wanted nothing more than to see Brister taken into custody and made to answer for his crimes. But at the same time, I dreaded the moment. Nothing I could envision would compensate for what he'd done to Lauren and her parents. When he was in prison, would I feel any better?

We turned onto the narrow asphalt dividing rows of tall white oaks, sweet gums, and magnolias. The trees were as thick as mosquitoes on the river, and their height nearly eclipsed the sun's last slanting rays. Ahead, the narrow road seemed to disappear beyond the first curve, and I found myself holding my breath, waiting, wondering if Brister waited for us just around the bend.

For the first time all day, the scorching heat began to lift almost magically along the shaded road. Within a few minutes, the asphalt turned to gravel, and trees lining the roadway thinned and allowed us to see into planted fields beyond. Cotton plants alternated with what Rand said were soybeans, separated by only thin rows of trees, and spanning to the point where sky met the fields and seemed to swallow them up in darkness.

"This must be part of the plantation," I mused aloud.

"Must be. And I'd say it's a pretty big operation."

"Looks big to me. But then I don't know much about plantations."

"You don't have to. By the time you finish writing about it, everybody'll know what the place where Glenn Brister met his match looks like."

"Thanks for that." I turned back to gaze over the expanse of crops. "Sure are a lot of places for him to hide around here though, aren't there?"

"I'm afraid so. But we've got the advantage of surprise, remember?"

"Yes, I remember. But right now, I'm not too sure about all this. What if he runs, and we lose him again? Then we'll really have some explaining to do to Mullen."

"It won't happen, Reagan. Trust me."

"I do trust you. Or I wouldn't be here."

"Good." He reached to take my hand and squeezed it lightly. "If Brister's hiding out back here, he's not leaving a free man."

Rand had slowed the car as we neared a curve. Just off the road, several grave markers, eroded and crumbling, jutted up from tall grass, followed by others that rose with the slope of the land up to a clearing. And in the clearing stood a small church, now surrounded on three sides by thick forest. Only the front of the building remained clearly visible.

If I hadn't known better, I would have thought we'd been suddenly and magically transported to an English village, so complete was the image. The church's weathered stone walls supported three Gothic windows filled with rich images, too dark at the moment to discern. Across the front, a slate roof rose sharply, straddled by what appeared to be a copper steeple, weathered and green. Totally missing were the elements that usually mark architecture in this part of the state. Somebody had no doubt wanted to mimic their ancestors, and they'd done so admirably.

"This place would make a great little article," I said wistfully. "Maybe we can come back some time when we're not looking for a murderer."

"I'd like that," he said softly. "I'd like most anything with you."

I thanked him for the compliment, but as we left that idyllic scene and made a final turn on the road, I felt a familiar chill. The sign proclaimed that we had entered the grounds of Springwood Plantation. Ahead, to the right, and occupying the center of an expansive lawn, the main house gleamed in the twilight. Its three stories looked even more graceful in reality than they had on the drawing of the brochure we'd seen in town. Lights positioned along a decorative balustrade emphasized a porch that covered the entire front of the house, and French doors all along the second floor sparkled with light from within.

A long carefully manicured drive, canopied by live oaks, veered sharply away from the road and led to the front of the white mansion before turning back to the public road.

"Gotta give it to Brister," Rand said. "He's picked some place to hide out."

"Yeah, no kidding." Then it hit me. "What are we gonna say to whoever lives in this place? We have to have some legitimate reason to search their property."

"I thought about that. We just need to be up front."

"You mean tell them we're looking for a murderer hiding on their property?"

"Why not? I mean, what better way to get somebody's attention?" He looked up at the huge antebellum house, every detail of maintenance up-to-date and gleaming with care. "Owning a place like this makes you responsible."

"Yeah, I guess they didn't get all this by being timid."

"Probably not."

I thought about that as we parked along the front of the house, between a sleek red convertible and a long black sedan with tinted windows. "We'll fit right in," I joked. "Maybe they're holding up the party for us."

"Could be." He grinned. "In that case, my lady, shall we?" He held out his arm to me. Enormous double doors made of etched glass twinkled and cast a glow over us as we rang the bell and waited for someone to answer.

Before long, a tall slender figure approached. Her dark shoulder-length hair silhouetted a slender face and even darker eyes, and she smiled graciously and said, "Good evening. May I help you?"

Rand introduced us and asked if we could talk with the owners of the property.

She glanced toward the source of chatter coming from an adjacent room, then turned back to us.

"I'm Sarah Atchison. This is my home. What is it you wish to talk to us about?"

Rand told her, "We're looking for someone, and we have reason to believe he's here on your property."

"You mean he's an employee?"

"Probably not."

She shook her head, puzzled. "But if he's not an employee, we wouldn't know anything about him."

I touched Rand's arm lightly, and I said, "Mrs. Atchison, it's entirely possible that no one knows this person is on the premises."

Again she glanced over her shoulder to the room beyond, then said, "Please, come in. If you'll have a seat, I'll get my husband."

We entered through a regal foyer, offset by a wide wooden staircase that rose then turned away from us at the landing. We followed her through a formal living room filled with antiques that, although probably museum quality, looked as if they'd actually been used. The room was huge, with a fourteen- or fifteen-foot ceiling. Groupings of chairs and a single floral silk sofa had been arranged around a black lacquered Steinway to allow for polite conversation while also listening to music. We accepted Sarah Atchison's offer to sit, and she excused herself, then disappeared into the room beyond.

Voices from the next room quieted only minimally, and Mrs. Atchison returned, followed by a bear of a man who towered over his wife's shoulder. He wore black dress slacks and a red-and-black-figured silk shirt that moved easily across his massive shoulders. His dark full beard more resembled a woodsman than a courtier, and somehow I knew this man would be more comfortable in jeans.

"Dave Atchison," he pronounced as he shook my hand.

I introduced the both of us, and Atchison led us to a pair of Queen Anne chairs, then took his place on the sofa opposite us. He crossed one leg over the other at the ankle, while his wife remained standing behind him, her hands resting on his massive shoulders. "Now, what can I do for you, folks?" he asked.

Rand told him why we were there, and Dave asked, "So you think we have a criminal on our property? That right?"

"That's what we've been told. The son of a man in town worked on your place for a while a couple of weeks ago, and he told his father he'd seen someone of Brister's description hiding out here."

"Why didn't this young man come to me about it?"

"I can't answer that for sure, but you know how kids are. If something doesn't affect them directly, they ignore it."

Dave nodded with a smile. "Yeah. Good point. So what exactly has this man done that has you out looking for him?"

Rand hesitated, and I spoke up. "Mr. Atchison, do you remember a family that disappeared on the parkway over twenty years ago?"

Sarah's eyes widened, but her husband answered, "Sure. We remember. We even had a friend at the time who was a friend of the father. He lived in Natchez, if I remember."

"Exactly," I said. "That's the family."

Now Dave's eyes widened. "Are you telling me this man on my property is the one responsible for that family's disappearance?"

"We believe he's one and the same. And we know now why the family disappeared. We know what made him do what he did."

Dave put the pieces together out loud. "Yes. I've kept up with that in the papers. Police found the remains up in Greenwood, didn't they?"

"That they did," I answered. "And he's also shot another man in Natchez, but luckily, that victim survived."

"How horrible," Sarah added.

Now Dave leaned forward in his chair. "I saw that on the news. He worked at the casino hotel, so I just assumed the shooter was somebody with a grudge. You know, somebody who'd lost a bundle."

Rand said, "I'm afraid it's not that easy."

"Well, whatever the reason, this man has to be stopped."

"That's why we came to you," I said. "Word around here has it that you don't put up with such, so we hoped you could help."

"Oh, I'll help. That's for sure. But I'm still a bit confused."

"About why we're here without law enforcement?" I asked.

"Right. This is serious business. What are two lay people doing trying to catch a murderer that a whole state hasn't found in twenty years?"

Rand answered, "I can see your confusion. Maybe I can explain. You see, Reagan came down here with an assignment for *American Byways* to write a piece on the Natchez Trace, and she stumbled on a suitcase with pictures of the missing family. After that she's followed one lead after the other, even risked her own safety. We're working with FBI, but we're also doing what we can on our own to help."

Dave seemed satisfied, but I added, "We happened to be nearby when we found out that Brister might be on your farm. So we came here first to ask you about it. If it pans out, believe me, we'll be the first to call in the troops."

"Well, that certainly puts a new slant on our little party tonight," he said, rising from the chair and turning to face his wife. "You go on back to the guests, my dear. Give my apologies, please. I'd find it difficult to eat my dinner while there's a murderer on the loose."

She smiled knowingly at him. "Of course. You go with these people. Do what you need to do. I'll take care of our guests."

He kissed her cheek and turned back to us. "Shall we?" he said and led us to the front door. "I've got a foreman who tells me the truth. If he knows anything about all this, he'll tell us."

Dave led the way, Rand and I close behind. He rounded the house and led us down a stone pathway toward a much smaller single-story wooden building not far from the main barn. Both were a hundred yards or so behind the main house, but well within the manicured expanse of lawn. Lights inside indicated that somebody was home, but when we knocked, we were met with only silence.

Dave knocked again, but again there was no answer. "I hate to do this," he explained and took out a key. "I've always given him complete privacy here." He slid the key into the lock and pushed the door open. "But I guess this is an emergency."

A light in the façade of an old oil lamp hung from the center ceiling and cast long shadows about the room, empty except for a heavy-looking leather sofa and two matching chairs. Offset to the right was a small kitchen and eating area. In the opposite direction, light fell onto a hallway from what had to be a bedroom.

Dave called out, "Amon! You in here?"

When no answer followed, he called again, this time louder. "Amon, it's Dave. Where are you? We need to talk to you."

He continued through the living room, into the kitchen, calling to his foreman, while Rand went the opposite way down the hall, to the place where light came from a second room. He stopped at the doorway, then called back to Dave. "I think I've found your foreman," he said simply.

Dave rushed to join him, but he, too, stopped short of entering the room. His wide shoulders slumped as he stood in the doorway, and I, too, felt helpless to turn away. The man lay prone on the floor of his bedroom with his arms stretched over his head. Blood still seeped onto the tile floor beneath him, but the body lay perfectly still and apparently lifeless.

Dave bent over the figure of his foreman and pressed two fingers to the side of the man's neck, then drew away. "He's gone," Dave said simply.

Dave looked about the room in despair, as if looking for the killer to still be there. "Amon was a good man. Who is this bastard?" he asked, staring back at us.

"A killer," Rand said simply, "who thought your man was about to give him away. He couldn't let that happen."

Dave's eyes glared as he stood up to his full height. "This is one killer that's gonna be sorry. And that's a promise." Then he stalked from the room and toward the door when he turned briefly back toward us. "You two wait here. I'm going to the house for a minute."

"What are you doing?" Rand asked.

"Getting my shotgun," he barked. "You just stay put." With that, he stormed out of the house.

"I guess it's time to call in Mullen," I said.

Wordlessly, Rand slipped the cell phone out of his pocket and punched in Mullen's number.

TWENTY-SIX

Mullen and his crew arrived within the half hour, and it seemed that all hell had now broken loose. The peaceful tranquility of the farm had changed into the aura of a battlefield. Guests' stylish cars were gone, replaced now by state and federal vehicles. Their lights flashed across the night sky, and everywhere I looked men and women in armor vests skirted about the premises. All had weapons drawn in anticipation of the fight to come.

When Dave had returned to the foreman's house with his shotgun, Rand tried to convince him to wait for reinforcements. It hadn't been an easy task. Poor Amon still lay in his bedroom in a pool of blood, but with the authorities summoned, Dave felt his attention was needed elsewhere. Determined to defend his castle and its inhabitants at any cost, he would have surely gone off alone if Mullen hadn't appeared when he did.

To Mullen's credit, he did an admirable job of calming Dave, and when combined forces began their search for Brister, Dave was allowed to go with them. We, on the other hand, weren't so lucky.

"I told you all along," Mullen said. "You're not going with us. No way. I can't keep the owner of the property from going where he wants, but you're another matter." He flashed his sternest look at me, but it cracked a bit around the edges, and he added, "Thanks for your help, but my head will roll if I let something happen to you."

I bit my tongue. I'd keep to myself that there'd be no fight if it weren't for Rand and me. And that I'd spent my life taking care of my own head, but when it came down to it, I really didn't want to become Brister's next victim. And I surely didn't want to see Rand take that role. We'd wait it out.

By that time, word that something big was going on at Springwood had created quite a stir among the local folks, who soon appeared on the scene. I had no idea where they all came from, but before long, state police blocked off the road about a half mile in both directions. Still they appeared on foot, eager to get a peek at what was going on. They talked in excited whispers but stayed out of the way. If Brister was in hearing range, he'd be out of there and on to the next spot.

It hadn't taken Dave long to figure out where Brister probably hid. Since the boy from town said that the man lived in an outbuilding, Dave immediately narrowed the search to two places. One was a concrete block storage building that seemed highly unlikely because it offered no ventilation, and the other was an old silo. Everything else had been visited in the last few days. They would have noticed if anything had been out of the ordinary there.

Mullen finally gathered his troops, and they headed out across the fields behind the house. Dave trudged shoulder to shoulder with Mullen. The two resembled a pair of old warriors off to rid the world of evil. If the noise created by the arrival of half the law enforcement east of the Mississippi hadn't warned Brister, they might indeed stand a chance of taking him alive. Even Brister had to recognize such force.

Rand and I were relegated to wait, and we chose to do that on the front steps where we watched as everybody except us took off. Actually, Sarah had insisted that we wait with her in the house, but neither one of us could do that. We wanted to be where the action was, even if it meant watching from the front porch. At least we could see for ourselves what happened.

All the days of waiting and searching might finally come to an end, but I wouldn't be part of it. Rand and I watched the last of the troops disappear into the darkness of the fields. The moon had waned to a thin crescent, and thick clouds blocked out all but the meanest light. From Amon's quarters, we had picked up the outline of the old silo that was now used only for storing extra chemicals used on the farm. Cool and away from the workers, it offered a perfect hideout.

Ten minutes passed, then fifteen. The only sounds were the occasional whispers of spectators who'd ventured too close and were being turned away, coupled with the now familiar sound of tree frogs. Dave had told Mullen that the old silo was less than twenty minutes away by foot, but we still hadn't heard a thing. No shouts, no gunshots.

In spite of the night's mugginess, the wrought-iron steps felt cold on the back of my legs, and I shivered, unnerved by the waiting. "Do you think this is another goose chase?"

Rand sat leaned over, with his elbows propped on his knees, as he stared across the front lawn at the amalgam of cars parked at odd angles. He didn't answer for a while, and when he did, it sounded more like a snort than anything else. "Hmmm. I'm not too sure those guys could catch a minnow with a ten-foot strainer."

I knew he was right, but so far I'd kept it to myself. He went on. "Look at this mess," he said, gesturing toward the cars, "You'd think we were after an army."

"I know, I know. But we can still hope."

"Yeah, guess you're right. Let's just say that Mullen's track record's not too good."

I held my wrist up the light again and checked the time. "They've been gone long enough," I concluded, and my hopes drooped. "They've lost him again."

Rand's head sagged, and he added quietly, "I think you're right."

It wasn't long before our prophecy proved all too true. Dave was the first to come out of the field, tromping with the agility that only one who spends his life there can afford. Mullen and the others trailed behind him. Frustration was evident in their gait. One by one, they dispersed to their separate cars. Mullen, when he saw Dave heading toward us, followed close on his heels.

Neither one said a word as they approached. They didn't have to.

"He's gone, isn't he?" I asked.

Dave waited stony-faced while Mullen explained, "He's been there all right. We found food and camping equipment. Without that, he can't hold out long."

"Forgive me if I disagree with that," Rand quipped.

Mullen shot him a look, but Rand continued. "He's somehow managed to evade everything we've sent his way so far. What difference could some camping equipment make? This man obviously knows how to live on the land. I'm betting he had a lot of practice with that in Vietnam. If we don't do something different, we'll never find him."

Mullen's jaw squared. "Tonight's not the time. Tomorrow in daylight, we'll find him. Count on it." Then he marched up the stairs past us where, at the doorway, he turned to Dave. "Mind if I use your phone, Mr. Atchison? Cell's not worth much out here."

Dave ushered him on, then turned back to us. "I'd a been better off going after him myself, like I wanted to in the first damn place."

"At this point, I'm inclined to agree with you," Rand admitted.

I took a deep breath and laid my hand on Rand's arm. "We're tired. We all are. It's been a long day, and there's probably nothing else we can do here tonight. Don't you think we should go back into Natchez?"

"I guess," he admitted. "This circus will still be here in the morning."

A faint smile crossed Dave's weary face. We found our car amid the official ones and wound our way through them to the road. The state police manned the roadblock and shone their light into our front seat.

"We're with Agent Mullen," Rand told them.

The man nodded, then said, "Have a good night. And be careful." He aimed the light away from us and back onto the road ahead. Its beam barely penetrated the black asphalt.

Driving away from Springwood, our headlights bored through the tunnel of darkness ahead. When we rounded the next curve, they cast an eerie glow over the grave markers we'd seen earlier in the day. Leaning with the weight of more than a century, they looked like something out of a Halloween movie.

I was about to make a comment to that effect when something else caught my eye. Higher up on the hill, in the church, I was certain I'd seen something.

"Stop," I ordered. "I saw a light in that church up there."

He braked the car and eased it to the right side of the road.

When he'd come to a stop, he leaned across to look up at the church. "Where? Reagan, I'm sure there's electricity in there now. Somebody must be working or maybe meeting in the church."

"No. Not that kind of light. It only lasted for a second. Like a flashlight that somebody turned off."

We were stopped now on the opposite side of the road, and Rand turned off the lights.

"I still don't see anything," he said. "Are you sure it wasn't just a lightening bug or something?"

"No. I know what I saw." I picked up the binoculars and focused them on the church, but they were useless in the dark. "I don't see anything now. But it was there. Take my word for it."

"Okay. Your word's good enough for me. So what do you think we should do?"

"I'm not sure, but I don't think we can leave until somebody checks it out. Do you?"

Rand's hands gripped the steering wheel, and his chin jutted forward. "Nope. You're right." Then he picked up the cell phone. "But let's be more careful this time."

In less than five minutes, Dave's truck, lights doused, pulled up behind us. He got out and came to our car.

"How'd you get away from Mullen?" I asked.

"I'm goin' to my brother's house. Lives up the road another couple a miles."

"Good. Dave, does anybody live up there near that church?"

"Nope. Nobody's got any business near that place. It's not even used for services on a regular basis. Mostly tourists and at Christmas. Now tell me exactly what you saw."

I repeated the incident for him again, and he looked back up the hill toward the church. "You know, I think we may just have our guy. Come on. Let's check it out."

Rand and I got out of the car and followed Dave back down the road a hundred yards or so, in the direction we'd just come from, then crossed over into a thicket of trees. The smell of cedar was strong, and I remembered seeing this stand earlier. Dave waited until we'd joined him in the thicket, then said, "We'll go 'round the back way. If he's in there, we'll catch him this time. You ready for this?" he asked, looking at me.

"Watch me," I said and fell into step behind him.

The jagged path he took up the hill wasn't easy. Blackberry vines caught at my clothes and pierced through to the skin. But I wasn't about to be left behind. I could hear Rand's breathing close behind me, but none of us talked as we made our way through the woods. At the top of the hill, Dave stopped, then edged forward to the perimeter of the woods.

The three of us huddled there at the edge of the woods, straining to see whatever was inside the little church. I started to move out of the woods, but Dave caught my arm. He shook his head and motioned for me to be quiet. Then he whispered, "Give him some rope."

And we waited. Minutes dragged by, and I thought that once again Brister had slipped through the noose. But then it happened. The light came on again. This time, it didn't waver, but moved in a slow arch from the back of the little church all the way to the front, then lapsed back into darkness. The door opened, and a figure emerged.

I thought my heart would leap from my chest. The size was right, the build was right. I knew that man was Glen Brister.

He stood in the doorway for a moment, probably surveying the hillside for intruders. Then seeing none, he took a few steps outside and began to descend the hill. A few steps down, though, he must have spotted the cars because he froze, only for a second, then turned and ran back toward the church.

"Let's go," Dave ordered, and he bolted out of the woods and headed straight for the church and the man we knew to be Brister. Rand and I followed, but I was no match for Dave. As we neared the church, Brister stopped on the doorstep, then quickly turned back toward us as he sent a flurry of bright gunshots in our direction.

Dave fell to the ground, but Rand continued forward as I screamed for him to stop. Luckily all bullets missed their targets, and the door to the little church slammed shut. Before the shooting could start again, Rand took cover behind a clump of bushes, and Dave and I slithered over to him, crouching as close to the ground as we could.

"We've gotta get him outta there," Dave said. "There's no way out except through that door he just went in."

"You mean there's no back door?" Rand asked.

"Nope. I've been to services there, and everything comes in and out the front."

"Got any ideas?" Rand asked in a whisper.

"Only two ways I know," Dave admitted. "Go in shootin' and blast him outta there or try to sneak up on him and hope he doesn't get us first."

Rand nodded agreement. "And I don't really think we wanna shoot this place up if we don't have to, do you?"

"Be a shame," Dave admitted. "It's been around here even longer than I have."

"Then that's it." Rand gripped my arm. "You stay here. Two of us in the line of fire is enough."

I was still covered with sweat from the uphill run, so I had no problem with that. Still, I didn't want to see either of them catch a bullet. "Be careful," I urged. "He's not worth either one of you getting shot."

Rand already followed Dave's lead through the bushes that connected to the woods behind the church. They'd been gone only for a minute or so when I spotted them coming out of the woods behind the church. From that angle, Brister had no way to see them, but still I held my breath as they crept along the side of the building.

The light I'd seen inside the church was absent now, and an eerie silence had taken its place. Even the tree frogs were silent. I knew Brister was in there because we'd all seen him rush inside when he spotted us. But the peaceful exterior betrayed nothing of the monster that hid inside.

Dave had crept to the first window of three stained glass that looked more black than any other color without light behind it. He knelt below its ledge and waited. Rand joined him, and they inched to the window's ledge. Shotgun poised, Dave raised up and peered into the stained glass. Where darkness had only a second before filled the interior of the little church, now a light emanated from the window and outlined the figure inside. Brister stared back at us.

The light lasted for only a second or two, but it was enough. Dave backed away slightly, took aim, and blasted through the glass toward the figure inside. In the shattering moment afterward, I feared that the shot had come from inside and that Brister had won again. But Dave still stood, Rand behind him. Again only darkness filled the little church.

Glass continued to fall as the men ducked beneath the ledge and waited for any form of retribution. When it didn't come, I rose from my cover and ran toward them.

"Get down," Rand shouted.

But I'd seen what they perhaps had not. When the shotgun blasted through the window, the figure inside bolted backward, as if lightening had knocked him from his feet. Brister was no longer a threat, and I wanted to see for myself.

Dave and Rand still insisted that I remain outside, but I knew what they'd find. Rand swung the heavy door back on its hinges. He took cover behind its thick wall of wood, while Dave entered the doorway and swung the shotgun in an arch around the church. But only silence met them as they slowly entered. We knew the murderer had taken sanctuary there, but where had he gone?

I had followed them in, and we all saw him about the same time. Brister lay crumpled on the floor in front of the altar, his hands clenched around the hole where blood now seeped from his chest. As we entered, his eyes turned up to us, but his mouth worked wordlessly.

Dave held the shotgun on him, and Rand approached, still aiming the pistol at the man's head. For a brief moment, Brister's mouth opened. "Lauren?" he asked. Then his head dropped forward, and all movement stopped.

With the pistol still aimed at Brister's head, Rand tapped the man's shoulder. The now-lifeless body slid sideways to the floor. Above him, over the altar, Jesus looked down at his fallen child. Glenn Brister would never kill again. But we would never know why he'd ever killed at all.

The three of us stood there for long seconds as we stared down at the man who'd caused so much misery. I half-expected him to rise, like the monsters in movies that require silver bullets. But Brister was clearly dead. Finally, Rand asked, "Does this place have lights?"

Dave nodded and walked toward the rear of the church. Immediately soft lights overhead lit up the sanctuary. I looked at Rand. "This isn't the light I saw."

"I know," he nodded. "Maybe he had a flashlight."

The three of us searched the little church, but all we found was a knapsack, the kind hikers use. We opened it and found the basic supplies we'd expected. Some packs of crackers, some water, a few bandages, two boxes of ammunition for the pistol he'd been carrying. That was it.

"It's gotta be around here somewhere," Rand urged.

We kept looking, but there was no flashlight. It simply wasn't there. Apparently, Mullen had by this time either heard the gunfire or gotten word from somebody else because while we searched, he appeared in the doorway of the church.

From the doorway, he shouted, "What's happened here?"

Dave glared back at Mullen. "We got our man. That's what happened."

Mullen came forward, and Dave met him in the middle of the aisle. "Why didn't somebody call for me?" Mullen asked, turning to include Rand and me in his glare. "You all could be dead right now."

"Luckily we're not," Rand answered calmly. "We didn't have time to call you. We were driving by when Reagan saw a light in here, and we came up to investigate."

Mullen turned back to Dave. "And I suppose Dave here just happened to be passing by too."

Rand shrugged. "It all happened too fast. We've lost him so many times, I didn't want him to slip through again."

"I see," Mullen muttered through tightly drawn lips. He then approached Brister's body and knelt to place his fingers on the throat of the man. He waited briefly, then stood up again and turned to me. "So you saw a light in here?"

"Twice," I said.

"Twice?"

"Yes. I saw it once when we drove by, and I saw it again when we were outside and Brister was in the church. The light was behind him. I saw him fall when Dave shot."

Mullen's eyes turned to Dave wordlessly. Dave added, "I saw it too."

Mullen sighed and took out his two-way. "I'm in the church at the top of the hill. Get up here now."

More cars stopped at the foot of the hill. We were about to be swarmed by federal and state agents, all there to witness Brister's death. As we waited on the porch of the little church, tree frogs resumed their haunting chorus across the woods. I turned to the forest behind us, half-expecting to see them, but I saw only a soft glow. And the little girl it surrounded as she disappeared into the forest.

EPILOGUE

Rand and I went back to Natchez long enough to pack up our belongings. That town had come to be a sort of home to us, and I admitted to a certain sadness in saying good-bye to our motel room perched on the hill.

I wanted to go home rather desperately, but I also wanted to be with Rand for a very long time. And for the moment, I wasn't exactly sure where home was anyway. But with Rand, I knew we could work it out.

As we left the room, Mullen called. He told us that Brister's past had become public information and that his wife now offered any help she might give to solve whatever remaining questions we had about him. "And in that light," he continued, "I'd really appreciate it if you two could stop by the local office on your way out of town."

We agreed, although neither one of us could imagine why. "I doubt he'd ask us to come by so he can arrest us," I joked.

Rand agreed with a laugh, and we soon found the office. Mullen stood up from the desk when we entered. He actually smiled and offered us a seat. Then he sat back down at the desk as his solemn face returned. "I appreciate your coming here. I know it's been a long time."

"Not a problem," Rand assured him. "What's going on?"

Mullen shook his head and reached to pick up something on the floor behind the desk. "I just wanted you to see this."

He laid the suitcase on the desk and opened it, then swiveled it around toward us.

My pulse raced instantly, and my stomach churned.

"Wasn't that suitcase at police headquarters in Jackson?"

His expression was unreadable as he said, "That suitcase is still in Jackson. Brister's wife brought this one in. Go ahead, look inside."

My hands shook, but I knew what I would find. One by one, I sorted through the same pictures I'd found on the Natchez Trace that now were fully developed. I handed the pictures to Rand, and he looked as I had done.

Mullen continued. "Mrs. Brutkiweicz said she found the suitcase in the attic."

"But how can this be?"

He shook his head in silence and said simply, "I guess we'll never know, but she said they were up there covered in dust. Looked like they'd been there a long time."

I looked at Rand, but he offered no answers either. Finally, he took my hand in his own and said, "Lauren wanted to make sure you found him. That's the only answer I've got."